As she enters her ninth season in the North American Hockey League, Sophie's pressure on herself to perform well has never been higher. Next season will mark a decade as the first woman in the League, a milestone no one will let her forget, especially as her expected replacement will be old enough to be drafted herself.

Sophie has the support of Coach Elison and her team behind her. She has come into her own on the ice as the captain and face of the Concord Condors. Off the ice, her life is looking good as well. She and Elsa are living together with plans to build a home, provided Concord signs them to contract extensions.

As always, though, it isn't enough. Sophie has her eyes set on the Maple Cup, the trophy given to the best hockey team each year. She has all the motivation she needs—a contract to live up to, a personal hockey hero on the team who has never lifted the Cup before, and a need to prove herself, again, before Emily Skelton is drafted and takes the League by storm.

I0597487

IN FLIGHT

Sophie Fournier, Book Eight

K.R. Collins

A NineStar Press Publication

www.ninestarpress.com

In Flight

© 2025 K.R. Collins
Cover Art © 2025 Jaycee DeLorenzo

ISBN: 978-1-64890-841-5

First Edition, February, 2025

Also available in eBook, ISBN: 978-1-64890-840-8

Chapter One

Sophie greets Armand Mason with a smile and a brief handshake. Mason is a middle-aged man with dark skin and even darker hair. He wears a green button-down, but the sleeves are rolled to his elbows in deference to the summer heat.

His grip is firm but not overpowering. He has callouses on his hands, in different places than Sophie does. She suspects his are from holding pencils or, maybe in this modern age, a tablet stylus. Sophie's callouses are from gripping her hockey stick and from all the weightlifting she does.

Elsa shakes Armand's hand next. "Thank you for agreeing to meet with us," she says.

Elsa, who normally only has a scant few inches on Sophie, has closer to four today, because she's wearing wedge sandals. They're open-toed to show off her lime-green toenail polish. The color clashes with Elsa's dress, a light-pink halter-top. The green-pink combination reminds Sophie of watermelon, but she's smart enough not to mention it to Elsa.

While her girlfriend—and that's still a thrill, thinking of Elsa as her girlfriend—is understanding of Sophie and her quirks, Sophie doubts that will extend to being compared to a watermelon.

Sophie doesn't wear a sundress like Elsa or business

casual like Armand. She wears black capri leggings and a black T-shirt boasting her team's name and logo.

The Concord Condors are New Hampshire's North American Hockey League team. Their logo is a condor with its wings stretched wide and a hockey stick clutched in its talons. Concord was one of the newest teams to be added to the league. The NAHL decided New England could support two teams, one in Boston and one in Concord, and that the proximity would create a rivalry which would sell tickets.

In the early years, there wasn't much of a rivalry. Concord was where Boston fans went because the tickets were cheaper. Now, though, Concord is a proper NAHL team. They have a Maple Cup to their name, having won hockey's most coveted prize in Sophie's third season. She hasn't managed to do it again, but she has a good feeling about this year.

Sophie gestures for Armand to sit at the booth she and Elsa picked out at the coffee shop. She and Elsa sit side by side opposite him. This year is going to be a good one, for many reasons. Yes, Sophie is chasing the Cup again, something she will do every year she's still playing in the NAHL, but there are other things she's focused on.

She has a girlfriend to take out on dates. She has a contract negotiation she wants done with before the summer is over. She has plans to go to Sweden with Elsa, then for Elsa to visit Sophie in Thunder Bay.

And, of course, she has this meeting with Armand Mason, a local architect.

Sophie and Elsa plan to sign contract extensions this summer, the two of them committing to Concord for as many years as they can. They've already committed to each other, for more than the eight or ten years their hockey contracts will last. Another declaration of their intent is this: planning a house together.

They're going to build their dream house. They'll

have enough bedrooms for when their respective families come to visit or for when their teammates need a place to crash. They'll have a sleek, modern kitchen where Sophie can cook when she has the energy and heat up team-prepared meals when she doesn't. They'll have an open living room with enough seating to host their teammates.

It will be perfect, and Armand is going to help them make it happen.

"Are congratulations in order?" Armand asks with a glance between them.

It isn't an unfair guess, and Sophie feels a twinge of guilt for lying to him, for using him, as she smiles and says, "Not yet. We're hoping by the end of the summer to have ironed out our new contracts. Once the ink is dried, we can begin building, but we wanted to start planning ahead of time. We think it will go well."

Armand's surprise morphs into a polite smile.

Sophie knows the assumptions people will make about her and Elsa. They see them together and think they're a couple. They *are* a couple, but Sophie doesn't want the wider world to know. So few things in her life are allowed to be hers, are private, that she clings to this one.

She was the first woman drafted into the NAHL. It means she's been the first for a lot of milestones in the league. She is the face of her franchise, and in some ways she's the face of the league. It's a lot of responsibility, and she accepts that it's part of the price of entrance.

She doesn't want to be the first hockey player to openly date their teammate. She doesn't want the pressure or the attention or the people who will dig into every detail of her life. She values her privacy. Even more, she values her relationship with Elsa, and she doesn't want to constantly defend it against people trying to twist it into something bad.

Armand won't be the only person to make assumptions based on Sophie and Elsa planning a house together, but there won't be a lot of people like him, either. For most of the hockey world, Sophie and Elsa are simply *Sophie and Elsa*. They shared an apartment in Elsa's first season in Concord, and they've shared a house every season since. There was a brief time when Elsa moved in with a boyfriend, but she was back with Sophie the next season.

Their relationship is teammates being teammates. Sophie is happy to feed into the misdirection, because it allows her to protect what's most important to her. She and Elsa will plan their house, and pictures will leak from today's meeting. The two of them will train with each other, first in Sweden then in Thunder Bay. At some point, they'll sit down with Concord's front office and sign matching contracts.

It isn't the first time Sophie has spun a narrative. It is, by far, the largest scale deception she's ever undertaken. Part of her feels guilty for it. There aren't many out athletes, and this is an opportunity for her to be a role model and a spokesperson. The thought of it exhausts her. Maybe, it's selfish. Or maybe, it's self-preservation. She isn't sure. She'll bring it up with Dr. Malone in her next therapy appointment. For now, though, her relationship with Elsa is a well-guarded secret.

Elsa's immediate family knows, and Sophie's brother knows. Soon, Sophie will have to tell her parents, but she doesn't intend to tell anyone else. Concord's front office won't be told, her teammates won't be told. One day, she'll tell a wider audience, either because it leaks or because she's ready to, but she isn't ready now. And Elsa isn't pressuring her.

"We'd like to stay within a thirty-minute drive of Concord," Sophie tells Armand once they each have their beverage of choice. Sophie has a smoothie which has too much sugar to be healthy, but there's fruit in it so she can pretend.

Elsa doesn't even make that small effort. Her iced

coffee has several syrup shots and a tall spiral of whipped cream. It's a toothache in a cup, but Elsa's happy with it so Sophie doesn't say anything.

"I don't know if that limits what we can do," Sophie adds because Armand is their architect, not their realtor.

"Are you looking to build a large house?" Armand asks.

"No," Elsa answers, and she grins at Sophie's look. "He's thinking McMansion. We want space, but not that much."

Armand smiles and ducks his head, almost bashful. "Large isn't exactly a precise word."

"A little bigger than what we have now," Sophie says. She slides the pictures and specs of their current house across the table.

The house is a good size for them, but its true benefit is the attached in-law apartment. It's the perfect place for their respective families to stay when they visit. They're close enough to see, but there's enough separation that Sophie and Elsa don't feel crowded. Would it be weird to have two in-law apartments in their future house?

"The biggest upgrade will be in the size of the yard," Elsa says. "We're looking to put in a saltwater pool."

"*We* aren't," Sophie says. She tries to frown at Elsa's impish look, but Elsa's too pleased with herself for Sophie to hold out for very long. They have playfully argued about their pool since they first considered the idea of building a house.

Elsa wants something whimsical and impractical, a saltwater pool with a grotto and a waterfall. Sophie thinks if she's going to have a pool, it should be a lap pool, something with purpose. Unlike their disagreement over toasters, which was solved by buying two, Sophie doesn't think this one will be solved by having a pool for each of their preferences.

Armand laughs at their antics and sips his tea before he pulls out a blank piece of paper. "Let's make a list. No judgements yet, anything and everything you might want. Next session, we can whittle it down based on practicality and preference."

"All right," Sophie says.

Her life is measured in milestones; from leagues she's broken into to hockey achievements, even to things like her first car, her first apartment lease, her first house. This is another milestone, planning a house with the woman she wants to live with for the rest of her life.

Under the table, where no one will see, Sophie reaches for Elsa's hand. Elsa meets her halfway, and they lace their fingers together.

*

Elsa doesn't linger long in Concord. She stayed longer than she usually does, because Sophie wanted at least two meetings with Armand before Elsa flew home to Sweden. Sophie tried, unsuccessfully, to convince Elsa to stay for the NAHL draft. And Elsa tried, equally unsuccessfully, to tempt Sophie to Sweden right away.

But Sophie has responsibilities to the league that Elsa doesn't have or want, and so Elsa goes to Sweden and Sophie goes to Philadelphia.

Even if Sophie didn't have obligations to Concord or the NAHL, she still would attend this year's draft. For the first time in far too long, there are women at the draft. There are three of them: Elizabeth Schatz, a Canadian forward Sophie played with at the Winter Games last year; Jordan Cassidy and Andrea Segura, both American forwards.

Being at the draft, even eight years removed from her own, brings back memories. Sophie's draft came on the heels of a season-long lockout that was blamed on her.

She spent the months leading up to her draft unsure if she'd even be allowed to attend. She was, eventually, invited, but to pacify those uneasy with her presence, the Commissioner and the league's owners agreed no team would be forced to draft a woman.

They had to opt-in by applying. That first season, only the Concord Condors were eligible to draft women. Concord took advantage of it and used their last pick, the last pick of the entire draft, to select Sophie. As Mr. Pauling, the team's owner, told Sophie, there was no sense in wasting a higher draft pick on her. It was a smart business decision.

It was, not even Sophie can argue it wasn't. But she was the best player in the draft, and she should have been selected in the first round, if not first overall. It's one of those things she isn't allowed to say. She's supposed to smile and be grateful she was given the opportunity to play at all.

She is grateful, but she's also angry, because it wasn't fair. She broke into the NAHL, and she's seen signs of change. Elsa, Gabrielle, and Lexie all went first round. Lexie—Alexis Engelking—holds the distinction of being the highest woman selected in NAHL history. The Indianapolis Renegades took her fourth overall. She wears the number four to remember it, maybe to drive her.

Her Indianapolis teammate, Chad Kensington, was the first overall pick at the draft. It's no secret Lexie believed it should have been her chosen first and not him. Sophie doubts this is the draft where a woman will be selected first, but she hopes she's still in the league when it does happen.

Sophie sits at Concord's table on the floor at the draft, and she observes the bustle and the chaos as teams try to make deals or figure out who they're going to draft when the person they wanted is taken by someone else.

She doesn't participate, beyond a few hellos.

Kansas City makes a deal with Quebec. They send Nathaniel Summers to Quebec and pick up a player, a prospect, and a pick at this year's draft. That pick is used on the second day to select Jordan Cassidy in the fourth round.

Two picks later, Elizabeth Schatz is drafted to the Boston Barons.

Sophie smiles and claps in case the cameras pan to her. Part of the rivalry between Boston and Concord is due to Sophie and Dmitri Ivanov, Boston's star player, entering the league in the same season. They're friends more than rivals, despite what the league wants. Schatz will be well taken care of there, but part of Sophie hoped Elizabeth would be her teammate in this upcoming season.

During the seventh round, Andrea Segura is drafted to the Edmonton Hydras. It's a good showing, and Sophie leans back in her chair and makes a note to get their phone numbers so she can add them to the group chat.

*

Sophie knocks on the hotel room door. When it opens, Segura is on the other side. Her hair is loose, today's curls almost completely gone. She wore a beautiful orange dress to the draft, but she's in her pajamas and barefoot now.

"You're Sophie Fournier," Segura says.

"Sophie?" Schatz sprints to the door. Her cheeks are flushed, more red than pink, and she sways into Segura's side.

"I see you've been celebrating," Sophie says.

"Come in, come in." Schatz grabs Sophie's hands and tugs her into the room. "I went to dinner with my family, and they're over the moon for me, of course, but you get it."

Sophie waves to Cassidy. Cassidy, who has a makeup

wipe in one hand and a beer in the other, nods in response.

"Do you want a beer?" Schatz asks.

Sophie accepts a beer from Segura and sits on the edge of one of the beds. Schatz and Segura sit side by side on the other while Cassidy removes her makeup in the bathroom with the door open.

"You'll tell us the real shit, right?" Segura asks. "Who should we be on the lookout for?"

Ah, Sophie's least favorite talk but one of the most important she'll have with any new addition to the NAHL. "Anthony Sinclair. He plays for Denver, and he won't hesitate to hurt you. And he spews some nasty shit." Sophie's been on the receiving end of his hits and his insults. "There are guys on your team whose job it is to deal with him. Let them."

"Do as you say, not as you do?" Cassidy asks with a grin.

"You break one guy's nose in your second season, and no one ever lets you forget it." Sophie mock sighs. She lost her composure, big time, against Sinclair in her early days in the NAHL. She cross-checked him in the face, broke his nose, and she faced the consequences for it. A couple years later, she didn't retaliate when he slammed the butt of his stick into her side and took her out of the final game in the International Hockey Tournament. She hasn't retaliated to any number of creative insults he's thrown her way. The closest she's come to losing her cool again was last season when he hit Elsa.

It was an open-ice hit, and Elsa landed awkwardly. Sophie thought she landed on her neck, maybe her head. It took two of Sophie's teammates to hold her back. If they hadn't, she would have dropped her gloves and hit Sinclair. She wouldn't have regretted it.

"Keep away from Chad Kensington," Sophie adds.

"He's the heart of American hockey," Cassidy says, not like she's arguing, more like she's curious.

It's Schatz who scoffs and says, "Not the heart. More like—" She makes a jerk-off motion with her right hand.

Sophie laughs, even though it isn't polite, and she probably shouldn't. She knows Chad Kensington likes to hit on younger women, ones who are more likely to be starstruck by him. There was a kerfuffle a few years ago involving a picture of him kissing one woman in a bar while his hand was up the skirt of another. There are rumors too. Rumors that he's a selfish teammate. That he puts people down in order to look better by comparison. All Sophie knows for sure is that she doesn't like him and there's a weird tension between him and Lexie.

Not that whatever inter-team trouble Indianapolis might be having kept them from winning the Maple Cup in back-to-back seasons.

"I can't believe I'm going to play for Boston." Schatz sighs and looks over at Sophie. "You're friends with Dmitri Ivanov, right? I guess you've only played against him, but I'll be able to play *with* him."

"No crushes on teammates," Cassidy says from the bathroom. "That's Hockey 101."

"A captain crush is different from a *crush* crush," Schatz insists.

Segura looks at Sophie as if her word is final on this. Sophie gives an awkward shrug. "Usually, I am the captain."

Segura laughs and nudges Schatz. "Fournier was your captain at the Games, right? Do you have a captain crush on her?"

"I'm not drunk enough for this," Schatz declares.

Cassidy wanders over, apparently done in the bathroom. She hands Schatz and Segura two glasses each, then wrestles with the cork on a bottle of champagne.

"You'll get better at that," Sophie says with a nod to Cassidy's efforts. "There's a lot to celebrate in the NAHL."

"Like the Cup?" Schatz sighs wistfully.

Segura waits for Cassidy to fill her glass then holds up her phone. "Selfie time!"

Sophie groans but before she can beg off, Schatz plants herself on Sophie's lap, keeping her where she is. Segura and Cassidy crowd in on either side of them.

"Lower your glasses," Sophie tells the women. "Social Media 101."

They take a picture with the four of them, and Sophie takes a picture of just her and Schatz. It isn't a great picture, but Sophie opens her text conversation with Dima, Dmitri Ivanov, and sends it to him anyway, with strict instructions to take care of Schatz now she's his teammate.

"Oh." Segura sounds disappointed and a little bit hurt as she scrolls through her phone. After a moment, she tosses it away with a disgusted noise. "People are dicks."

"Fuck 'em and drink," Cassidy says. She tops off each of their glasses.

"There isn't anything wrong with protecting yourself," Sophie says. "You can stay off social media entirely. You can curate your platforms. You can have everything pass through your PR team before it reaches you." She wishes the evening could be all champagne and giggles, but there are some hard truths she should share with these women before they enter the NAHL. "If they think it will hurt you, they'll say it. And if it does hurt you, they'll say it more."

"Is it worth it?" Segura asks.

"That's a decision you have to make for yourself." Sophie curls an arm around Schatz's waist, for her own comfort more than Schatz's. There are ways the league is better for women than when Sophie first entered the league, but there are many ways in which it hasn't changed.

Johanna Achenbach is put down, because she isn't as good a goalie as Gabrielle Gagnon, but none of the male goaltenders in the league are measured against Gabrielle. If they were, they would all fall short too.

Sophie and Lexie are pitted against each other, because they're both women. Sophie's labeled a failure because she only has one Maple Cup to Lexie's two. And Lexie is a failure, because she doesn't have the scoring titles or international success Sophie has.

More women in the league means more competition, more ways for the talking heads and analysts to highlight how they aren't good enough, but Sophie won't allow that to divide the women who have made it.

"I should add you to the group chat," Sophie says.

"That's real?" Cassidy asks.

"It is. None of you will have another woman on your team. This helps us keep from feeling alone. I have Elsa, and I'm grateful for it, but I still call Lexie sometimes so we can shout at each other. I listen to Mads talk about playing in New Mexico. Gabrielle and I exchange stories about suffocating media."

Sophie's phone dings, but it isn't a message from one of the other women in the NAHL. It's a Snapchat from Dima. In the video, Dima grins and waves at the camera. His black hair is a mess, and there are dark circles under his eyes.

"I will care for your little sapling," Dima promises. He crouches down next to a small plant and pours some clear liquid over it.

Segura sounds judgmental as she asks, "Did he just water that plant with vodka?"

"Probably." Sophie saves the video for future blackmail. "There will be ups and downs in the league. We share the good stuff and talk through the bad stuff. And we look out for one another."

"Like when Madison Plante fought Alstead for taking Gabrielle Gagnon out," Schatz says.

"Exactly." Sophie cards her fingers through the tangles of Schatz's hair. "We compete against one another, and none of us will go easy on you on the ice. But off the ice, we're here for one another."

Sophie was the only woman in the NAHL in her rookie season. It was lonely and when her sophomore season rolled around, she thought she'd have Elsa on her wing and Gabrielle in her division. But Elsa stayed in Sweden and Gabrielle played for Quebec's minor league team, and Sophie spent another season as the only woman in the NAHL.

There still aren't very many of them, but she isn't alone, and she wants to make sure none of them ever feel alone either.

Chapter Two

After the draft, Sophie flies out to her parents' house in Thunder Bay. It's a short stopover before she goes to Sweden. She would avoid it, but there's an important conversation she needs to have, and she knows it's one she should have in person.

"Do you want to go shopping with me?" Sophie asks her mom.

They've never done the traditional mother-daughter bonding. Sophie has always been more tomboyish than stereotypically girly. And, for most of her life, hockey has taken up all her time and focus.

Maybe, at twenty-six, it's too late for this kind of request, but Sophie finally feels as though she can take the time to do something indulgent. Clothes shopping with her mother isn't at the top of her wish list, but it's something.

"Shopping?" her mom echoes.

They're in the kitchen. Sophie's mom is a restless person, like Sophie, but instead of only feeling settled when she's on the ice, her mom just needs something in her hands. Right now, her mom is reorganizing the Tupperware drawer, but she pauses in order to give Sophie her full attention.

Sophie has always felt a bit intimidated by her

mother. For as long as Sophie has known her, she has had a husband, children, a job, and a house. It's all seemed effortless. Maybe it's the nature of being a parent, but in comparison to her mom, Sophie has always felt as though she was falling short of her mom's example.

Her mom would be devastated if Sophie ever admitted it but for all the incredible things Sophie has done with her life, when she compares herself to her mom, she only sees what her mom's accomplished that Sophie hasn't.

Sophie's mom loves her, something Sophie has never doubted. Her well-meaning attempts to set Sophie up with her neighbors' sons or coworkers' daughters is because she believes everyone else should love Sophie too. Sophie never understood it, and she didn't particularly want it. But now that Sophie has Elsa, she wants to tell her mom.

"I want a few sundresses," Sophie says. She tries not to be offended at her mom's shocked expression. "You know I'm only here for a week. It's because I'm flying to Sweden."

"Sweden?" her mom repeats. Then, questioningly, "Elsa?"

"Elsa," Sophie confirms, rather than saying there's no other reason for her to go to Sweden.

"And you want sundresses for your visit?" her mom asks slowly, her words measured. She sounds as if she's drawing conclusions and is giving Sophie the time to tell her they're wrong.

"I do. I'm—we're—" Sophie planned what she was going to say. She *practiced*. And now, all those carefully chosen words are gone.

"You're..." her mom prompts.

"Dating," Sophie says in a rush. "Elsa and I are dating."

Sophie's mom draws in a sharp breath. She covers her

mouth with her hands. Her eyes fill with tears. Sophie hopes this is a positive sign.

"Oh, sweetie." Her mom holds her arms out. "Will you hug me?"

"Mom," Sophie groans, but she submits to the hug.

"I'm so happy for you. Will the two of you visit us as well?"

"That's the plan. We're going to train in Sweden and then stop by Concord to sign our extensions and then I'd like to bring Elsa here to meet you and Dad. I mean, she's met you, obviously, but *meet you* meet you."

"Sophie." Her mom cuts off her babbling by cupping Sophie's face between her hands. "We'll be happy to host the two of you. Maybe Elsa will tell me the truth about these house rumors."

"I'll tell you," Sophie says. She hasn't yet, because she wanted her mom to know the honest answer and not the story Sophie and Elsa are spinning to the press. "We're building a house. And after we go to Sweden, we're going to sign matching contracts."

Her mom's eyes shine with tears, but Sophie thinks they're happy tears. "You don't do anything by halves, do you?"

"I love her," Sophie says. Her mom knows what a monumental confession that is.

What her mom doesn't know are all the details. She doesn't know that Sophie first met Elsa at a U-Tournament in Zurich. She doesn't know that if Sophie hadn't been invited to the NAHL draft, she was going to Sweden to play with Elsa. Her mom doesn't know that after Elsa signed her first extension with Concord, Sophie tattooed Elsa's number on her hip.

Sophie has known since Zurich that Elsa was special. She didn't realize the degree to which Elsa was special to her until recently. They were teammates, and Sophie thought that was all she wanted. But she wants Elsa to be in her life after hockey. She wants Elsa to be more than hockey.

Hockey is where it began for them, but it won't be where it ends.

"We're keeping it quiet," Sophie tells her mom. "Immediate family only, for now. I don't want my relationship to be a headline or a talking point."

"I won't tell anyone," her mom promises. Then she hesitates, and Sophie knows the question she's about to ask.

"I'm going to tell Dad," Sophie says.

"He'll support you. It might take him some time to come around, but he will support you. He loves you as much as I do."

He does but he shows it differently. Sophie knows she wouldn't be in the NAHL without her dad pushing her to be better. But all he does is push. Somewhere, they went from hockey being the thing that bonded them to hockey being the only thing that bonded them.

"It can wait for tonight," Sophie's mom says. "You and I have some important shopping to do. Are you planning to sightsee while you're in Sweden?"

"We're going to train," Sophie says. Then, at her mom's frown, she sighs and says, "Yes, we're going to do some sightseeing as well."

*

Sophie gets on a plane at seven in the morning and lands in Linköping at ten in the evening. She hates time zones. She hates airplanes too, with their cramped seating and subpar food. She kept up with the hockey news on the flight to keep herself from sleeping.

Quebec picked up Johanna Achenbach. It was

obvious she wasn't going to play for Regina this season. They made her the starter last season when they traded Scott Pearce to Philadelphia. It should have been a moment for celebration, but in Jo's first start, she was booed by her own fans. Regina's front office chose her, but the fans rejected her.

And now she's in Quebec. It's a tough market to play in, especially for a goalie. Quebec's legacy is Five-Hole Billy. There's even a statue of him outside Quebec's arena. William Loiseau backed the team to their record-tying five back-to-back Maple Cup Championships. Then, in Game Seven in what would have been their sixth win, the puck trickled through Loiseau's legs. It was overtime and his mistake cost Quebec the game, the championship, and a record. Loiseau was driven out of the province and supposedly Canada itself.

The only reason Sophie believes Quebec won't be a disastrous landing spot for Jo is that Gabrielle plays in Quebec. She is the best goaltender in the world, and if anyone can mentor Jo, it's her.

It does mean that Quebec picked up Nate Summers, a talented center, at the draft and now Jo at the start of free agency. They're gearing up for a serious run at the Cup. It isn't a surprise. Every team in the league wants to win the Cup, but Quebec has taken some definitive steps toward it. Sophie can't help but wonder who Concord will sign or trade for in order to shore up their own chances.

Sophie takes a cab to Elsa's house, because she didn't want their reunion to happen in a crowded, public airport. The sidewalk outside Elsa's house is a better place for it. This late at night, it's too dark for even any lurkers to see much.

It means Sophie can fall into Elsa's hug. She tucks her face against Elsa's neck and inhales deeply. "Hi," she mumbles.

"Hi." Elsa wraps her arms around Sophie.

"I hope your family isn't waiting up for me." Sophie's body thinks it's mid-afternoon, but her mind is exhausted.

"They're excited to see you."

"In the morning?" Sophie asks hopefully. She needs a long sleep, a hot shower, and a solid breakfast before she's up to seeing anyone.

"All right. I'll smuggle you in." Elsa laughs and picks up one of Sophie's bags. "Come on. I'm in the in-law apartment. The house is for my parents. I'm not here enough to need an entire house."

The house is moderately sized, and the in-law apartment is similar to the one Sophie and Elsa have back in Concord. It's difficult to see any details of the house in the evening light. Elsa opens the front door to the apartment and ushers Sophie in first.

The door opens into a living room with a plush beige carpet. Sophie's feet sink into it. She can't wait to feel it on her bare toes. She pauses long enough to take her shoes off, then Elsa leads her through the living room and into a hallway. Sophie catches a glimpse of mismatched artwork on the walls before Elsa turns her into the first bedroom.

Sophie isn't surprised by the clashing styles, of the artwork or even the furniture. Elsa has a Dalí and a Pollock hanging in their room in Concord. She likes what she likes, whether it goes well together or not.

Sophie leaves her bag on the floor and goes to look at the pictures hanging on the walls. There's a framed picture of the Condors after their Maple Cup win. Next to it is a picture of Sophie and Elsa holding the Maple Cup between them. Sophie is staring at the Cup as if all her dreams have come true. Elsa looks at her with the same expression.

They're so *young* in that picture. Elsa doesn't even have an A on her sweater yet, marking her as one of Sophie's alternate captains.

"This year," Elsa says. She comes up behind Sophie, and Sophie gratefully leans back against her.

"This year," Sophie agrees.

*

After an early run and a joint shower, Sophie and Elsa join Elsa's family for breakfast in the main house. Elsa's mom looks like Elsa except half a foot shorter and her blonde hair is going white. Elsa's dad has a mischievous glint in his eyes, which must be where Elsa gets her impish behavior from.

When Sophie tries to shake Elsa's dad's hand, he pulls her in for a hug instead. And then Elsa's grandmother, a woman with short gray hair and a welcoming smile, kisses Sophie's cheeks. Afterward, she pushes Sophie toward one of the chairs at the table.

"I can help," Sophie says, because it seems rude to sit and wait for someone else to cook for her, then serve her.

Elsa's grandmother waves her off, as if she doesn't even need Elsa to translate to know what Sophie said.

"Has Elsa told you the best places to visit?" Elsa's mom asks.

"We've picked some places to go," Sophie answers neutrally.

This, apparently, is an invitation for Elsa's parents and grandmother to talk over one another as they name their favorite sights in Sweden. Sophie's overwhelmed at the first few and by the time they wind down, she is looking at Elsa with a hint of fear. There's no way they can visit all those in one summer, but she doesn't want to disappoint Elsa's family.

Elsa smiles as if she can hear Sophie's panic. "We don't have to do it all this summer."

"Oh," Sophie says. Then, "*Oh.*" There isn't anything

to do but draw Elsa in for a kiss, something brief and sweet, because it's early in the morning and they have an audience. She squeezes Elsa's hands. "What do we want to do on this visit, then?"

"Today, we're going to a museum," Elsa says. "Someplace quiet and cool. Once you've adjusted to the time change, we'll go for a bike ride around Roxen Lake. Maybe we'll even have a picnic and go for a swim."

Sophie wrinkles her nose. "A bike ride and swimming in the same day?"

Elsa laughs and dips in for another quick kiss. "Fun swimming. Like we'll do in our saltwater pool."

"We aren't going to have a saltwater pool," Sophie says, but she's pretty sure she's already lost this fight. Armand's latest designs had a sketch of the backyard with three different sized pools. To distract herself from Elsa's smug face, Sophie turns toward Elsa's family. "Has Elsa told you we're designing a house?"

"It's very nice," Elsa's mom says politely, with the tone of someone who hates it but doesn't want to offend anyone.

"She thinks it's too big for only the two of us," Elsa says.

"We need room for our families to visit," Sophie says. "And we need the space to host team events. I guess most of the time it'll only be the two of us. We could petition the front office for a rookie?"

"No," Elsa says. "It's for us. Everyone else is only allowed to visit."

Sophie shrugs and doesn't push. There are times she's wanted a rookie or two, people to make her home seem less echoing and lonely. All those times have coincided with a lack of Elsa in her home. She doesn't mind their house being only for the two of them.

She and Elsa exchange a smile which Elsa's family

politely ignores, then they sit down at the table to eat breakfast together.

After breakfast, Sophie and Elsa train. They eat again, have a short nap, then they go into Linköping to view the Linköping Castle. The castle is a museum now. They go on a tour and walk side by side. Their hands brush, but Sophie isn't daring enough to hold Elsa's hand, not even in Sweden.

They eat dinner in a quiet corner of a bustling restaurant. It takes most of Sophie's remaining energy to lift her silverware, so Elsa carries the conversation for the two of them. Sometimes, her words trail off and when Sophie looks up, Elsa is staring at her with a fond smile. It never fails to make Sophie squirm, embarrassed and pleased to be the focus of Elsa's attention.

By the time they're done eating, the sky is beginning to grow dark. The day's activity and the time change catch up with Sophie on the trip to Elsa's. Sophie is happy to change into her pajamas once she's in the room she and Elsa are sharing. She covers a yawn and waves Elsa off when she reaches for her own pajamas.

"You should hang out with your family," Sophie says. "I'm going to be boring and sleep."

"Sleep in this instead." Elsa tosses a shirt at Sophie's head.

Sophie catches the shirt and shakes it out to look at it. It's dark green with the logo of Gothenburg's hockey team. Sophie can't help but laugh as she turns it over to see NYBERG and the number 13 on the back. "I'm in your apartment, in your bed, sleeping with you, and it isn't enough?"

It's a teasing more than a scolding because Sophie switches out her current sleep shirt for Elsa's. Elsa grins as she slinks over to Sophie. She hooks her fingers in the waistband of Sophie's pajama pants and tugs lightly on the elastic.

They're close enough that Sophie can feel the heat from Elsa's body. Elsa's telegraphing her intentions obviously enough for Sophie to pick up on them. And Sophie had said she wanted to get into bed. Of course, she planned to sleep, but she's adaptable. She can put sleep off for a little while.

"Did I put your shirt on so you could take it off again?" Sophie asks.

"You could leave it on," Elsa suggests. She guides Sophie down onto the bed, until Sophie is laid out for Elsa's greedy eyes. Before Sophie can become self-conscious at being on display like this, Elsa kneels on either side of Sophie's thighs. She rucks up Sophie's shirt and presses a kiss to the sensitive skin just below Sophie's bellybutton.

It isn't new to her, the way Elsa likes seeing Sophie in her clothes. Sophie spent years not understanding the kind of relationship Elsa wanted with her. And even now that they're together, there are still boundaries, because they're keeping their relationship private. In these moments they have alone, if Elsa wants to see the proof of her importance to Sophie, if she wants Sophie to wear shirts with Elsa's name, then it's an easy thing for Sophie to give her.

Sophie will even admit that it isn't only for Elsa's benefit. Sophie likes it too, the way Elsa stakes her claim. Of course, Sophie did it first, when she inked Elsa's importance on her skin. With a grin of her own, Sophie tugs down her pajama pants until her crossed hockey stick tattoo is visible. She brushes her thumb over the 93 on one side and the 13 on the other.

Elsa nudges Sophie's hand out of the way to press a kiss there as well.

"You and me," Sophie says, and it's a fact as much as a vow.

Elsa's next kiss has the sting of teeth.

*

As much as Sophie enjoys her time in Sweden, sightseeing, spending time with Elsa's family, and having Elsa to herself without the pressures of a hockey season, they do eventually have to leave. The farewells happen at the house, which Sophie quickly realizes is because it would cause a scene at the airport if they did it there.

Elsa and her mom hug each other tightly and talk for a long time. Elsa and her dad both tear up for their goodbyes. For Sophie's part, she exchanges an awkward half-hug, half-handshake with Elsa's dad which makes the man laugh and shed more tears.

Elsa's grandmother presses a full winter set of knit gear into Sophie's hands. There are mittens, a scarf, a hat, and socks. Unlike the previous gifts Sophie's received, the crowns aren't hidden, tucked away inside a pattern or flap. Everything is a rich blue with bright, bold, yellow crowns.

"These are lovely," Sophie says, because it's polite to thank someone for a gift. "But I'm Canadian."

"For now." Elsa's grandmother pats Sophie's face and shuffles to hug her granddaughter.

Sophie sighs and thanks Elsa's grandmother in Swedish before she accepts a hug from Elsa's mom. Even if Sophie and Elsa get married one day, she won't wear anything so blatantly nationalistic. Sophie's proud to represent Canada at the Winter Games, and she'll grudgingly do it at any future International Hockey Tournaments. The headlines she would cause by wearing Swedish knitwear aren't worth it.

But she takes the gift in the spirit that it's meant; as far as Elsa's family is concerned, Sophie is one of them now. It makes her think about commitments. Sophie and Elsa are dating, and they're building a house together. When they return to Concord, they're going to sign matching contracts, a commitment to Concord, yes, but also each other. It isn't anything as binding or recognized as a marriage, but it's a step in that direction.

Does Elsa want to get married? Does *Sophie*? Thoughts about marriage and family and kids have always existed in a nebulous *after hockey* state in her mind. It's become more relevant now. When she's done playing, is her future not just a life with Elsa but one where they exchange promises and rings?

Sophie glances over at Elsa to see if any of these thoughts are reflected on Elsa's face as well. But Elsa's face is guarded. She's turned toward the window as they drive through a familiar landscape. Her cheeks are still splotchy and there's a tell-tale swollenness around her eyes.

It hits Sophie now, what a big deal it was for Elsa to leave the Swedish Hockey League behind for the NAHL. When Elsa didn't come over the first season after she was drafted, Sophie had been devastated, betrayed and angry, a whole riot of emotions. But she understands now. Gothenburg, where Elsa played, is only a three-hour drive from Vikingstad. She and Elsa took a day trip to see the city where Elsa played her first professional hockey game. It was three hours for her parents to see her. Now, it's a nine-hour flight and a six-hour time change.

Yet.

Elsa chose Concord. She chose *Sophie*.

"I love you," Sophie says softly. It doesn't seem like enough, and the words themselves aren't. But Sophie backs them up by holding out a hand to Elsa. She backs them up with plans to create a life together, to meet Elsa in the middle wherever she can.

Elsa chose Sophie, and Sophie chose her back.

Elsa slides her hand into Sophie's and squeezes it briefly. They hold hands for the rest of the ride to the airport.

Chapter Three

The contract negotiations aren't as onerous as Sophie expected them to be. Sophie and Elsa's agents handled most of it. Sophie and Elsa made it clear what they wanted; term and no movement clauses, and they were willing to be flexible on price. To an extent, of course.

Sophie struggles with that aspect of her contract. On the one hand, she doesn't live an extravagant lifestyle. She doesn't need multiple millions of dollars. But the number on her contract is a reflection of her value. Or, rather, how much her team values her.

She was paid less than she deserved on her last contract. Part of her wants to demand double digits, to push for the largest contract in NAHL history, but she holds back. One, Concord wouldn't give a deal like that to both her and Elsa. Two, tying up so much money in Sophie would make it more difficult to sign and extend other players. Sophie has to find the balance between a respectable salary and putting her team at a disadvantage.

The final numbers come in at eight million a year for ten years. Sophie and Elsa have their matching contracts. This upcoming season will be their last on their current contracts, then the season after, when their new contracts kick in, they'll be Condors for another decade.

It's everything Sophie wants, and there isn't anything faked about her smile as she makes a show of signing the contract for Derek Napoli and his camera crew. Elsa sits next to her and signs as well. Surrounding them are important people in the franchise, including the owner Martin Pauling and the general manager Ron Wilcox.

Off to the side, watching everything with a sharp eye, is Mary Beth Doyle, Concord's PR manager. Her hair is up in its customary bun and, given the importance of today, she doesn't have a pen or a stylus sticking out of it.

"This was a formality, but an important one," Martin Pauling says once the photo-op is over. "Unless all this business with an architect and a house was a negotiating tactic."

Sophie suspects he'd be proud if it had been, but she shakes her head. "Elsa and I are planning a house together. Concord is where we want to play. Obviously, we've held back on any major decisions until we were sure this is where we'd be, but we can start the next level of discussions with Armand."

"Can we bring a crew to one of these discussions?" Napoli asks. Derek Napoli is the producer for *In the Nest*, the behind-the-scenes glimpse into the Concord Condors. It's an opportunity for fans to see the team off the ice, in addition to on it. Sophie understands the importance of Napoli's job even if she hates how it feels as though he's always intruding on her life.

"I'm sure we can arrange something," Sophie answers.

"You two make the perfect story," Napoli continues. "Two players who met at a U-Tournament but played for different teams. Elsa was drafted to Concord and then didn't come the first year. And then she did come over, and you've gone from roommates to linemates to now signing matching contracts and building a house. Disney would pay serious money for a plot like this." Napoli blanches. "Not that I'm saying this is a happily ever after kind of story. I—"

Sophie cuts him off with a gentle smile and by saying, "If we're talking happily ever after, then this season should end with another Maple Cup."

Napoli seems relieved that Sophie isn't angry he implied their story ends with a wedding or storybook kiss. Because Sophie's invested in this misdirection, she allows him to sweat a bit, instead of telling him he's hit the nail directly on the head.

"Do you have time for a celebratory dinner?" Ron Wilcox asks.

"We do," Sophie answers. She allows Mr. Wilcox to pull her into a conversation about his wife and his two daughters, Kaylee and Jessi, and tries to ignore the prickling on the back of her neck which means Mary Beth is watching her closely.

*

Sophie and Elsa arrive in Thunder Bay while Sophie's family is at work. It means they have the house to themselves as they unpack. Sophie guides Elsa through the familiar house without giving her a tour. They can do that later or, even better, she can push it off on her mom who seems to like that sort of thing.

Sophie pauses in the doorway of her room. Her childhood bed is a twin, and it won't fit two grown hockey players. She hadn't thought this through. "There's a guest room across the hall," Sophie says, but she frowns, because she's used to sleeping with Elsa these days.

Technically, the room was Colby's, but now that he's grown up and moved out of the house, it's been converted into a generic guest room. Sophie wonders when her room will be converted into a guest room as well.

Elsa drops her suitcase near the bed in the guest room. She looks around, and Sophie wonders if Elsa finds the bland decorations boring. "I can make this work," Elsa says. "I can sneak into your room when everyone else is asleep."

"You want to sneak into my room?" Sophie asks. She laughs because she's pretty sure Elsa is serious. Sophie didn't have a typical childhood. All her free time was taken up by hockey. The only time she snuck out of her house was to skate on the backyard rink, but she's pretty sure her dad knew and let her do it, because he approved of the extra practice. "I could stay in here with you while we're visiting."

Elsa smirks, as if she knows Sophie doesn't want to be away from her, and she's pleased about it.

"Ugh," Sophie says, because she can't argue. "Let's unpack so we can go for a run before everyone gets home."

"A run? You work me so hard."

It's Sophie's turn to smirk. "You like it when I work you hard."

"No hockey talk," Elsa says.

"Who said I was talking about hockey?" Sophie laughs and dodges Elsa's swat. It's easy between them, and Sophie can almost forget where she is and the enormity of this visit. Sophie has never brought someone home before. And even though she's told her parents and her brother about her relationship with Elsa, and they've been supportive, or grudgingly accepting in her dad's case, Sophie's still nervous.

These nerves send Sophie into the kitchen after she and Elsa have run, done two core circuits, and showered. Sophie slides the ham into the oven to bake while she tackles the side dishes. She tops off Elsa's glass of lemonade and considers the bag of potatoes on the counter.

"What do you think?" Sophie holds up a potato. "Mashed? Cubed? Should I go to the store for potatoes better suited for baked potatoes?"

"Sliced, seasoned, and baked," Elsa answers easily.

"We aren't having French fries." Sophie tracks down a cutting board and a knife. She'll cube the potatoes and cook them. It'll be easy enough to mash them if people prefer them that way. And by people, she means Colby. Sophie's mom will politely tell her whatever she's made is fine, Sophie's dad won't have an opinion, and Charlotte, Colby's girlfriend, probably won't have one either.

"I didn't say anything about frying," Elsa says. She tracks Sophie's movements with a slight frown. "Are you sure I can't help?"

"I'm sure," Sophie answers. She carefully cubes the potatoes and drops them into a casserole dish. "Vegetables next. Asparagus, you think? Green beans? Salad? Two of the three?"

"I think you should tell me what's bothering you," Elsa says.

Sophie isn't sure if she's glad Elsa knows her so well or annoyed that she does. "Nothing is bothering me. Butter-glazed green beans with roasted almond slices for the family and salad for us?"

Elsa doesn't answer, and her silence weighs heavily as Sophie bustles around the kitchen to prepare the green beans. Once she has put both the potatoes and the green beans in the oven alongside the ham, Sophie is out of distractions.

"I haven't talked to my dad since—" Sophie gestures between the two of them. Her breath comes faster, and it ratchets up her anxiety. Tears gather at the corners of her eyes, and she glares at the counter as if she can hold them back. "He seemed, well, I guess he didn't have a choice but to accept it. But he didn't seem that mad? Except he hasn't talked to me since. Normally, my inbox is full of training videos by this point in the summer. I know we can always leave. We have a home in Concord waiting for us, but your family was so nice to me. I want mine to be nice to you."

Sophie might as well be talking to herself with all the

response she's getting from Elsa. She takes a deep breath and slowly releases it. "I'm sorry. I'm fine. I shouldn't have dumped all of that one you."

Elsa rounds the island until she can stand behind Sophie. She sweeps Sophie's hair off the back of her neck and presses a kiss to where Sophie always carries the majority of her tension.

"You don't have to be fine," Elsa says. "I'm here with you. We can do this together."

"What if he doesn't come around?" Sophie asks. She isn't relaxed, but Elsa isn't either, both of them drawn tight.

"Then he doesn't," Elsa answers. "I won't break up with you, because your dad is a jerk. I knew he was when I started dating you."

"He isn't—"

Elsa reaches around Sophie to place a finger against her lips. "He is. I know you don't complain and that it seems normal to you, but the way he treats you is more tough and less love."

"I'm going to make him love you too," Sophie says. She was the first woman to play in the NAHL, in large part because her dad taught her never to let a barrier stand in the way of something she wanted. She'll apply the same strategy to him.

*

Sophie's mom is the first one home. She pauses in the entryway to the kitchen, no doubt able to smell the cooking food. "You didn't have to cook," she says. She drapes her cardigan over the back of one of the island chairs, then she hugs Sophie. "Welcome home, sweetie."

"You had a long day," Sophie says. "It really wasn't that much effort."

Sophie's mom hugs Elsa next. "I'm glad you visited. It's time and past we hosted you here." She doesn't wait for a response before she joins Sophie at the sink. She gently nudges Sophie's hip with hers. "Sit and relax. I can do the dishes."

"You've been working all day," Sophie protests. She holds her ground.

"And you've been on a plane all day."

It was hardly all day but before Sophie can point that out, Elsa says, "Is this a family thing or a Canadian thing?"

"A little of both," Sophie admits.

Her mom opens the oven to look inside. "Ham? Green beans with almonds?" Her voice has lost some of her earlier cheer. "Your father will be happy." She closes the oven again and checks the timer. "I'm going to change out of my work clothes. Elsa, be a dear and don't let Sophie do the dishes. I'll do them once I'm back."

"Will do, Mrs. Fournier," Elsa promises.

Sophie's mom smiles as if Elsa's said something funny. "You can call me Ellen." She plucks her cardigan off the back of the chair on her way upstairs.

Sophie glances at Elsa and waits for Elsa to bring up their earlier conversation about Sophie's dad and how Sophie is trying to either bribe him or soften him up with his favorite meal.

Elsa, however, doesn't bring it up. She boxes Sophie out, away from the sink, and turns on the water.

"What are you doing?" Sophie asks. "You're a guest."

"Is Charlotte allowed to do the dishes?" Elsa asks.

Sophie smiles and waves her hand to give permission. "Yeah. Wash away."

It took time for Charlotte to transition from guest to family adjacent. Sophie missed most of it, because she was in Concord, but Charlotte is practically family these days.

She wants Elsa to reach the same status.

When Sophie's mom returns, she's in a pair of jeans and a long-sleeved shirt. She looks at Elsa but before she can scold, Elsa jumps on the offensive. "I promised Sophie wouldn't do the dishes and she didn't."

While Sophie thinks she takes after her father more than her mother, she and her mom share the ability to dig their heels in over seemingly inconsequential things. Colby and Charlotte's arrival spares them all an involved discussion over dishes and the distribution of household chores.

"Hey, sis," Colby greets, then he lobs a bag of Snickers at her head. He tosses a bag of candy at Elsa as well, but hers is a bag of Swedish Fish.

"Seriously?" Sophie asks.

Colby grins, as much of an obnoxious older brother now as an adult as he was when they were kids. It was Colby who first took Sophie out on the ice. She played hockey because he did, and she wanted to do everything he did. Then she fell in love with it, and she's made a career and a life out of it. Colby stopped playing competitively after college, but he's in a local beer league which he claims is enough for him.

"I tried to talk him out of it," Charlotte says. "We also have a cheesecake platter."

"I like cheesecake," Elsa says. She approaches Charlotte, ostensibly to take the platter and set it down, but Sophie's pretty sure it's a bid to sneak a piece.

"Don't spoil your dinner," Sophie says absently. At Colby's smirk, Sophie punches his shoulder, and she doesn't hold back.

"Ow!" Colby rubs his arm and glares at her. "The rules are if you're doing something mockable, I'm allowed to mock." He jumps back before she can hit him again. "Fine, fine. Let's talk hockey. There were women at the draft this year. But next one is the big one, right? The wunderkind is eligible."

"Do you mean Emily?" Sophie asks.

"Personally, I like Skeletor better," Colby says.

Emily Skelton is draft eligible next summer. For years, she's been heralded as the next Sophie Fournier. She isn't. She isn't the next Sophie Fournier or the wunderkind or Skeletor. She is Emily Skelton, and she's a damn good hockey player.

Sophie met her the summer after Concord won the Maple Cup. Emily and her mom flew out to Thunder Bay to meet Sophie and see the Cup. Sophie and Emily have exchanged letters ever since. Emily was eleven when they first met. It's hard to believe she'll be eighteen next year.

Emily will be eighteen and the league will be one hundred. The centennial season could see the first woman drafted first overall. Has Emily dared to let herself think about it? Sophie thought it for herself. Even though for the longest time, she wasn't sure if she'd even be invited to the draft, she dreamed about what it would be like to be selected first overall. Even once she was invited and only Concord was eligible to draft her, she still had idle daydreams about it. The reality was that Sophie was drafted last, the two-hundred forty-fourth pick.

"Her name is Emily Skelton," Sophie says and if her voice is too sharp, it's because she's done her best to look for out for Emily. On Sophie's side, the letters they exchange are full of advice, everything Sophie wishes someone had told her as she set her sights on the NAHL. They talk about the heavy weight of expectations, what it's like to be an elite player, how best to deal with angry fans.

The garage door rumbles as it opens, and Sophie isn't the only one who goes still. Even once Colby breathes again, he isn't relaxed. Sophie's mom is bustling around the kitchen with the kind of restlessness which means she isn't completely at ease.

Sophie's stomach twists, and she hates that she's the one who brought this discord into her house.

The third step on the stairs creaks, because it needs to be replaced. It's needed replacing for ten years, and Sophie expects it'll still need replacing ten years from now. Then her dad emerges from the garage with a briefcase in one hand and a Tim Hortons cup in the other.

"I thought you were cutting back on caffeine," Sophie's mom says.

"It's decaf," her dad says.

"I wasn't born yesterday." Sophie's mom plucks the cup out of her husband's hand. She kisses his cheek and goes to the sink to dump the rest of his coffee down the drain. "Sophie made dinner. It's just about done."

"All right." Sophie's dad looks around and seems surprised at all the people here, even though he had to have known the plan for tonight. His eyes slide right over Elsa and when he says, "Hello," it's directed in Colby and Charlotte's direction.

Her dad goes upstairs to change. By the time he returns, dinner is on the table. They all sit and begin the complicated dance of passing dishes around while trying to also fill their own plates. It doesn't take long for the silence to grow stiflingly thick.

Sophie glances at the head of the table. Her dad's complete focus is on cutting his ham, more attention than the meat deserves. Sophie clears her throat. "Girls' day on Saturday?" she asks. She looks across the table at Charlotte, hoping for an ally. "Are you busy?"

"I'm in, especially if massages are on the schedule," Charlotte answers.

"Shopping," Sophie's mom adds.

"Froyo," Elsa contributes. She grins before Sophie can protest. "It's yogurt! Once you add fruit, it's basically a parfait."

"No, it isn't," Sophie says, "but okay. Massages, shopping, and froyo. I can plan a day around that."

"And what am I supposed to do?" Colby asks.

"Go golfing with your father," Sophie's mom says. "Or mow the lawn. It's getting as long as your hair."

"Aw, I like it long," Charlotte says. She ruffles Colby's brown locks to back up her point. She looks at her hand afterward and hums. "We should get our nails done as well."

"Yes," Elsa agrees.

Sophie knows when she's outnumbered. "I'll sit outside and wait for you, but I'm not doing my nails. I always chip them the next time I'm in the weight room." Two summers ago, Sophie trained with Lexie Engelking. It was a weird summer, at turns aggressive, competitive, and friendly bonding.

Lexie liked to paint their nails. The more outrageous the color, the better. Sophie figured that if it was something Lexie did, then she could do it more often as well. But her nails never lasted longer than two days before there was a chip or a scratch and she had to scrub all the paint off.

Sophie's dad clears his throat. "Is there any training in these plans of yours?"

"I have a schedule written up," Sophie says. "We can go over it after dinner."

"I saw a few drills I think you should incorporate. You're almost back to your pre-surgery speed."

Sophie nods and manages not to wince at the reminder of the season she spent sidelined thanks to an ACL tear. Under the table, Elsa knocks her foot gently against Sophie's, an offer of support.

*

It takes Sophie a few days to realize her dad isn't picking any fights about Elsa, because he acts as if she isn't here. Elsa hasn't said anything about it, but she's noticed. It's obvious by the way her spine stiffens whenever Sophie's dad is in the same room as them, the way she raises her voice as if determined to make herself difficult to ignore.

For someone who earned herself the on-ice nickname The Bully, it's an indirect approach to dealing with the problem. Why hasn't Elsa confronted Sophie's dad? Is she afraid Sophie will take her dad's side over Elsa? Is she waiting for Sophie to fight on her behalf?

On Saturday morning, Sophie wakes up early to talk to her dad before he joins Colby to go fishing. Sophie slips out of Elsa's embrace and pulls a Condors sweatshirt over her head before she heads downstairs. She doesn't realize until she's in the kitchen that her sweatshirt boasts a thirteen rather than a ninety-three on the sleeve.

"Good morning," Sophie says as her dad pours himself a decidedly not-decaf cup of coffee.

"You're up early," her dad says. His eyes dip to the number on her sleeve, then he returns to contemplating his coffee.

Pierre Fournier is a man who has always wanted the best for his kids. He pushed Sophie when she was growing up, and he still pushes her now, because he believes the heights she'll reach will be worth the pain of getting there. Sophie isn't sure he's wrong. But she also knows he isn't always right.

"Quit treating Elsa like she doesn't exist," Sophie says. "She is a real person, and I love her, and you can't change that."

Her dad takes a long sip of coffee as if he needs the fortification. "I'm not upset you're interested in women."

"Elsa," Sophie corrects. "I'm interested in *Elsa*."

Her dad's eyebrows pull together. He doesn't understand the distinction, but a mean part of Sophie thinks he doesn't deserve an explanation. Sophie's mom does. She was delighted when Sophie gave her the pamphlets she had received in turn from Dr. Malone.

Romance, sex, Sophie was never overly interested in either of those. The former seemed like a hassle and the latter was something she could handle just fine on her own. When, after years of knowing Elsa, Sophie found her feelings changing, she panicked. It was Dr. Malone who gave her a word to fit to them. *Demisexual.* There are nuances and degrees to it, but Sophie doesn't care about them. All she cares about is that how she feels, how she *is*, is common enough to have a label.

"I told you relationships were for after hockey, because they're a distraction," Sophie's dad says. "Dating a woman is an even bigger distraction than dating a man, and, on top of that, she's your teammate. If this gets out, you have a hard road in front of you."

"You think I should break up with Elsa, because it might be hard?" Sophie knew this was the issue, but even hearing her dad say it, she can't quite wrap her head around it. She'd laugh, except she isn't sure she'd be able to stop. "The way you thought I should set my sights on the NAWHL because the NAHL would be too hard? Oh wait. That isn't what you said."

Sophie stares her dad down until he meets her gaze, because this is important, and she only wants to have this conversation once. "You told me if the NAHL was worth it, I had to pursue it no matter how hard it was. I put the work in there, and I'm willing to put the work in here. If Elsa and I are outed, yes, it will be a shitshow, but I won't break up with her because I'm scared of a possibility. Elsa is the best thing to ever happen to me, and you were there the day I was drafted so you know what I'm saying."

"I—" Her dad sounds choked up. He clears his throat

as if he can hide that he's emotional. "I'm sorry. I'm trying to protect you."

"I know," Sophie says. It's why she hasn't gotten mad the way she suspects Elsa wanted her to. It's why she rarely vents her frustrations with her dad. Because behind all his decisions is the fact that he loves her. "But I don't need you to protect me, I can do that myself. I need you to support me."

"Okay." Her dad clears his throat again. "Colby's waiting in the driveway for me."

"I hope the fish are biting," Sophie says.

Her dad nods and practically flees with his coffee. Sophie rubs her eyes and her hands come away damp with tears. She lingers downstairs until she feels more settled, then she returns to Elsa.

When she slips back into bed, Elsa curls her arm around Sophie's waist and pulls her closer. "Love you too," Elsa murmurs.

Chapter Four

Sophie and Elsa don't stay in Thunder Bay very long. They return to Concord where they continue to train together. They meet with Armand more frequently, as well as the general contractor he recommends. Slowly, but surely, their idle thoughts about a house become more concrete.

In the midst of their summer, Concord signs Mikhail Figuli to a one-year, $750,000 contract. Sophie stares at the notification on her phone for a long time. This year is the league's ninety-ninth. Figuli has played in twenty-nine of them. For all those seasons played, he doesn't have a Maple Cup to his name.

Everyone jokes he won't retire until he wins the Cup, but he'll be forty-eight this season. At some point, his body will give out on him, Cup or no Cup. But more than any of that, he is a NAHL legend. Figuli and Stucki were an unstoppable pair, Figuli at wing and Stucki at center. Then Stucki suffered a career-ending injury and Figuli started bouncing from team to team, searching for that kind of chemistry again.

Sophie still has a poster of him in Thunder Bay. She keeps it in a drawer, because it's weird to have his face on her wall now that she's an adult instead of a kid. But the point is, she grew up idolizing him. In her first season in the NAHL, the two of them battled for the Maddow

Trophy, the award given to the player who scores the most points during the season. He has been an inspiration and a quasi-rival, and now he's going to be her teammate.

"Figuli?" Elsa asks. She must have gotten a notification as well, but she doesn't sound properly awed. "Isn't he old?"

"He *is* the NAHL," Sophie says. Yes, he's at the tail end of his career, but he's still a good player. Concord wouldn't have signed him if he didn't have anything to offer. "This is—"

"Hey," Elsa says, and she sounds distinctly unhappy.

No, Sophie amends as she looks over at Elsa. She's *jealous*. "I suppose we shouldn't offer him our in-law apartment, then."

"No," Elsa says.

Sophie isn't sure whether to be flattered or annoyed by Elsa's grumpy jealousy. "He was playing in the NAHL before I was born. I want to win the Cup with him this season, because he deserves it, but you're the one I signed a matching, ten-year contract with. *You're* the one I love."

Elsa looks slightly mollified, but she's sneaky and Sophie wouldn't put it past her to leverage this into Sophie saying more nice things or backing up those nice things with kisses or a return to bed. Given that Elsa is currently in bed and is a temptation even in a T-shirt and her underwear, Sophie expects that she is going to succeed.

Sophie does her best to ignore her as she searches through her closet for what to wear today. Her eyes catch on a bright splash of color. She looks at the green sundress, the one covered in white polka dots. Next to it is a navy-blue dress with little white anchors stitched onto it.

"I can't believe you talked me into these," Sophie says. She bought them on the Saturday shopping trip, after their massages but before the nail appointment. "They aren't the kind of thing I can wear on gamedays." Even if

Sophie was the kind of player who wore dresses on gamedays, these aren't formal enough.

"Are you looking for reasons to wear your dresses?" Elsa asks. She props herself up on her side and watches Sophie with obvious fondness. "It sounds like you want me to take you on a date."

Sophie blushes. "I'm not—it's not like that."

"Mmm," Elsa says. Her eyes are bright with mischief. "So, you don't want to date me?"

"You are the worst," Sophie tells her. "I don't even like you."

"Liar. Tomorrow, we're going to lunch, somewhere with outdoor seating. You'll wear one of those dresses and your new sunglasses, and we'll enjoy the weather and a nice sangria."

It sounds...kind of perfect, actually. Sophie has too much pride to admit it. "What are you going to wear? One of your short-shirt things? You bought a floral one when we went shopping."

Elsa's amusement only increases. "Are you talking about the romper I bought? And it's paisley, not floral."

"Whatever, you knew what I meant."

"Yes, I've learned to decipher Sophie-speak."

"I had one as a kid," Sophie says. She leans against the doorframe of her closet. "But it was pants instead of shorts and it was made out of denim."

"You owned a denim jumpsuit? Why didn't anyone show me pictures while I was visiting?"

"Because my mom loves me," Sophie answers and laughs. "I'm sure you'll be able to convince her to show you pictures next time we visit. I had to wear it for school pictures like three years in a row."

Sophie's phone pings again. This time, it isn't a Concord signing. The Los Angeles Orcas signed Buchanan as their back-up goalie. The Team USA goaltender is officially the first woman to sign with the NAHL, rather than be drafted. She's also the first woman to leave the NAWHL for the NAHL.

Another notification follows on the heels of this one. Another Team USA player has been signed. This time, it's Shea, picked up by the Atlanta Lancers. A third notification provides an article on the signings. Sophie opens it and skims its contents.

She frowns as she reads part of it out loud to Elsa, "Both women acquitted themselves well in Team USA's bronze medal finish at the Boston Winter Games. Whether they can make the transition to the NAHL is still in question, but at $800,000 a year for a two-year contract, it's an affordable gamble." Sophie makes a disgusted sound. "At least they didn't say Atlanta and LA were taking a chance on them."

When Sophie was drafted, reporters loved to say Concord took a chance on her as if she hadn't set records at every level she played at. Not to mention, Concord chose her last. It was the opposite of taking a chance.

There's a small but talented number of women in the league. Their struggle has been to be good enough to play but at the same time, not be treated as anomalies. Three women drafted and two signed so far this summer means another five women in the league. It's another step in the right direction. Sophie tries to focus on the positives, rather than the steps still remaining.

*

Concord's Fan Convention takes place over a weekend, beginning Friday afternoon and going through Sunday evening. There are planned autograph sessions, player meet-and-greets, and panels with various Concord Condors. It's a packed weekend, but Sophie loves it.

Most teams have a version of the convention, a way

to connect with their fans and drum up support ahead of the new season. Concord didn't start hosting a convention until Sophie was drafted. They simply didn't have enough dedicated fans to make it worth it. Now, they have one every summer, and Sophie has the opportunity to talk to hundreds of people who love her team, and hockey, as much as she does.

There's an extra buzz in the air this year, because of the Figuli signing. Sophie, while looking out over the crowd, spotted more than one jersey with a prominent number nine on the back of it. Some of them were even Concord jerseys, but Figuli's fans wear jerseys from a number of different teams; Montreal and Milwaukee to name a couple.

Sophie's on the hunt for the man himself. She's played against him, and she's even played with him at a couple of All-Star games, but she hasn't spoken with him since he became her teammate.

Her first glimpse of him is while he's on one of the panels. His hair is thinning, and there's no mistaking the fine lines creasing the skin around his eyes and mouth. But his eyes are sharp and bright, and his suit is a riotous plaid, because he once told a reporter if the league was going to force him into suits, he was damn well going to have some fun with it.

Figuli is on the Around the World Panel. The placard in front of him has his name, number, and below them, his country. Slovakia. Next to him is Kevin Faulkner, Canada. Also on the panel are Theodore Smith, United States, and Christian Spitzweg, Germany.

Kevlar and Theo are Concord's top defensive pairing. Like Sophie and Elsa, they live together, and Sophie's talked to Kevlar more than once about the struggle of competing on the international stage against a NAHL teammate and friend. Spitzer holds his own on the panel, receiving nearly as many questions as the others.

Sophie has to remind herself that Spitzer isn't a kid anymore. She looks at him and sees the chubby cheeks and wispy blonde hair from his first season. But it's been years now, and his face has sharpened into prominent cheekbones and an angular chin. He still can't grow facial hair for love or money, but he's far from the nervous rookie Sophie first met.

Spitzer answers a question about the best part of being in the NAHL, and Sophie feels her first twinge of regret that she and Elsa are keeping their relationship a secret from their teammates. In the early days, when Sophie set the expectation that the Concord locker room would be a safe place, she got some pushback and a few eyerolls from her teammates. Spitzer was the one who asked her if she was so adamantly against homophobic slurs because she was gay or because she had realized he was. Has Spitz found someone who makes him as happy as Elsa makes her?

"A question for Figuli," the moderator says. "This was submitted via Twitter. Suzie from Thetford wants to know how it feels to be older than your new franchise?"

Figuli laughs, loud and unrestrained. It's hardly the first question he's gotten about his age, because Figuli is older than every one of his teammates and even some of the staff. Sophie hadn't thought about how he was older than the franchise itself.

"First, you ask me about rookies who were born in *my* rookie season and now you're asking about the franchise?" Figuli shakes his head, but he's still full of good cheer. It isn't as though he doesn't know how old he is or that it's going to be a major storyline. "Here's the thing, Suzie. You're lucky enough to be a fan of the Concord Condors, which means you've had a front seat to Sophie Fournier's career. You saw her break Kyle Sorkin's rookie point streak record in her first season and then Bobby Brindle's point streak record in her seventh season. If I don't play for decades, how else am I going to keep my records safe?"

"No hard feelings about the Maddow competitions, then?" the moderator asks.

"Would I have liked to win one or two more? Of course. But here's the thing about being in the league as long as I have been. I've learned to tell the difference between a skilled player and an elite one. We use elite too casually these days, but if ever a player in this generation deserved the title, it's Sophie Fournier."

Sophie's glad she's creeping on the panel, so no one is around to see her blush. But when she meets up with Figuli after his panel and before her next one, she confronts him about it.

"Laying it on a little thick there?" she asks.

Figuli slaps a hand to his chest as if she's wounded him. "I spoke only the truth."

"I can't believe you took Elsa home before me," Merlin complains as he joins their conversation. His red beard is trimmed short, but the hair on top of his head is longer, almost to his ears. He was Sophie's first friend on the team, way back in her own rookie season. He tried to convince her his nickname was Merlin because his hands are magic and not because hockey players aren't particularly inventive and Merlin isn't a huge leap from McArthur.

"You had quite the summer," Teddy says. "Training in Sweden, contract signing, training in Thunder Bay." For all that Teddy's tone is light, Sophie knows there's something pointed beneath it. Theodore Augereau is a goalie, and goalies are sharp. If anyone was going to see through Sophie and Elsa's carefully crafted narrative, it would be him.

"You forgot house planning," Sophie says with a smile. Then, before anyone can comment, she turns to Merlin and asks, "How's Skylar?" because his daughter always makes for a good distraction.

*

It's Saturday morning, and Sophie has a quick break between panels. She takes full advantage in the team kitchen, sitting at the table with a bowl of apple cinnamon oatmeal. Her phone is tuned in to the convention footage so she can grin at Bechs and Jonny's shenanigans during their panel.

Tanner Bechtol is a player who is stuck as a permanent rookie in Sophie's head with the energy and youth he brings to the team. Jonathan Kellman, on the other hand, is a veteran player known more for his fists than his skill. Sophie has seen Jonny drop the gloves and bloody another player for skating too close to Bechs. Right now, on the panel, Jonny has Bechs in a headlock, and he cheerfully teases the younger player as Bechs tries to squirm free.

Mary Beth strides into the kitchen, and her heels click unevenly on the floor. Between that and the pink dusting her cheeks, Sophie deduces that Mary Beth was in a rush to get here. And if Mary Beth is in a rush...

"What happened?" Sophie asks.

"Lauren Rizzo signed with the Cleveland Presidents," Mary Beth answers.

Boston is Concord's divisional rival, but Cleveland is their rival in the truest sense of the word. Michael Hayes, Sophie's longtime prep school rival then Concord teammate, was traded to Cleveland in their first season. In Sophie's second season, one of Cleveland's forwards took a run at Benoit Delacroix and wrecked his knee. And, of course, two years ago, Sophie tore her ACL in a game against Cleveland.

Any news about Cleveland will make waves, especially here in Concord, but there's something else. Mary Beth wouldn't be flustered by a simple signing. Yes, Rizzo is a veteran d-woman, and she was a pain in Sophie's ass at the Winter Games, first in Helsinki then last year in Boston, but, again, there's nothing panic worthy about the move.

"Denver wanted her," Mary Beth says and now Sophie pays close attention. "She declined to sign with them. According to Rizzo, the word's spread and no woman will play in Denver."

Well, shit, Sophie thinks. She stands up and tosses the rest of her oatmeal in the trash. "I assume there are reporters waiting for me. What do you want me to say?"

"The truth, of course," Mary Beth says.

Sophie snorts. When she was still shell-shocked from the draft, Sophie met Mary Beth for the first time. Mary Beth was straight with her. She told Sophie they would spin stories and craft narratives to everyone outside the room—to management, the team, the reporters—but between Sophie and Mary Beth, they would always speak the truth.

Sophie knows what Mary Beth means here. It's always better not to lie to the reporters, because it makes it difficult to keep track of what she said and when, but telling the truth doesn't always mean answering their questions.

She can't help but wonder if word started to spread after the draft this summer, when Sophie talked to this year's draftees about Anthony Sinclair. Or maybe Denver was a no-go zone before that. Sophie certainly has no love for the team, its style of play, or its coach.

She tucks all those feelings behind a carefully neutral face as she stands in front of a small assembly of reporters. She recognizes most of them. There's Ed Rickers from *The Granite State Sports Network* and Marty Owen from *The Concord Courier*. Rickers is a welcome sight. Marty Owen, as always, is not.

"Is it true what Lauren Rizzo said?" Marty Owen asks. "Women are boycotting the Denver Boulders?"

"I can't speak for every woman," Sophie says, and this

is the delicate dance of speaking to reporters. "From Rizzo's comments, it's clear she doesn't have an interest in playing for Denver. I don't, either, so that makes two of us. Does that extend to every woman in the league and every woman who might one day play in the league? I can't speak to their thoughts."

"You don't want to play for Denver?" The reporter who asks the question isn't one of Sophie's regulars. She has a lanyard proudly stating she's from *The National Sports Network*.

"I signed a ten-year commitment to Concord this summer," Sophie reminds her. "I'm exactly where I want to be."

The reporter from *TNSN* seems to recognize a conversational dead-end when she hears one. She pivots to a new topic. "Lauren Rizzo makes the sixth woman added to the NAHL this summer."

"We doubled our numbers," Sophie says. "Twelve women on ten different teams. It's representation on almost a third of the league's teams. We're making progress."

"Where do you think you'll be in your tenth season?" Rickers asks.

Sophie smiles politely and gives a bland answer. She, of course, is invested in the numbers. She wants there to be enough women in the NAHL that she doesn't have the numbers memorized. And she doesn't want her career measured by how many women are in the league. When Sophie plays in her tenth season, and that's just around the corner, she wants the focus to be on what *she's* achieved in that time; records, point totals, number of Cups.

*

On the Monday after the convention, Concord announces a trade. Golovin and Dunbeck have been traded to Cleveland for Drew Bowen, a prospect, and Cleveland's 2020 fourth round pick. Sophie's still reading through the details when her phone dings announcing that Cleveland has already flipped Golovin to Vancouver.

Sophie is glad Mr. Wilcox waited to finalize the trade until after the convention. She'll still have to answer questions about it, but it didn't cause a disruption to the convention itself.

Elsa is napping on the couch so when Mary Beth calls, Sophie waits until she's in the memorabilia room to answer. The memorabilia room is just that, a room dedicated to Sophie and Elsa's hockey achievements. One of the rookies described it as a shrine which isn't far off.

There's an entire wall devoted to international hockey with pictures and framed jerseys representing Sophie's time with Team Canada and Elsa's with Team Sweden. There's a wall displaying gifts from other players; signed sticks, signed jerseys, and other collectibles. The final two walls are for Condors hockey. There are milestone pucks for both Sophie and Elsa, the accomplishment and date noted on each puck in Ben Granlund's careful handwriting.

There are more milestones coming up this season. Sophie could hit five hundred career assists and eight hundred career points. Elsa is on the doorstep of three hundred career goals, and it isn't out of her reach to hit three hundred career assists and six hundred career points. That could be another five milestone pucks added to the collection. They'll need another display case to hold them all.

"I saw the trade announcement," Sophie tells Mary Beth when she answers the phone. Her gaze is drawn to the framed jerseys above the puck displays. There is one for Sophie, in the home red, with her captain's C in stark white. Elsa's is the home red as well, and it has her alternate's A.

"This isn't the first time a trade with Cleveland worked out well for us," Mary Beth says.

"Are you reassuring me or feeding me lines for the interviews you're scheduling?"

"Both." Mary Beth laughs lightly. "I'm a multi-tasker."

"I understand that when Bowen was a Cleveland President, he played true to his team's identity. I trust that within a few weeks of being a Condor, he'll play true to ours," Sophie says in her bland media voice.

"You're a superstar," Mary Beth tells her.

"Will you send me Bowen's phone number?" Sophie asks. "Unless you think he'll be flipped."

"From what I've heard, he's staying. It's only a matter of time before Kuzmich retires."

Sophie doesn't want to think about anyone retiring. She says her goodbyes to Mary Beth and gives Drew Bowen a call.

He picks up on the third ring. "Hello?" he asks warily.

Sophie doubts she's the first call from an unknown number Bowen has received today. "Hello. This is Sophie Fournier."

There's a long pause. "Word gets around quick, huh?"

"I wanted to welcome you to the Condors and make sure you have my phone number in case you need anything. I'm sure you have a lot to do, but you're part of our organization now."

"Uh, thank you."

Sophie puts them both out of their misery and wraps up the conversation quickly after that. Bowen isn't the first player to come to Concord via Cleveland. It's how Teddy became part of the team, after all, and Sophie's glad to have him as a teammate. Bowen isn't even the first player who doesn't like Sophie to come to Concord. Jonny played her tough when he was a Boulder, and she'd braced herself after his trade, prepared for him to carry the same attitude into Concord's locker room.

He didn't, though. She can only hope that Bowen is like Jonny in that way. She's fought too long and too hard to make a place for herself in the NAHL. She won't let someone like Bowen make her uncomfortable.

Chapter Five

"What's the plan for today, Cap?" Theo asks. He sits in his stall, his eyes closed, as he waits for the locker room to fill up.

The first day of training camp is Sophie's. There will be a meeting with management and the training staff later on, but the morning and afternoon workouts are hers to plan.

Training camp always follows a predictable pattern: captain's choice on the first day, the first skate of the season on the second day. As a veteran of the team, Theo knows what's on the schedule for today. But, as Sophie looks around the room and sees so many unfamiliar faces, she realizes a portion of the team doesn't know.

And some of them, like Bowen, eye her with suspicion. It sparks a bit of mischief, and Sophie adopts an airy tone. "Oh, you know, the usual. Trust falls, holding hands, singing about our feelings."

Kevlar laughs, then, after seeing the look of horror on Bowen's face, laughs even harder. "It's a joke. Sofe has a sense of humor."

"You'll *wish* we were doing trust falls," Merlin mutters.

"What was that?" Sophie asks. "Are you disrespecting a Concord tradition?" For the benefit of the newcomers in the room, she explains, "We have an annual historical run through the city. It was started by the captain before me, Dan Mathers. We see the historical landmarks, wave at a few fans, and get a light run in at the same time." Sophie reaches over to flick Merlin's ear. "In ten years, when you're in a rocking chair with only your memories to keep you company, you'll think on these runs with fondness."

"I'll be a spry forty-three in ten years," Merlin says. "If Figs can play until he's fifty, I can manage forty-three."

"I'm not playing until fifty," Figuli says, "I'm playing until I win a Cup. Which means I'm done after this season."

Half the players in the room hurry to knock on the nearest stall. Sophie's never held to superstitions. She couldn't afford to. She does, however, look over at Figuli. "Figs?" she echoes.

Figuli shrugs. "I've had worse names."

"Merlin tried to saddle me with Absalom after a late-night Wikipedia binge," Kevlar says. "It didn't stick. Unlike Marinara Man."

"Fuck you!" Peets calls from across the room.

Sophie laughs as Theo and Kevlar pull Figuli into a well-told story about Ivan Petrov's rookie season and how he fell asleep in his spaghetti at a team dinner. Sophie looks around the room as her teammates, or potential teammates, chat and prepare for the day. There are a few notable absences. Elsa isn't next to Sophie and Teddy is missing as well.

They scoot in just before they'd be considered late. Sophie's still tempted to let Merlin fine them for the offense. They're both veteran players, and Elsa has a letter on her jersey. They're supposed to be setting an example to others.

"It isn't my fault," Elsa says as soon as she spots Sophie's scowl. "Teddy ambushed me."

"He has chicken legs," Sophie says.

"Yeah, but he's scrappy," Elsa says. She crosses the room to where Sophie is. She smiles winningly, as if she expects Sophie to be so happy to see her that she forgives her.

The worst part is, Sophie feels her resolve weakening. "You're Merlin's partner for the run."

"Hey now, why am I a punishment?" Merlin asks.

"I thought I was your favorite," Elsa says.

"Captains don't have favorites," Sophie tells her. "But if they did—"

"Teddy would be your favorite," half of the room choruses.

"I can't argue with that," Sophie says. "Elsa and Merlin are together. Everyone else pair up, and we'll head out."

They run through downtown Concord and loop back to the facility for an extended core circuit in the parking lot. They end the morning session with another Concord tradition, a plank circle. Sophie keeps her title as last player planking, but Alex Jacobs, one of the young guys at camp, gives her the toughest competition she's had in a few years.

They return to the locker room for showers and a fresh change of clothes, then head to the team kitchen for a group lunch. Sophie's done this drill enough to fill a plate before scanning the room for a good mix of new and old players.

She sits at a table where Jacobs, Woodsy, and Zehavi are already sitting. Danny Zehavi, aka DZ, came to them from the Regina Rapids. He's a d-man with a protective streak that falls somewhere between hovering and suffocating, depending on the day. Sophie understands why he's like this, Pearce and Jo didn't have the healthiest relationship when both goalies played in Regina, but Sophie doesn't need DZ to protect her from her teammates.

"How did you like Dayton?" Sophie asks Jacobs. He played for the Dayton Demolishers when he was in Juniors. He might play for them again this season, depending on how training camp goes. When Sophie watched the Demolishers play, she was more focused on his teammate, Elizabeth Schatz, than Jacobs himself.

"How can anyone like Ohio?" Woodsy interjects. "It's flat and boring."

"Like your girlfriend!" someone calls out from another table.

Woodsy doesn't bother to turn and see who said it. Sophie glances over long enough to see that Kevlar has the situation well in hand before she turns her attention back to her table.

"We don't tolerate that kind of shit here," Woodsy tells Jacobs. "I played in Juniors, so I know what it's like. The NAHL is different. *Concord* is different," he amends. "You won't find a better place to play."

Sophie doesn't know the details of Woodsy's time in Juniors. She knows it was far from fun, both from what she's observed of Woodsy and the rumors she's heard about his team. The general consensus was hazing that went several steps too far. Sophie knows a thing or two about that. As the only girl on her teams growing up, she was often the target of not only the other team but her own as well.

She has worked to make Concord a better place to play than any of the teams she had growing up. She doesn't want anyone to step into Concord's locker room and feel afraid or like they have to hide part of themselves. From what Woodsy just said, the work has paid off.

"I'm glad," Jacobs says. He glances around as if he's nervous. "Uh, Bechs told me Elsa threatened to kill him because he high-sticked you at training camp."

"Bechs needs to stop spreading lies," Sophie says. "It was an accident."

"The high-stick or the death threats?" Woodsy asks. He grins because he knows he's stirring shit up.

"Eat your lunch," Sophie tells Jacobs. "We have another session this afternoon, and it doesn't get easier."

"Captain Mom," DZ mutters.

Sophie slowly looks up from her plate. As the color drains from DZ's face, Sophie allows a smile to stretch across her face. "What was that?"

"Nothing," DZ quickly says.

Sophie nudges his plate to the side so she can place his neglected bowl of salad in front of him. "Eat your vegetables. They're good for you." Sophie turns to wink at Jacobs, who bursts into surprised laughter.

*

On the second day of training camp, Teddy corners Sophie in the weight room. Everyone who knows her knows she likes to hop on the stationary bike and do some stretching before she steps onto the ice. It makes her predictable.

Teddy isn't the first teammate to join Sophie for part of her warmup. He won't be the last. But when he unrolls a yoga mat next to hers, Sophie feels the hairs on the back of her neck stand on end. Her body tries to warn her, but it's too late, because Teddy fixes her with an intense goalie stare.

"So," Teddy begins.

And Sophie knows in that moment that Teddy knows. She isn't sure what gave her and Elsa away. Maybe it was the way they stumbled to Sophie's car last night after dinner, exhausted and leaning on each other. Maybe it was the joke Kevlar made about Sophie and Elsa acting like a married couple as they negotiated who was going to drive.

It doesn't matter what clued Teddy in. What matters is that he knows, and no one is supposed to know. It isn't fair. Teddy was the one Sophie panicked at the first time she and Elsa shared a bed and she didn't know what it meant. He's the one she panicked at last year when she showed up to training camp and realized she wanted to kiss Elsa. He deserves so much more than the deflection Sophie's going to give him.

She looks around to make sure their part of the room is clear. "We aren't telling anyone," Sophie says softly.

"You—"

Sophie shakes her head and cuts off his questions. "We aren't telling anyone so I can't tell you anything."

Teddy is quiet, considering, long enough for Sophie to move into her next stretch. And then, equally quietly, he says, "Okay, then. Are you happy?"

Sophie's smile is an answer in itself, but she nods as well. "We are."

"Good." Teddy squeezes her shoulder. Then he makes a show of looking at the clock mounted on the wall. "You better hurry up if you want to be the first one on the ice."

"Like anyone else would dare," Sophie says, but she does rush the last of her stretches.

Something about a fresh sheet of ice resonates with her. The way it's smooth, without a single skate line etched into it. It's infinite possibilities stretching out in front of her, and there's something powerful in being the first to mark it.

As captain, it's Sophie's right to be the first one on the ice. She takes a moment to stand at the bench gate and look over the practice rink. She imagines all the drills she'll do here, all the goals she'll score, and even all the posts she'll hit. She hears the laughter of her teammates as they goof off between drills and their ragged breathing as they recover from bag skates.

Sophie draws in a lungful of frosty air and steps onto the ice. She skates two full loops of the rink before her team comes up the tunnel. Elsa stands guard at the gate and prevents anyone else from joining Sophie.

"Are you good?" Elsa asks.

"It's hard to play hockey by myself," Sophie answers.

With permission given, Sophie's teammates all join her on the ice. They have five different games of keep-away going by the time Coach Elison blows his whistle.

They all turn to him. He's by the benches in a Condors tracksuit. His whistle hangs down around his neck again. "I wanted to see if it still worked. It's been a long offseason, but we have hockey back."

Cheers go up through the rink.

*

Sophie's conversation with Teddy about Elsa or, rather, her non-conversation with Teddy about Elsa should have prepared her for having a similar conversation with Mary Beth. She's known since the contract signing that Mary Beth was going to want to have a talk about Elsa. The way Sophie deflects questions from the media and spins narratives, she learned those tricks from Mary Beth. It means Mary Beth is well-suited to seeing through them.

Over the summer, Sophie avoided the conversation by avoiding Mary Beth, which was easy, given the distance between them. It's much more difficult to avoid Mary Beth now that the season has begun.

Still, Sophie manages for a good five days, mostly because Figuli is the talk of the city, and Mary Beth spends most of her time wrangling him into interviews. But Mary Beth eventually corners Sophie in the equipment room. Sophie can't help but flick her gaze toward the door behind Mary Beth's shoulder. What are the chances someone will realize they absolutely have to have another roll of stick tape before they leave for the day?

Not likely.

"We need to have a chat," Mary Beth says.

"We really don't," Sophie says.

Mary Beth's eyes widen in surprise. "You've been difficult to find on purpose."

Sophie has been a model player for Concord's PR team. She entered the league with media training, she always does what she's asked, whether it's a one-on-one interview in a cashmere sweater, her hair gently curled to make her look soft, or opening her home to a camera crew who wants to do yet another special on the NAHL's first female player.

Sophie doesn't run her mouth to the cameras. She's mastered the art of deescalating stories before they can become a PR nightmare.

"I respect your wish for privacy," Mary Beth says. She speaks slowly, one word at a time, as if she's reworking the conversation she intended to have. "But we need contingency plans."

"We don't," Sophie says. "This isn't a topic available for discussion."

Sophie's heart beats faster, and she begins to sweat, under her arms and even the palms of her hands. She's never talked to Mary Beth like this before. She first met Mary Beth after her draft. Mary Beth led Sophie into a room full of men and stayed at Sophie's side so she wouldn't be on her own. They aren't friends, but they've been allies since Sophie entered the league.

"I have—" It's Sophie's turn to pause and think through her words. "I have given everything to this team. I have never complained. I have never made your job more difficult. I know what my role is, both on this team and in this league, but this topic is off limits. It's mine and I don't have any intention of sharing it with a wider audience."

Mary Beth pinches the bridge of her nose. "No matter how careful you are, you're going to slip at some point. We have to be prepared."

"Prepared for what?" Sophie asks. She schools her expression into her best blank look. After a moment, she lifts one shoulder in a shrug. "When we first met, you told me there couldn't be any lies between us. I am asking you not to push me on this. If you ask, if anyone asks, I will lie. This is the most important thing in my life, and I'm prepared to protect it."

Mary Beth looks as though she's marshalling another argument, but then the door opens behind her. Sophie has never been so happy to see Kevlar before in her life. He actually looks a little surprised at whatever is on her face, but he rallies quickly. "Are you almost done? A group of us are going to lunch together, and we didn't want to leave you behind."

"We're done," Sophie answers.

"We'll finish another time," Mary Beth says.

Kevlar looks between them, as if he isn't sure he wants to insert himself into this fight.

"We're done," Sophie repeats, firmer this time.

Mary Beth sighs and steps out of the way so she isn't blocking the door. "Go. Enjoy your lunch."

Sophie hooks her arm around Kevlar's when she reaches him. She half-drags him out of the room, and she doesn't slow down until they turn the corner, and the door is out of sight.

"Do you want to talk about it?" Kevlar asks.

"Not even a little bit," Sophie answers.

"All right. You know we have your back, no matter

what?" At Sophie's nod, Kevlar says, "We picked that Italian place you like. I told Theo to make sure Teddy was on the other end of the table, because he's stingy when it comes to sharing rolls."

Sophie leans in until she can bump her shoulder against Kevlar's. "Thank you."

*

Training camp gives way to preseason, and the number of people in the locker room dwindles as players are reassigned to Juniors, to Concord's minor league affiliate in Manchester, or cut entirely. Jacobs and Bowen both make it through the first round of cuts.

Sophie still hasn't talked to Bowen much. They exchanged more words during their phone call than they have since he arrived in Concord, but she doesn't know how to change that. He hasn't been hostile toward her, and there haven't been any leaks to *The Sin Bin* or *The Concord Courier* which might be associated with him. She doesn't need to be friends with everyone on her team, but she does need to have a better relationship than *don't outwardly despise each other*.

"Has anyone seen Bowen?" Sophie asks, one day before practice.

"The equipment room," Woodsy answers.

Sophie leaves to find him. She's hosting a team get-together at her house, and if she personally invites him, he'll feel obligated to go. She approaches the equipment room, but she slows her steps as she hears voices come from inside.

"Is this supposed to be intimidating?" Bowen drawls.

"No," Theo answers. "It looks like you're going to be a part of this team, so we wanted to make something clear to you."

"What's that?" Bowen asks.

It's Kevlar who answers. "No matter how much you hated her when you were in Cleveland, we've loved her more. Sophie is our captain, and if you have a problem with her at the helm, you should ask your agent for a trade now."

Sophie turns away from the door and returns to the locker room before she's caught eavesdropping. Her chest is tight with emotions she can't show. Her team loves her. She knew it but doesn't mind hearing it confirmed. Years of being on the outside, of only being accepted when she put up big numbers during games, they took their toll on her.

At Chilton Academy, her teammates' protection was conditional based on her performance. Concord is different. Part of it, she's sure, is that at the NAHL level, they recognize scoring isn't the only way to contribute. Sophie helps her team by winning faceoffs, by her defensive play, by a dozen little things.

But part of it is that this is *her* team. Her team supports her because she's her. She smiles to herself and only tones it down slightly as she enters the locker room.

"Did you find him?" Woodsy asks. He doesn't look up from the careful way he tapes his socks.

"Find who?" Jonny asks.

"I was looking for Bowen," Sophie answers. She notes who looks alarmed—Jonny, Teddy, and Merlin—because it means they knew Theo and Kevlar were cornering Bowen for a chat. "I couldn't find him. The weight room was empty."

Jonny visibly relaxes from where he's sitting next to Woodsy.

"That's because he's in the equipment room," Woodsy tells Sophie. "You looked in the wrong place. What did you need?"

"I wanted to invite him to the Mario Kart party,"

Sophie answers.

"Oh, he won't come," Bechs says breezily. "It's at your house and girls are scary. I bet your couch is covered in cooties."

"How are you only two years younger than me?" Sophie asks.

When Bowen enters the locker room, trailed by Theo and Kevlar, Bechs bounds over and grabs his arm. "Circle, circle, dot, dot." Bechs draws two circles on Bowen's skin with his finger and pokes him twice. "Now, you have your cootie shot. Which means no excuses to skip out on the party tonight."

Bowen rubs his arm and frowns at Bechs. "Seriously?"

"I have a lot of cousins," Bechs answers. "Brad was upset when Jilly reversed his cootie shot, and he thought he wouldn't be able to go to the tea party. I explained to him the shot was fake, and he could go to the party as long as he wasn't a dick, and then I got in trouble for saying dick in front of a bunch of kids." Bechs sighs.

Bowen, wisely, sidesteps Bechs's story. "Should I bring anything?" he asks Sophie.

Sophie points to Teddy, because volunteering her house means she absolves herself of all other responsibilities.

"Juice boxes?" Teddy asks. "Since apparently our team is made up of children?"

"Capri-Sun?" Bechs asks, excitedly.

"Children," Teddy repeats.

"I'm bringing popsicles shaped like rocket ships," Figuli says.

*

True to his word, Figuli brings four boxes of popsicles. There are two boxes of rocket ship popsicles and two boxes of crayon popsicles. Sophie shakes her head but makes space in her freezer for his offering.

"It's important to remember how to have fun," Figuli says, as if he's offering sage advice on hockey and not making up a bullshit excuse for his shopping.

"I know how to have fun. Come and watch this." Sophie brings Figuli back to the TV room where her teammates are setting up their tournament bracket. The TV room boasts seven different TVs and even more seating. Sophie leans over Spitz's shoulder, because he's writing down each player for the bracket. "Figs is in and he's Yoshi," Sophie says.

"What?" Theo's voice cracks on the word. "It's my turn!"

Sophie shrugs. "Seniority."

"You're still doing the dishes for the rest of the week," Kevlar says.

"No," Theo tells his d-partner. Then he points a finger at Sophie. "Did you plan this with him? That's fucking cheating."

Sophie didn't plan this with Kevlar, but Kevlar's laughter won't dissuade Theo. In fact, Theo takes this as confirmation, and he tackles Kevlar off the couch in order to wrestle and determine whether or not their deal about the dishes will hold up.

"This is why I don't have anything with sharp corners in here," Sophie tells Figuli. All the TVs are mounted on the walls where they won't be knocked over or broken by the frequent wrestling matches that happen in this room.

Figuli laughs and claps her on the shoulder. "You're going to be all right, Fournier."

Now that Figuli has taken the coveted Yoshi avatar, the next fight is over who gets to be Princess Peach.

Spitzer has to make a new bracket, and Sophie despairs, because her team is arm wrestling over who gets to be Princess Peach riding on a motorbike in a silly racing game.

"Wait, Bowen is Bowser?" Bechs asks after they finally assign characters to everyone.

"Heh." Jonny nudges Bowen with his elbow. "Bowser."

Bowen rolls his eyes. "That's the best you can come up with?"

"Trust me and take it," Kansas advises. Eric Minei was stuck with the nickname Kansas after he compared Concord to his former team, Detroit, one too many times. Of course, the most embarrassing part of that is that now whenever the rookies get drunk, they try to serenade him with "Somewhere Over the Rainbow".

Again, this is Sophie's team, the one she hopes to win the Maple Cup with this season.

Elsa comes up beside Sophie, and she slides an arm around Sophie's waist and tugs her against her side. "They're great," Elsa says.

"I wouldn't trade them for anything," Sophie says, and she means it.

Chapter Six

The preseason kicks off in Washington DC. Sophie is one of several players who stay in Concord while the rest of the team fly out. The preseason is designed as a tune-up for those guaranteed to make the team and a final test for the players still on the bubble. As the captain and the cornerstone of the franchise, it isn't important for Sophie to play in every game.

She makes her debut in the home game against Philadelphia, and she embarrasses Scott Pearce as he makes his first appearance of the preseason. The next game is in Vancouver and Sophie, once again, is left behind.

Even worse, Elsa makes the flight to the west coast which means Sophie's house is too big and empty. HGTV isn't as fun to watch without Elsa criticizing every choice the house hunters make. Sophie can't watch any of their other shows, either, because she relies on Elsa to remind her what happened in the last episode and whether Sophie likes certain characters or not.

After a brief on-ice session with the assistant coaches then a longer stint in the weight room, Sophie isn't ready to go home. Instead, she puts on a light jacket, fills her pockets with Sharpies in case she runs into any fans, and drives to the grocery store.

Sophie is recognized around the city. Especially with the season on the horizon, her face is on billboards, in commercials, and even on a set of memorabilia cups on sale at one of the local gas stations.

There are times when Sophie has her groceries delivered, because she doesn't want the hassle of going to the store or she can't afford the distraction of being noticed, but she doesn't mind it today. She's staring at a wall of various kinds of bread when someone clears their throat next to her.

"I don't like sesame bagels."

Sophie turns to see a little boy standing next to an even younger girl. The girl is the one who spoke and, encouraged by Sophie's acknowledgment, she continues, "My mom says they're better for you than plain bagels, but I pick all the seeds off."

"Are plain bagels your favorite?" Sophie asks.

The girl shakes her head, and her bangs fall into her eyes. She impatiently pushes them back. "Blueberry is the best."

"Only if you put peanut butter on them," the boy says.

"Ew. That's gross."

"I like peanut butter on my cinnamon raisin bagels," Sophie tells the kids. She's almost certain they are siblings. They have the kind of back-and-forth that reminds Sophie of her relationship with Colby. "But if I buy English muffins, I can put eggs on them."

"Eggs are icky," the girl says.

"They're a grown-up food," the boy says, "but you're a grown-up so it's okay."

"And you're a hockey player!" The girl beams at Sophie, proud of having this knowledge. "You can get *both*. Mom says we can't play hockey, because she doesn't know how she'd feed us. Are you really a garbage disposal? That's what she calls Uncle Dan."

Sophie laughs and pulls a sleeve of bagels and a sleeve

of English muffins off the shelf. "Elsa and I do eat a lot, but it's the fuel we need to play hockey." She looks around in search of the mother they mentioned.

The girl also looks around and frowns at whatever she sees—or doesn't see. "Where's Elsa?"

"She's in Vancouver," Sophie answers. "There's a preseason game tonight."

"Why aren't you with her? Are you fighting?" The girl sniffs loudly and wipes her nose, as if she's prepared to burst into tears if Sophie and Elsa are indeed fighting.

"We aren't fighting," Sophie promises. "During the preseason, Coach Elison is still determining who will be on the team so there are too many of us to play every night. I'm sitting this one out, but I'll play against DC in two days."

"The games are too late for me to watch." The girl's tears threaten to spill over.

"We have an open practice tomorrow afternoon," Sophie says. She crouches down so she's on the same level as the girl and her brother. "You could ask your mom if you can go after school is over. You'll be able to stand against the glass and wave to us while we skate."

"Can we bring a sign? People always have signs on TV." The girl claps her hands together at Sophie's nod. "I'm going to wear my Fournier shirt. Will you sign it if I do?"

"Of course," Sophie promises. She holds her hand out. "I'm Sophie Fournier."

"I know that." The girl giggles and shakes Sophie's hand. "I'm Alicia. This is my brother Dan."

Sophie shakes Dan's hand next, then stands up. She's about to suggest they go find their mother when a harried-looking woman rushes over.

"We found Sophie Fournier!" Alicia says before her mom can scold her. "Can we go to practice tomorrow?

Everyone's invited. We need poster paper so we can bring a sign."

"I don't remember saying yes," the woman says, but she smiles at both her children, which they recognize as a yes. "But I suppose if you've been invited, we can make time to go. Now, say goodbye to Ms. Fournier, and we'll pick out the bread you were supposed to be getting."

Sophie grins and meanders over to the fresh produce where she is asked for three autographs in the time it takes her to pick out the perfect eight apples.

*

Sophie puts the groceries away when she gets home, then she naps, because she wants to stay up for the game tonight, and it's starting at seven west coast time. She passes the rest of the afternoon cooking several dinners that she then stores in the fridge or freezer to heat up later this week when she doesn't have the energy to cook.

Time still drags. By the time the game starts, Sophie is settled into her bed. She's already brushed her teeth and changed into her pajamas so she can fall asleep as soon as the game is over. The bed is too big without Elsa in it. Sophie turns up the volume on the pregame coverage and feels sorry for herself.

Before things can get too bad, her phone rings.

It's Dima.

"Hello," Sophie says, answering the call. "Doesn't Boston have a game tonight?"

"They left their captain behind," Dima says with a fake sniffle.

"Ah. This is the Sad Captains Club?"

"Yes. We play Denver tonight. Hertz is there. He'll protect our sapling."

Sophie doesn't like playing against Hertz. He's a

heavy hitter who finishes checks most players would pull up on, and he always has one or two borderline hits per game. But she's glad he's on the ice with Schatz tonight, because Dima isn't, and she needs someone looking out for her.

"Do you actually call her that?" Sophie says.

"Team calls her Lizard. Sapling is my special name."

"She's a good kid," Sophie says. Then she groans as a picture of her face pops up on the TV. "I'm not even playing. Why are they talking about me?"

The panel shows Sophie's statistics from last season and the season before. They compare her historic start two seasons ago with her start last season and come to the conclusion she's reached her peak and is now in the decline of her career.

"Ugh," Sophie says. "Apparently, I'm not living up to my own standards, my career is over, and Concord should trade me before my no movement clause kicks in."

"Bullshit," Dima says. "What would I do without my best rival?"

"Fade into obscurity and mediocrity, probably." Sophie mutes the TV. She knows better than to listen to this garbage.

"You know how to make me feel good," Dima says sarcastically.

"Not that kind of phone call," Sophie tells him.

Dima chokes on his laugh.

They fall into a companionable silence as they watch their respective teams play. Sophie cheers when Elsa scores a goal, and Dima cheers when Hertz and Rawlings fight. It isn't as good as watching a game with her teammates and it isn't nearly as good as playing, but it isn't lonely, at least.

*

Sophie has a vague recollection of waking up when Elsa came home. She thinks she may have fought Elsa for the pillows and lost. In the morning, Sophie is no longer clutching the pillow she fell asleep with in her arms. She does, however, have Elsa curled up behind her with an arm wrapped tightly around her waist.

It takes some time to extricate herself from Elsa's grip, because she doesn't want to wake Elsa up. She slips downstairs, eats a light breakfast, and reads quietly on the couch until Elsa makes her way downstairs.

Elsa's hair is tousled from sleep, and her eyes are half-closed as she shuffles into the room. Her shirt skims the top of her thighs, and she isn't wearing pants. Elsa's toes still have flecks of gold nail polish from their trip to the salon in Thunder Bay. Her thin ankles give way to strong calves and even stronger thighs.

Sophie has seen Elsa use her legs to power her from one end of the ice to the other. She's seen the bulge and strain of muscle as Elsa does squats in the weight room. She knows what those thighs feel like clamped around her waist. And she knows how easily Elsa spreads her legs when Sophie runs her hands up them and parts them.

Elsa smirks a little, looking more awake once she catches Sophie staring. "Come back to bed."

"I'll start the coffee maker," Sophie says instead.

Elsa groans. She makes another valiant attempt to persuade Sophie back upstairs. She tugs her to her feet and twists her fingers in Sophie's shirt. "Bed," she repeats. "I promise I won't sleep. You won't either."

Sophie is tempted, but then she remembers the big hit Elsa took in the third period of last night's game. "Lift up your shirt."

Elsa obediently pulls up her shirt. There's a dark bruise blooming against her side. As much as Sophie would like to return to bed with Elsa, she isn't going to risk hurting her. Sophie drops Elsa's shirt and heads for the kitchen. "You should eat breakfast and then you should ice."

"All right," Elsa says, and the bruise must ache if she's giving in so easily. She follows Sophie into the kitchen and hovers by her side as Sophie starts the coffee machine. Once Sophie isn't touching the coffee maker, Elsa pinches her side. "You should eat too."

"You sound like your mother," Sophie says.

Elsa grins, as if this is something to be proud of. "My mama's smart."

Sophie bypasses Elsa to grab the eggs and a few Tupperware containers of chopped vegetables out of the fridge. "What kind of eggs are we having?"

"Scrambled," Elsa answers.

Sophie slices two English muffins and puts them in the toaster.

"Don't turn it on," Elsa says. "You have to time it correctly or they'll be overdone."

Sophie holds up her hands and backs away from the toaster. "As always, I defer to your breakfast expertise."

"You're a brat," Elsa tells her.

Sophie laughs and blows her a kiss.

*

Sophie arrives earlier to open practices than regular practices because she wants a chance to interact with the fans who came to show their support. She isn't the only one to show up early. She chats with Jonny and Kuzy in the locker room as she changes into her Condors gear.

Merlin bursts into the room with Theo on his heels. They're both red-faced, and at first Sophie thinks it's because they sprinted here, then she realizes they're *laughing.*

"There's—" Merlin laughs too hard to finish.

Kevlar pushes through Merlin and Theo and while he looks amused, he isn't speechless because of it. "Wait until you see one of the signs," he tells her.

Sophie's stomach sinks, and she worries about what's waiting for her out there. It can't be too bad if Kevlar also thinks it's funny, but Merlin's crying now because he's laughing so hard. Sophie follows her teammates up to the practice rink to see what's caused all this commotion.

It doesn't take her long to find the culprit. It's a pink poster reading *I hope you make the team!* and it has Sophie's number carefully stenciled in each corner.

"Oh, fuck," Sophie says, too quietly for her voice to carry beyond her teammates. Then Alicia and Dan pop out from behind their poster to wave at her.

"Wow, you must be really worried Coach Elison is going to cut you if you're recruiting the cute kid vote," Jonny teases.

Sophie is never going to live this down. She's prepared to brush past her teammates and go say hi to Alicia and Dan when Coach Elison comes over to join them. He looks uncharacteristically solemn, and he rests a hand on Sophie's shoulder to claim her attention.

"Are you feeling unsure of your place on the team?" Coach Elison asks.

Sophie opens her mouth, prepared to answer, then she realizes he's joking. He catches the outrage on her face and he laughs, openly and loudly. Sophie is glad for this obvious sign that Coach Elison is nothing like the coach she had for her first six seasons.

Coach Butler preferred his players off-balance. Sophie never felt entirely comfortable with her place on the team, not even after her first contract extension or being named the captain. Coach Butler wanted to be the ultimate authority, and he wanted to make sure everyone felt dependent on him. He also didn't have a sense of humor.

Coach Elison does, even if Sophie isn't too fond of it at the moment. She can't openly scowl at her coach, so she reserves her dark look for Merlin instead. Over Merlin's shoulder, she spots Dan and Alicia still waving enthusiastically at her.

Sophie waves back, then she grabs Merlin's arm. "You wanted a front row seat to this? You have it now."

"Wait, what?" Merlin protests, but Sophie is already dragging him up and into the stands.

They make quick progress on their way to Dan and Alicia. Once they reach the two kids, Sophie crouches down so she doesn't loom over them. "Thank you for coming," she tells them.

"Do you like our sign?" Alicia is in a red T-shirt with the Condors logo on the front. It's a couple sizes too large and it hangs down like a dress. She taps the large 93s on the corners of the sign. "Mom outlined the numbers and then I colored them in."

"I do like it," Sophie says. "So does Merlin. Did you know that he saw your sign and then ran all the way to the locker room to tell me about it?"

"Really?" Alicia asks. She turns her youthful earnestness on Merlin, and Sophie feels a vicious bite of satisfaction at the guilt which briefly crosses his face.

There was a time when Sophie wasn't confident enough to handle the inevitable joking that will come from this sign. Her teammates will give her a hard time about it for a few weeks, and she's sure one or two hockey outlets will run with a story. Sophie doesn't blame Alicia and Dan for the sign, and she can't even muster up more than vague annoyance with the storylines it will spawn.

Despite Coach Butler's best attempts to tear her down, Sophie knows her importance to Concord. She is their captain. She is the face of the franchise. She led them to their first Cup, and she signed a ten-year extension this summer, because Concord wants her at the helm for the next decade. This is her place, her team, her *home*.

It doesn't mean she won't use this opportunity to make Merlin squirm. She smiles sweetly at him before she turns back to Alicia. "Do you want to tell Merlin how long you worked on your poster for?"

"Hours!" Alicia chirps, missing the interplay between Sophie and Merlin. "Do you think it looks good, Mr. Merlin?"

"It looks very good," Merlin tells her.

"Will you sign it after practice?" Alicia asks.

"I can sign it now," Merlin tells her. Sophie hands him a Sharpie, and he kneels to scrawl his name on the sign. "After practice, I can probably round up the rest of the team so they can sign it as well. We're glad you came to watch."

Sophie can't help but smile as she takes the marker from Merlin so she can add her own name. Merlin does tease her, but she puts up with it, because he's a good guy. She's almost certain he'll use this as chirping material for the next month, but he doesn't direct any of that at the kids. He's kind to them, generous, and she's pretty sure he now has two new fans in Alicia and Dan.

"Have you made the team yet?" Dan asks. "Because we can cheer for you too if you need it."

"I would love it if you cheered for me," Merlin answers.

*

After practice, Sophie's asked by their local reporters about her passionate fans. Unlike Sophie's teammates, whose teasing was mostly fond, there's something darker lurking beneath the reporters' questions.

Or, in Marty Owen's case, plain fucking stupid.

"You seem to like kids," Marty Owen says, which is a lead-in to the *when are you quitting hockey to have babies?* question. If he dares to ask it, Sophie is walking out. Fortunately, even Marty Owen recognizes there's a line he shouldn't cross, and he pivots to, "They seem concerned you and Nyberg won't make the team. Is this a concern you share?"

"It isn't," Sophie answers.

"There were two kids in particular who were very enthusiastic," Ed Rickers says. "I think I heard some adapted softball cheers mixed in with their chanting."

"They're passionate and they love what they love," Sophie says.

"What about Figuli?" Marty Owen asks.

"I don't think anyone can doubt his passion or love for hockey," Sophie answers.

Marty Owen huffs as if Sophie's being difficult. "He's only played in one preseason game, and he isn't set to play in anymore. Is he in danger of not making the team?"

"Preseason is for Coach Elison and the rest of the coaching staff to evaluate their players and test different line combinations. Figuli has enough of a résumé that he doesn't need to play in every preseason game."

"Will we see you two on a line together this season?" Rickers asks.

"It's an eighty-three-game season," Sophie says. "So, my guess is yes, at some point you'll see us on a line together, but I doubt we'll be regular linemates. Figuli's time in the league has honed him into a precision passer. He's a playmaker, first and foremost, which is also my primary strength. We'll be more effective on different lines."

"Does Coach Elison share your view?" Marty Owen asks. Before Sophie can answer, he calls out, "Coach Elison, do you expect Fournier and Figuli to be linemates this season?"

Sophie looks over her shoulder, and she's surprised to see Coach Elison headed toward her scrum. Few people in the North America Hockey League enjoy being in front of the reporters, whether they're players, part of the coaching staff, or even management.

Coach Elison still has his whistle around his neck from practice. He's in a black tracksuit with red piping and the Condors logo over the left breast. He comes to a stop next to Sophie, and he offers a mild smile to the reporters. "The season is too long for me to say they'll never play together, but it won't be common."

Sophie doesn't successfully hide her smile. Coach Elison spots her expression and chuckles softly. "How close were our answers?"

"Not an exact match," Rickers answers, "but close enough to be boring."

Coach Elison laughs a little louder, clearly in a good mood today. "We save all our excitement and pizazz for when we're on the ice."

"Pizazz?" Danielle Rossetti echoes.

"You know." Coach Elison wiggles his fingers in what might be an impression of jazz hands.

Sophie isn't entirely sure what he's doing, but Danielle Rossetti's judgmental eyebrows mean he'll be the one teased instead of Sophie, at least for the rest of the day.

Chapter Seven

Sophie could play ten thousand games and never grow tired of hockey. She stands on her defensive zone blue line as the Canadian national anthem is played, in deference to their opponents tonight, the Quebec Bobcats.

The Canadian anthem fills her with pride. Faint memories of receiving her gold medals at the Winter Games drift through her as she listens to the words she's known by heart since she was a little girl. She doesn't feel the same pride for the American anthem, but it's become familiar to her. "The Star-Spangled Banner" means Condors hockey which, in its own way, reminds her of home.

The singer holds the final note, voice echoing through the stadium.

Then the fans cheer, the public address announcer thanks their singer, and Sophie steps off the blue line.

It's time for hockey.

She takes the first faceoff of the season against Coderre, Quebec's top line center. She wins it, then both teams spring into action. Kevlar chips the puck into the offensive zone, and Sophie chases it down.

Sophie and Taylor Sorkin race for the puck. Sophie sees Elsa coming from the side, a stride ahead of them. She knocks Sorkin into the boards and pins him there as Elsa snaps up the puck. Sophie keeps Sorkin out of the play until

Elsa has possession of the puck and is on the move.

As soon as Sophie lets Sorkin up, he slashes her ankles with his stick. She ignores the stinging pain and drops down to Gabrielle's net. She doesn't force her way into the blue paint yet, but she keeps her stick on the ice as a target for Elsa to pass to.

Elsa's pass lands right on the white tape of Sophie's blade. She twists and shoots the puck, but Gabrielle shifts, and the puck hits her solidly in the logo on her jersey. The puck drops to the ice, and Gabrielle covers it before Sophie can take a second jab at it.

The official blows the play dead. LG, one of Gabrielle's d-men, cheerfully shoves Sophie out of Gabrielle's crease as the goalie hands the puck over to the official.

Sophie skates the bench for a line change and so someone else can try to score on Gabrielle. Sophie will have plenty more opportunities before the game is over.

The next line with a shot at Gabrielle is their third line. When Sophie told her reporters she and Figuli wouldn't make good linemates because their style of play was too similar, she meant it. She didn't tell them she's glad they aren't linemates because it means she can sit on the bench and watch him play.

Figuli has lost most of the speed he used to be known for, but he makes up for it with economical movement. He looks faster than he is because he's precise. The players defending him have to stop and start as they try to predict his movements and cut them off while he slides through their clumsy attempts.

Alex Jacobs, the other winger on the third line, gets caught watching Figuli, and he fumbles the puck when Figuli passes to him. The puck jumps over his stick and it's Quebec's player who reaches the loose puck first.

When Jacobs returns to the bench, he knows he had a bad shift. He doesn't need Coach Elison's barked, "Quick gawking and play!" but he nods dutifully as he shuffles down the bench to sit. He blanches when he realizes the only seat is next to Sophie. He takes it and hunches his shoulders as if he expects her to lecture him as well.

"He's pretty good, eh?" Sophie asks.

Jacobs stops staring at his skates. He glances at her uncertainly.

"Figs," Sophie says. She isn't a stranger to awed or even cowed rookies. She still remembers her first NAHL season, and the first game in that season. It's as overwhelming as it is exhilarating. Coach Elison has already set himself as the disciplinarian which means she can be the nice captain. "There's a reason Figs has played for so long. He has the talent. I wouldn't mind scoring off one of his passes." She gives Jacobs a significant look. "It would be a hell of a way to score your first NAHL goal."

Jacobs meets her gaze and nods, agreeing with her.

"So do it," she tells him. "The next time you step on the ice, expect that he's going to get you the puck. Make sure you know what you're going to do with it once you have it." She nudges his shoulder with hers. "Once they're replaying your goal on the jumbotron, you can stare as much as you want."

"Elsa scored four goals off your assists in her first NAHL game," Jacobs says, which means he's watched footage of the team.

Elsa, hearing her name, joins the conversation by draping a heavy, possessive arm over Sophie's shoulders. "Sophie is *my* center."

Sophie laughs and elbows Elsa gently in her side. "Quit trying to scare him. It's you and me. This season and then ten more."

Elsa bumps their helmets in acknowledgement.

*

Gabrielle and Teddy each stand tall in their nets. Elsa

scores an ugly goal in the second period which stands as the only goal as time winds down on the game. With a little over a minute left, Quebec pulls Gabrielle for the extra attacker.

With six attackers on the ice, Quebec launches an assault on Teddy's net. Kevlar lives up to his name and blocks a number of shots. When the puck makes it through the defense, Teddy kicks it harmlessly out of the way.

Another shot makes it through. Sophie watches from the bench as Teddy, fed up with the fuss in front of his net, gets his paddle on the puck and flings it down the ice. Figs chases the puck out of the zone.

He reaches it before LG does, and he dances around the defenseman and sends the puck toward the empty net. Without Gabrielle to protect the net, Figs scores an easy goal.

The crowd chants for him, as loud for his first goal as a Condor as they had been when Elsa scored the first goal of the season. Sophie leaps to her feet with the rest of the bench to welcome Figs and his line with a fist bump.

Coach Elison sends Sophie's line out to finish the game.

*

The second game of the season is against Toronto. Before the game, when they're still in the locker room getting ready, Teddy stands on one of the benches and clears his throat to gain the room's attention.

"A moment of silence, please," he requests. "After tonight, I will no longer be tied in the points race with Sophie Fournier." He bows his head.

Sophie wads up a ball of tape and throws it at his head. She laughs as it bounces off the part of his brown hair and falls to the floor. "You're so full of shit."

"And you shouldn't doubt yourself," Kevlar tells Teddy. "How do you know you won't assist on every goal this game?"

"Maybe Sophie won't get on the board," Bechs says.

Sophie grabs Elsa's arm before she can throw the entire roll of tape at Bechs.

*

Merlin scores the first goal of the game, and Teddy has the secondary assist on it. They're up 1-0 over Toronto late in the first period, and Sophie's spirits are high as Teddy plays up his assist. He pulls his mask off so every camera in the building can pick up on his exaggeratedly shocked face.

Sophie laughs as Merlin and his line skate by the bench to celebrate the goal.

"Teddy for the Maddow?" Figs jokes.

Sophie only laughs harder, then she takes her line over the boards for a chance at the second goal of the game.

The honor ends up going to Toronto when Matty opens up the second period with a wrister that beats Teddy high glove side. It ties the game, but Sophie won't let that stand. She plays a hard shift following Matty's goal, and she slides a cross-ice pass to Woodsy, which ends with the puck in the back of the net.

Concord has the lead back, and Sophie has tied Teddy in the points race. Still bubbly, because the season is new, and her team is playing well, Sophie decides to have a little fun. She points down the ice at Teddy so he knows they both have two assists on the season.

He points back with two fingers as if to say *I have my eye on you.*

When Figs notches a power play goal off a pass from

Elsa which originated with Sophie, Teddy removes his mask and wipes away fake tears. It's ridiculous and the kind of fun they would never have if Butler was still their coach. It isn't the kind of fun they'd have if the game was tighter than it was or if they were deeper in the season.

But everyone is light with the new season and winning always keeps everyone relaxed. Of course, it isn't subtle, and Sophie isn't surprised when Napoli grabs her for the second intermission interview.

The CondorsTV crew crowds her and Napoli, pressing close even though she's sweating profusely and no doubt reeks. She wipes her face with a towel, only for new sweat to bead up and takes its place on her skin.

"Everyone is wondering, what is with your goaltender tonight?" Napoli asks.

"He's a goalie," Sophie answers, as if that explains everything. And it does. Goalies are weird. It's a basic fact. But just as basic, and even more important, is this: always love your goalie. And Sophie does. She loves Teddy, shenanigans and weird habits included.

"This is odd, even for a goalie," Napoli says, unwilling to let her off the hook.

Napoli is only trying to do his job, and while there are times Sophie aims to make it more difficult, this isn't one of them. Her team is having fun, and there's no harm in inviting the fans to join them. "After our first game, Teddy and I were tied in the points race, and we were joking about it. He's mourning the fact that Figs's goal put me ahead of him."

"An offensive-minded goalie? There's a first." Napoli chuckles and claps Sophie on the shoulder. "Congratulations on your five-hundredth assist, Sophie."

"Thanks, Derek." Sophie wipes her face with her towel again and joins her team in the locker room. Five hundred assists. Another milestone to add to her growing collection.

*

After the two home games to start the season, the Condors have an extended road trip. The day before they fly out, Merlin hosts a Leftover Party at his house. Sophie didn't ask questions, too relieved to have someone else hosting a team event. The general idea was that everyone would show up to Merlin's house, bring with them any food that might go bad while they're on the road trip, then they'd prepare and eat all of it.

Sophie thinks maybe she should have asked more questions. Or imposed some rules.

"Hey, it was Figs's idea," Merlin says when Sophie and Elsa arrive, as if he can sense Sophie's judgement. "Also, no need to watch your fucking language."

Sophie isn't a stranger to hockey players or swearing, but even for them, she thinks that was an unnecessary use of the word fuck.

Merlin just grins and says it again. "Skylar's on a play-date so I can swear as much as I want."

Skylar is Merlin's daughter. She'll turn two soon, and as cute as she is, Sophie's glad she doesn't have a kid. Marissa has had to cut back on her hours (she works as a nurse at Dartmouth-Hitchcock in Concord), and Merlin isn't as involved with the team as he was when he didn't have a kid.

Sophie must still be making a face, because Merlin feels the need to defend himself. "Once you have kids, you'll understand." Now it's Merlin's turn to make a face, because Sophie and her relationships and prospective progeny are forbidden topics. "I mean, whenever you decide to have kids. Uh. *If* you decide to have kids."

"I would quit digging now," Elsa advises. She breezes past Merlin and heads into the kitchen with her box of perishables.

"What about you?" Merlin asks, because if he isn't

sticking one foot in his mouth, he's cramming the other one in instead. "Are you ready for a miniature shitting machine?"

"How does having a baby even work if you're an active player?" Theo asks, as if Sophie is the expert.

Now that they're in the kitchen, they're surrounded by teammates, and all of them are invested in Sophie's answer. She offers up a shrug, then, because it's inadequate, adds, "Stewie did it, but she plays in the NAWHL. I'm not sure if I'd be able to take a season off, have a baby, and then be back in hockey shape in time to make the roster for the next season."

She knows what it's like to go down with injury partway through a season. In her seventh season, she tore her ACL. It took her the rest of the season to recover enough to be allowed back on the ice. And even with her offseason training, she wasn't at her best last season. Would recovering from pregnancy follow a similar trajectory? If so, she won't be having any babies until after hockey is over. If she even decides to have a baby. Maybe Elsa wants to be pregnant. Maybe they'll adopt. Maybe they won't even have kids.

Sophie scowls at Merlin, because it's his fault everyone's thinking about this now.

"What would you even do with the baby?" Bechs asks. Kevlar elbows him, too sharp for it to be friendly. Bechs whines and rubs his side. "Ow! What was that for?"

"For assuming our captain is getting herself knocked up and then abandoned by some rando," Kevlar answers.

"Oh." Before Bechs can apologize, his face twists in a way that suggests he's remembering it takes *two* people to have a baby and in order for Sophie to be pregnant, she'd probably have to have sex.

Kevlar elbows Bechs again. "And that's for thinking about our captain having sex."

"And, new topic of conversation," Sophie announces, because this is veering too close to territory she wants to remain firmly forbidden. She ignores her teammates who are clearly bristling with more questions in order to sift through the various fruits, vegetables, meats, and other food assembled on the counter.

She frowns as she holds up a loaf of white bread that has blue-green mold creeping up the side. "This is already past its prime. Why give birth to children when I have a team full of them?" She picks up a package of salmon steaks and studies it from various angles. "Is this party going to end with food poisoning? What's the expiration date on this?"

"Is that for me?" Figs asks. He comes in from the patio. He has a grill brush in one hand and a tool belt around his waist with other utensils, proving that hockey players of all ages can be idiots.

"Will it offend the King of the Grill if we use the oven for some of this?" Sophie asks. She finds a bundle of asparagus and sets it aside with the salmon.

"King of the Grill?" Figs echoes.

It's a tradition left over from when Matty was captain. He was the King of the Grill and after he left, there was an opening. It wasn't until Jonny came to them from Denver that anyone settled into the role. There don't seem to be any bruised feelings or hurt pride over Figs taking over while he's here.

"How do you have a king without a crown?" Jacobs asks.

Theo looks over at Kevlar, stricken. "A crown? How come we never realized we needed a crown? We need to fix this. Merlin, you have a kid, right? You must have crafting supplies."

"She's too young," Merlin answers.

"All right, new plan," Theo says. "Jacobs, this was

your idea, so you're in. Kansas, you're coming too. Kevlar, obviously. There's space for two more."

"Where are you going?" Sophie asks but none of them answer.

She doesn't find out until they return from Burger King with one hundred chicken fries, minus the few they ate on the ride back, and a cardboard crown. Sophie lends a permanent marker to the cause, and Spitzer writes KING OF THE GRILL in surprisingly neat block letters on the crown. And then, crown acquired, they have to conduct a ceremony where they officially name Figs King of the Grill.

Jonny records the whole thing and sends it to the group chat. Sophie has a feeling it'll end up in one of Napoli's segments or on the team's Twitter feed.

"This is our team," Elsa murmurs, coming up behind Sophie so she can talk quietly in her ear.

Sophie leans back against Elsa and watches as Bechs claims the Sharpie. Then, because he's a boy with a Sharpie, he starts trying to draw dicks on anyone who stands still long enough. Sophie's team scatters, and she shakes her head at the chaos.

"We committed to another ten years of this."

Elsa takes advantage of everyone's preoccupation to squeeze Sophie's hips. "I wouldn't choose to be anywhere else."

Neither would Sophie, and she inked that promise for all the hockey world to see this summer. She turns her head until her cheek brushes Elsa's. It isn't quite a kiss, but it's an intimate gesture, one they can get away with even at a team event.

Chapter Eight

Sophie's thoughts have centered on her injury and her slow recovery from it, but she isn't the only one reflecting on her past seasons and performances. The first game of their road trip is in New York City. They're handed their first loss of the season, and Sophie doesn't notch so much as a secondary assist.

"There's no point streak to start this season," Marty Owen says. "At least, not one worth talking about."

In Sophie's seventh season, the one where she tore her ACL, she set a NAHL record before her injury. She had a point streak which lasted twenty-one games. Then she tore her ACL against Cleveland, and she was forced to sit up in the press box and watch as Chad Kensington broke her record with a twenty-two-game point streak. Last season, when Sophie was healthy again and cleared to play, she picked up her point streak where she had left it. She opened the season with at least a point in another twenty-one consecutive games.

According to the record book, Sophie once again is the holder for most consecutive games with a point or more. According to assholes like Bobby Brindle, Sophie's streak doesn't count because it spans two seasons.

Then there's Marty Owen who will find any way he can to tear her down. Well, that isn't quite fair. He does the same to everyone on the Condors. This is Sophie's ninth season with the team and Marty Owen has been here for all nine of them. She still isn't sure he even likes hockey.

"Chad Kensington is off to a hot start," Marty Owen continues, as if Kensington should be the name associated with point streaks and not Sophie's. "Indianapolis as a team is. They're three-for-three in the win column. With back-to-back Cups and now playing with this kind of fire, do you think they're making a bid for the consecutive Cups record?"

Sophie's lips thin out, but she limits her reaction to that small movement. Back in the eighties, the Montreal Mammoths set a NAHL record by winning five Maple Cups in a row. Right off the back of their streak, Quebec started their own. They tied Montreal with five Cups, then had the opportunity for a sixth. So now the bitter rivals share a record no one's even come close to since. Indianapolis is the first to win even back-to-back Cups since that era.

Sophie doesn't intend to let Indianapolis win a third Cup this season, but she knows better than to say that to a reporter.

*

Sophie may not be setting records to start this season, but she isn't sitting useless on the bench. She picks up two assists against Orlando. She feeds Merlin on the power play to open the scoring, then she assists on Elsa's goal, the one which ties the game late in the third. That tie pushes them to overtime where Figs scores the game-winner and earns himself another run of headlines.

In their next game against Atlanta, Sophie improves on her performance, and she sets Woodsy up for three goals. She celebrates his hat trick with the rest of the team, their enthusiasm making up for the fact that they weren't on home ice so there wasn't a deluge of hats raining down on the ice after the third goal.

After the game against Atlanta, Marty Owen continues to cement himself as Sophie's least favorite reporter. "You hit Shea a few times tonight," Owen says to open Sophie's scrum.

Shea, who Sophie has competed against in the Winter Games, is now an Atlanta Lancer, which means she's competition. Of course, Sophie hit her. Sophie doesn't say it, but she implies the answer with the arch of her eyebrows.

Marty Owen isn't cowed. "Were you taking advantage of her lack of experience with physical play?"

Sophie can always count on Marty Owen for a bullshit question every scrum. She glances past her crowd of reporters. She wants to send them over to Woodsy's stall, because he scored a hat trick and that should be the talk of this game. Instead, Marty Owen is trying to stir up drama between the women in the league, as if Sophie hasn't spent her entire tenure in the league suppressing those kinds of stories.

"If you think women's hockey isn't physical, then you haven't watched Team Canada and Team USA compete enough," Sophie tells Marty Owen. "I hit Shea, because she's dangerous with the puck. They were strategic hits, meant to knock her off the puck or force her to pass before she was ready."

Sophie doesn't hit other players for the sake of hitting them. If it isn't going to advance the play, she won't do it. After eight seasons covering her play, Marty Owen should know that.

"You don't think you should have gone easier on her in solidarity?" Marty Owen asks.

He doesn't know her at all, Sophie thinks. She smooths her expression into something less homicidal and gives a light, non-controversial answer. Privately, she hopes someone asks Lexie a question like this. Lexie won't hesitate to unleash on the reporter.

*

Sophie notches two assists against New Orleans and another two against Memphis. She isn't stringing together the kind of point streak which will eventually break her own record, but she isn't playing poorly. Twelve points in seven games is an average of 1.7 a game. It's a pace she can't sustain throughout the entire season, but it's damn impressive.

The reporters obsess over her lack of goals, as if the zero in that category invalidates the twelve in the assist column. There's a slew of articles suggesting that women simply don't have the drive or killer instinct to be goal scorers. They're better suited to support roles, a play-maker like Sophie, or a defensewoman like Madison Plante. Someone is even stupid enough to write an article about how Johanna Achenbach has found her game again as Gabrielle Gagnon's backup, and that maybe some players were never meant to play in the spotlight.

The articles bother Sophie more than her own stats. She went goalless for a long stretch in her rookie season. She obsessed over it then, but she barely thinks about it now. She contributes more to her team than scoring goals. Until she feels as if she's stepping on the ice and bringing her team down, she won't be bothered.

After New Orleans and Memphis comes Detroit. Sophie isn't letting the coverage about her play get to her, but someone clearly thinks she needs a pep talk, because Elsa sends Sophie to fetch her a roll of tape for her and Teddy just so happens to be the only person in the tiny equipment closet when Sophie enters.

Sophie huffs but she doesn't roll her eyes. "I'm not fragile."

Teddy holds his hands up as if he and Elsa aren't the resident Sophie-Managers. "No one is saying you are. You hit five hundred assists at the start of the season. With this pace, you're going to hit six hundred before the season is over."

Sophie does roll her eyes this time, but she's feeling fond now, rather than exasperated. "That's a bit optimistic, but it's a nice change from the doom and gloom. You'd think I was having a point drought, not a goal one. Why isn't anyone talking about *you*? Your point production has dropped off a cliff. And after such a strong start to your season. It's sad, really."

Teddy laughs and shoves her shoulder. "Will that be your deflection in your next scrum? You're going to throw me under the bus?"

"Never," Sophie says, too seriously to match Teddy's teasing tone. "And you clearly need Media Training 101 if you think that is considered a deflection. It isn't nearly subtle enough."

"I bow to your media expertise," Teddy says.

"More like you don't want to feel guilty for abandoning me to the sharks."

"Oh, I never feel guilty for that. Didn't you know the C on your jersey stands for chatty?"

Sophie shakes her head, but she's grinning as she plucks a roll of Elsa's favorite tape out of Ben Granlund's supply. Sophie has heard Elsa rant about the difference between white and eggshell enough to make sure she has the white tape.

When she returns to the locker room with Teddy, she tosses the tape to Elsa and starts her rounds, checking in with each of her teammates to see where their heads are at before the game. The rookies, as always, need settling. Talking to the veteran players helps center Sophie as much as she helps them.

Kansas waves Sophie off when she approaches him, because he's locked in and ready. Detroit was the team he played for before he came to Concord. There was a time he thought he'd retire with Detroit. He always finds an extra gear when they play his former team. Sophie can't relate, and she hopes she never can.

She's a Concord Condor, and she wants to be one for life.

*

Early in the first period, Woodsy passes the puck to Sophie. She's by the hashmarks, one of her favorite places to shoot from. She shoots. The puck ricochets off a d-man's skin, and it sparks a breakaway for the other team.

The next time Sophie has the puck near the net, she passes.

And again, the time after that.

She doesn't realize how many looks at the net she's ignored in favor of passing the puck until Coach Elison pulls her aside when they're headed down the tunnel for first intermission.

"You stopped shooting," Coach Elison says.

"I didn't hit five hundred assists by scoring goals," Sophie says.

Coach Elison doesn't look impressed with her answer. He doesn't yell at her the way Butler would have. Of course, Sophie wouldn't dare talk back to Butler like this. "When you have a good look at the net, shoot. You know what a good scoring chance looks like. Stop passing on them."

"Yes, coach," Sophie says. She'll never break her goalless streak if she doesn't shoot the puck. And yes, her career stats are heavily tilted toward assists over goals, but it isn't as though she's a slouch in the scoring department.

Sophie follows Coach Elison's advice, and she opens the second period with a shot on goal. The goalie kicks the puck aside. Kevlar gathers up the rebound, and he drives the second chance home.

This is why she should shoot the puck. Because even if she doesn't score, her teammates might.

Of course, even though Sophie is content with her place, it doesn't mean everyone else is. Her lack of goals is, once again, the topic of her post-game scrum.

"You have more than twice the number of assists than you have goals on your career," Marty Owen says. "Does that concern you?"

"I've never been a pure goal scorer," Sophie answers. When she was very young, maybe, because she emulated the players she saw on TV and because every kid liked scoring goals. But as she grew up, she learned her teammates liked her better if she set them up for goals rather than scoring them herself. She developed into a playmaker, and she has a case for being the best one in the NAHL. Marty Owen's comment is a reminder that there is no such thing as good enough.

She doesn't let it bother her. Because yes, there will always be people who criticize her play, who tell her she's fallen short and to do more, but she has a ten-year contract extension that says Concord believes in her. They looked at her play since she first laced up her skates as a Condor, and they said they wanted her to be a part of them for another decade.

So, fuck Marty Owen and fuck Bobby Brindle's snide comments about her stats. Her team believes in her, and everyone else is just background noise.

*

Concord closes out their road trip against Milwaukee. It's one of the many teams Figs has played for during his extended NAHL career, and he puts on a show for his former fans. He notches himself a goal, an assist, and the shootout winner, which should quiet everyone who claims he's too old to still be playing.

After the game ends, Sophie takes up her post at the entrance to the tunnel and sees each of her teammates down to the locker room. She hands out back slaps and compliments in equal measure.

Sometimes, Elsa lingers so she and Sophie can walk down to the locker room together. Sometimes, it's Coach Elison who takes the opportunity to chat about the game with Sophie. Tonight, it's Mary Beth who acts as Sophie's escort.

Their relationship is still strained after Sophie's stubbornness about Elsa. Sophie regrets that she and Mary Beth will probably never have the easy professionalism they had before.

"You have a free night," Mary Beth tells Sophie. "Figs is doing the lion's share of the media tonight."

Normally, Sophie would be excited to have the night off from media. No hockey player enjoys media scrums. Part of being captain is that Sophie always has to stand in front of the reporters and answer for her team, good or bad. She knows there isn't anything new for her to say. If she had reporters in front of her tonight, they would rehash the same things they've covered for the past two weeks. Still, part of her doesn't like having a free night.

Elsa lingers by Woodsy's stall, cheerfully giving him shit over a play in the second period. Sophie gives her a slight nod to let her know she has the time to shower today. On the nights she has the time before media, Sophie will jump in the shower quickly. On other nights, she has to wait until her media responsibilities are finished.

Given that there's only one shower allocated for Sophie and Elsa, they have to communicate to determine who gets to use it first. The woman's shower is a curtain around one of the showerheads in the main room. In Concord, they have a semi-permanent shower set aside, but it's different when Sophie and Elsa visit other teams.

It makes Sophie wonder if Concord has a designated

woman's shower in their visitors' locker room. Of course, it also makes her wonder when Concord's home locker room will upgrade to two showers, or at least expand their partition to include two showerheads.

Sophie retreats to the shower and stands gratefully under the hot spray. She considers who she would even bring up the issue of showers with and laughs at the inevitable fallout when word got out that Concord's Sophie Fournier was complaining about the shower facilities. She certainly wouldn't have any more nights off from answering questions.

But these are the little things that slip through the cracks. It's easy to count the women in the league, to see their spread across the divisions and teams. Stats nerds can run analytics on how the women perform. But no one is thinking about whether there are enough showers in the locker rooms for them.

As if on cue, Elsa parts the curtain in order to join Sophie in the shower. She drapes her towel over the curtain rod to keep it from getting wet and frowns as Sophie takes the shampoo out of her shower caddy.

"You're slow tonight," Elsa says.

"I'm not in a rush," Sophie says. She rubs her shampoo into her hair and steps out of the spray so Elsa can stand beneath it. It isn't efficient to share the shower, and they aren't home, so they aren't even sneaking kisses or touches.

Sophie claims the water again to rinse out her hair, then she takes her towel from where she had hung it earlier. Elsa reaches out to touch Sophie's wrist. "Is everything okay?"

Sophie is unsettled, but there's nothing wrong. It doesn't seem entirely truthful to say, "Everything's fine," but it doesn't feel like a lie either. She leaves Elsa to finish her shower and heads back out to the locker room.

Figs still has a cluster of reporters around him, but

everyone else is changing into their game day suits. Sophie glances around the room and makes eye contact with Bowser. His gaze darts to the shower room then back to Sophie, and the look on his face suggests he just realized that Sophie and Elsa must have been in the shower at the same time.

Sophie bares her teeth in a smile that is far from friendly. Bowser hurriedly drops his gaze. Sophie will have to talk to him. Or maybe she'll delegate and have Theo and Kevlar chat with him again. Or she could make DZ's day and let him have a threatening talk with Bowser.

*

They return home and face DC. Sophie played well against them in the preseason, even finding the back of the net, but she doesn't have the same success in the first period. Neither team scores, leaving the giant zeros on the jumbotron for each team as they head down the tunnel for first intermission.

Sophie slipped the puck through two defenders to put it on Elsa's stick late in the first period, but Doherty snapped it out of the air with a quick glove save. On Sophie's next shift, she left a no-look drop pass for Kevlar. His shot hit the crossbar, hit Doherty's back, and somehow didn't fall into the net.

They've had plenty of chances, but none of them have crossed the goal line.

"Doherty isn't this good," Elsa mutters. She drops onto the bench in front of her stall. "How hard is it to put the puck in the back of the net?"

Sophie flinches even though she knows Elsa isn't blaming her. Still, this is Sophie's tenth game without a goal. A good captain would start the second period off with a strong shift and an early goal.

She doesn't understand what's wrong. She has the

promise of another ten years with Concord, her team is solid, she's living with the woman she loves. For once, everything in Sophie's life is good, except for hockey.

And honestly, she isn't playing poorly. She just can't score a damned goal. How long until that becomes the focus? The media have been fixated on it, but the fans haven't turned on her. Yet. It's only a matter of time. If her drought stretches long enough, will her team turn on her as well? Will Elison?

Sophie shakes her head to clear it. She has a commitment from the front office, and her team isn't as fickle as others have been in the past. Concord is her team in a way Chilton never was. She is their captain, and she is more than her ability to score goals.

Sophie doesn't score on the opening shift of the second period.

She doesn't score on the next one or the one after that. The second period passes without a goal for either team. Then the third period passes the same way.

They go to overtime with the score tied at zero.

Coach Elison sends Sophie out for the faceoff. Sophie wins it. They drive into the offensive zone. Sophie and Elsa pass the puck back and forth until Elsa snaps the puck on net. Doherty pushes off his right post, and the puck hits him in the chest. He slaps his glove down on the puck before anyone can take a second whack at it.

Sophie's recalled to the bench, but Elsa stays out as Coach Elison sends Peets and Figs to join her. Sophie chews on her mouth guard. She never likes seeing Elsa on the ice with a center who isn't her. She fought one of Elsa's Swedish teammates at the IHT, because Sophie was angry and jealous and didn't know what else to do with all her feelings.

Peets is tossed from the faceoff, and Elsa steps in to take his place.

You can win this, Sophie thinks at Elsa. *We've been practicing, and you're much better. Quick reaction.*

The official drops the puck. Elsa reaches it first, and she sweeps it back to Figs. Figs fires the puck on net. It's the muscle memory and instinctive trust of a goal scorer, and the puck whips past Doherty.

The goal light flashes.

Sophie stands and holds her fist out so she can give her teammates the credit they deserve for their win.

*

Sophie is already out of her game day suit and in her pajamas when her phone rings. It's her dad. Sophie takes a moment to rest her head against her refrigerator before she takes a deep breath and answers. "Hey."

"Your passes were sharp tonight," her dad says. "It's a shame no one could convert on them."

"It happens," Sophie says. She opens the pantry door and studies the nutrition chart on the inside of it. It's a precise breakdown of what she should eat and when, depending on where in the season it is. She relies on it when she's too tired to think or when she isn't motivated to eat but knows she has to.

Tonight is the kind of night where she'll eat the minimum necessary. Hopefully, she'll feel better tomorrow.

"Ten games without a goal," her dad says, as if Sophie doesn't already know. "Goal scoring has never been your strength, but do you know how you turn weaknesses into strengths?"

"Practice," Sophie answers.

"Practice," her dad repeats.

"I *am* practicing." Sophie can't keep the bite out of her words. "It isn't as though I want to be dead weight."

"You aren't dead weight." Now, her dad sounds

annoyed as well, which doesn't bode well for the rest of this conversation. "Fishing for compliments isn't how you get praise. You earn praise by playing well."

Sophie sighs, hopefully too quietly for her dad to hear. She grabs the peanut butter out of the pantry and tracks down the loaf of bread. For some reason, it's in the microwave. This is another one of Elsa's habits that Sophie doesn't understand. Instead of a breadbasket like Sophie had growing up, Elsa was taught to keep bread in the microwave.

"Elsa's faceoff win in overtime was clutch," Sophie's dad says. "Clearly, she's been practicing what I showed her this summer. She and Figuli looked good together."

"It was barely five seconds," Sophie snaps.

"And they scored the game winner," her dad says, unbothered by Sophie's outburst.

And you couldn't manage in sixty minutes what they did in five seconds, Sophie tells herself, a thin, insidious voice she shouldn't listen to. But she's tired, and her defenses are down, and she bows her head. Maybe a change is what they need. Elsa is Sophie's linemate, but only as long as it's good for the team. If it isn't working, Sophie can't be selfish.

"Do you think I should talk to Coach Elison about switching up the lines?" Sophie asks, because she can't trust herself to be objective about this.

"It can't hurt to try," her dad answers.

He's right and Sophie knows it. Sophie is struggling right now. Maybe a shake-up is what she needs to reorient herself. It won't be forever. Sophie and Elsa signed matching contracts, because they wanted to play together. But Sophie won't be the one to drag Elsa down.

Sophie rubs her forehead, hoping to dislodge the headache building behind her eyes. Elsa isn't going to like this.

Chapter Nine

Sophie puts it off. The season is only ten games in, which is too small a sample size to introduce what she can admit is a radical change. Maybe, all Sophie needs is the threat of losing her favorite linemate in order to find her scoring touch again.

After she talks to her dad, chokes down a peanut butter sandwich, then puts in the bare minimum at the bar with her teammates, Sophie goes home and visualizes. She should be focusing on sleep, but instead she runs through all her shifts from the game against DC, and she tweaks them to see herself scoring.

She'll do this again tomorrow in video review with the footage from the game, but she can do it well enough on memory alone. On that shift, she should have shot instead of passed. In her mind, she shoots the puck, and it goes past Doherty. Another shift where she did shoot but Doherty stopped her. In her second chance, she elevates the puck more, so it sails over Doherty's shoulder and hits the back of the net.

By the time Sophie falls asleep, she's scored fifty times.

She goes to practice with a renewed sense of purpose. She gives every drill her all, and she hands out encouragement and praise to her teammates as they follow her lead.

Instead of the usual drag after an overtime game, every-one is sharp, and both their passes and skating are crisp.

They end practice with a scrimmage, which is always a favorite. Sophie catches a pass from Elsa on the tape of her stick blade. Sophie has an open shooting lane, but Teddy's in goal, and he's tough to beat on a good day, let alone when she isn't feeling her best.

She glances around at her other options. Spitzer drifts down, an option if she needs him. But Elsa lurks on the edge of Sophie's vision, and Sophie slides the puck back to her. Jacobs curses, because he hadn't thought So-phie could make the pass, and he's out of position.

Coach Elison's whistle pierces the air. Elsa bobbles the puck, and she glares at their coach for interrupting the play before she can shoot.

But Coach Elison doesn't look at Elsa. He looks at So-phie, and he points his whistle at her. "You won't score if you don't shoot the damn puck."

It isn't the first time Sophie's been called out in prac-tice, and it won't be the last, but it still stings. She grits her teeth and says, "Yes, Coach."

She ends the scrimmage with two shots on goal, but it isn't good enough. She grabs a couple of loose pucks as Jacobs and another one of the rookies skate around with a bucket, doing clean-up.

"No," Coach Elison says, and Sophie turns to glare at him, but he's unmoved. "There's no extra ice-time today."

"Of course, Coach," Sophie says, and she buries her anger and her frustration deep enough that it doesn't show on her face. She drops her pucks in Jacobs's bucket and skates to the far end of the rink to grab the two pucks over there.

She isn't surprised when Elsa follows her.

"You're frustrated," Elsa says.

"I'm not playing well," Sophie says. "And I feel as

though he's keeping me from improving. I'm never going to find the back of the net if I don't practice."

"You will," Elsa promises.

"When? Next game? Next month?" Sophie shakes her head. "I haven't scored a goal yet this season. I'm supposed to be leading this team and instead I'm—" She cuts herself off before she can finish her thought.

"Instead you're what?" Elsa challenges. Her eyes are flinty, hard, as if she knows Sophie was going to say "useless."

Sophie isn't useless. She knows she isn't. She's still winning faceoffs. She's still making good passes. Her defensive game is the best it's been in her NAHL career up to this point. She's the fucking captain. She contributes every moment she's on the ice, whether it's practice or a game. But there's more she can do, a glaring hole where her goal scoring should be.

She takes a deep breath and looks around. Jacobs, wisely, spotted Sophie and Elsa in the corner and left the bucket of pucks on the bench for them. Sophie raps her fist against the glass. "I'm not where I need to be right now," she says.

"No," Elsa says. She grips Sophie's face between her gloved hands. "Whatever you're thinking, no."

Sophie knocks Elsa's hands away. "I'm trying to be better at communicating, so I'm talking to you first, but I'm going to Elison's office after this, and I'm going to suggest he switch up the lines."

Elsa groans. "It doesn't count as communicating if it isn't a conversation. Do I get any say in this?"

"No," Sophie answers, and she flinches because it's harsh, but it's also true. Sophie and Elsa knew it would be a difficult balance to be in a relationship while being teammates, especially since Sophie is the captain. If she can't keep Elsa on her line because she selfishly wants to, she certainly can't do it because Elsa selfishly wants them to stay together.

"I'm not playing well enough," Sophie says. She holds her hand up before Elsa can say anything. "I'm not. It's a fact. But I will get better. This isn't the end of my career, no matter what Marty Owen and Bobby Brindle wish. But I can't drag you down with me too."

"You play better with me," Elsa argues. "I don't want another center. I want *you*."

It's unfair for Elsa to play on Sophie's weaknesses. Sophie doesn't want Elsa centered by anyone but her. Sophie would gladly play with Elsa every shift for the rest of her career, but she can't. She and Elsa are a team within a team, but Concord comes first. It has to.

"Our no-move clauses don't kick in until next year," Sophie says. "We don't get our ten years if we don't earn them this season. We can't falter. I can't—" She turns away. "I can't drag you down."

Sophie doesn't think Concord will drop her for a goal drought. She's pretty sure she could go without a goal for the entire season and if the rest of her game was strong enough, Concord would keep her. There would be criticism, of course, and with it would come pressure, but she's earned a bit of faith from them. But if Sophie spreads her struggles to Elsa? Keeping both of them would be a risk.

Sophie won't jeopardize her and Elsa's future.

"Fine," Elsa says, and it's biting and grudging, but it's agreement, and Sophie can't help but look to her with shock on her face. "Someone else will center me, but it will be temporary." Elsa stares Sophie down until Sophie nods in agreement. "I'll work hard for whoever it is, and when I have you back, I'll work just as hard."

"Okay." Sophie nods again and she feels a bit like a bobblehead. She steps closer, until she can rest her helmet against Elsa's. It isn't as good as hugging when they aren't in all their padding, but it's enough. "I'm going to get through this."

"Faith and patience," Elsa says. "And give it a few more games? The season is still early."

Elsa's been more reasonable than Sophie expected, and Sophie doesn't actually want to change the lines. "All right," she agrees. "But only a few. I can't let this spread."

*

After the fifteenth game of the season, Sophie is still goalless. Even worse, Elsa is now passing on scoring chances to try to help Sophie score. It's selfless and yet, it's wrong. Because now neither of them is on the score sheet, and with Concord's top two players struggling, the team begins to lose games. It doesn't help that in that stretch before Elsa stopped shooting, she hit three hundred career goals. She has more goals in fewer seasons than Sophie. Instead of her stats driving Elsa to score even more, she's limiting herself for Sophie. And Sophie can't allow that.

The practice after they lose to Quebec, Elsa is grumpy, because she knows Sophie is going to talk to Coach Elison after practice. Sophie has let this go on long enough, and there needs to be a change.

Coach Elison isn't surprised when Sophie knocks on his office door after she's changed out of her practice clothes. He gestures for her to come in. She closes the door behind her and doesn't dance around why she's here. "You should switch up the lines."

Sophie was never this direct with Butler. He didn't want her opinion and, when she gave it, he was as likely to do the opposite to spite her than to listen. Of course, if Butler was still the coach, Sophie would have been a healthy scratch by now in order to teach her a lesson.

"What are you thinking?" Coach Elison asks.

"Have Peets center Elsa and Figs. Elsa has a goal scorer's touch, and Figs will be able to get her the puck. I'll take Woodsy and Jacobs. Woodsy and I are solid together, and Jacobs has settled enough that he could learn something from being on my wing."

"It will be a media feeding frenzy," Coach Elison says.

It isn't a no, but it could be. Coach Elison won't throw her to the sharks without her okay. Sophie appreciates his concern, but she can handle it. It's her own fault she isn't scoring goals. She'll take the responsibility and the extra scrutiny for it.

"I can handle it," Sophie promises. "I'll leave the final line combinations to you, but Elsa and I need to be separated until I find my game again. She's started prioritizing my game over hers, and it'll hurt us in the long run."

"It won't be a problem?" Coach Elison asks. "You two signed matching contracts this summer, and you're living together."

"I talked to her before I came to you. She isn't happy, but she understands. And neither of us expect this to be permanent. The team is better when we frontload our top line, but only if the top line is producing."

"I agree. I'll announce the change at practice tomorrow. I'll give Mary Beth a heads-up in case she wants to prepare a few responses." Coach Elison shifts from coaching mode to something softer. There's a warmth in his gaze there wasn't before. "You'll make it through this, Sophie. None of us here doubt you."

It—that means more to her than she'll ever admit. Sometimes, it feels like her entire career has been marked by doubt. As though people only watch her to wait for her to stumble and fall and prove she was never good enough. Maybe that's why this drought is hitting her so hard. It feels as if she's failing and giving her doubters ammunition.

She has to remember their opinions mean nothing.

What does her front office think of her play? What does her team think? What does she think? Those are the opinions that matter.

"Thank you," she tells her coach, then she heads to the locker room where Elsa is waiting for her so they can drive home.

*

Sophie still hasn't scored a goal when they travel to Boston for the twentieth game of the season. She is grateful for the opportunity to skip out on team lunch and visit Dima. She and Elsa are adjusting to not playing on the same line, and Sophie appreciates the support from both Elsa and her coach, but she needs time away from her team.

Dima is her best friend, and she knows part of it is because he doesn't expect anything from her. He isn't her teammate, and she isn't his captain. She can simply be Sophie when she's around him.

It's her first time at his house, an off-season acquisition. She's seen pictures of course, but none of them did the house justice. The house is green with white shutters, and it stretches up and up, at least three floors. Instead of a standard front door, there's a set of almost medieval-looking double doors that don't match the Grecian columns lining the front of the house.

The house is a mix of modern and medieval and colonial and something else entirely, and it clashes, but it's also the perfect house for Dima.

The man himself opens the door wearing a pair of pants patterned with sharks and a bright yellow T-shirt that has one of the Minions from *Despicable Me* on it. Dima's smile is boyish, but his hug is firm, and it has the strength of years of friendship behind it.

Sophie hugs him back and tries not to breathe too

deeply, because he always overapplies his cologne, as if he's hoping Alina and Alexander will be able to smell it all the way in Russia.

"Next time, come in," Dima tells her as he steps back and ushers her inside. "No knocking or doorbells. We are friends, yes?"

"Of course," Sophie says. They have been ever since they met for NAHL promotionals ahead of their first season. Sophie was awkward, and Dima blew right past it, badgering her until she stopped being self-conscious. They celebrated his birthday with chocolate cake ordered from room service, and they made a pact that they wouldn't let the NAHL draw them into any kind of rivalry bullshit. Their relationship would be defined on their own terms.

They've ranted to each other about the expectations and pressures on players who don't fit the mold of good Canadian boys, and they've visited each other during injury, and sometimes, when they're very lucky, they even get to see each other when things are going well.

Dima gives her a haphazard tour of the house, and she doesn't realize it's on purpose until he says, "Best for last," and ushers her into the living room.

Sprawled across Dima's couch with her phone in one hand and the TV remote in the other is Elizabeth Schatz. Sophie's never been good with surprises, but years of media training have taught her to smile on command. She smiles now and gives Schatz a little wave for good measure.

It isn't that she doesn't like Schatz, but she's someone who looks up to Sophie, which means Sophie has to be worthy of being looked up to. Sophie had hoped for a quiet lunch with Dima. She wanted to ask for his advice on dealing with reporters who are out for blood with each game that passes without a goal for her.

Sophie can adjust. She pops back into the kitchen to

pour herself a glass of water, then she joins Schatz in the living room. Schatz pulls her knees toward her chest so there's room on the couch for Sophie to sit. Once Sophie is comfortable, Dima drops onto her lap, even though there's a loveseat and two armchairs all empty.

Sophie grunts at the extra weight, but she doesn't shove Dima off.

"How are you liking Boston?" Sophie asks Schatz. "Have you been to the aquarium yet?"

"You haven't watched *Being a Baron*?" Dima asks. He twists so Sophie can see his offended expression. "We have a whole episode at the aquarium."

"I keep up with your hockey, not the other shit," Sophie answers.

"It's like you don't care about me," Dima says. He sniffles for effect.

"You're so fucking dramatic," Schatz says. "You should've been an actor, not a hockey player."

"Why be one when I can be both?"

"Oh no," Sophie says, because she isn't going to sit here while Dima lies to Schatz's face. "He isn't an actor, and NAHL promos don't count. I was with him while we filmed those. It's just standing awkwardly with your stick and half your padding. And no"—Sophie fixes Dima with a look—"saying *hockey is back* doesn't count as memorizing lines."

Dima huffs. "So mean to me. I bring you a friend, and you repay me like this."

They catch up on each other's teams, then talk about what's going on in the rest of the league. Schatz makes lunch and after they eat, Sophie makes Dima do the dishes, because it's rude to make the rookie cook and clean up after.

"Do you want to nap here?" Dima asks as he flicks water at her.

"And help you throw Elsa off her game? No, thank you," Sophie says, wise to his tricks.

"Elsa's easy, just poke her a few times." Dima jabs his fingers into Sophie's stomach to demonstrate, and Sophie laughs as she knocks his hands away.

"Why do you enjoy antagonizing her so much?" Sophie asks. She tries not to feel self-conscious as Schatz watches her and Dima interact. "She hits you hard."

"And then we have power play. I am team player, willing to sacrifice my body."

"You're an idiot," Sophie tells him. "A lovable idiot, but still."

Dima turns to Schatz and in a stage whisper says, "Do you hear? She *loves* me."

"I'm going to hit you tonight," Sophie grumbles, but she's smiling so Dima doesn't take her seriously.

*

The joke's on Dima, because Sophie's line is given shutdown responsibilities since Peets's line is tasked with scoring. Sophie is out against Dima's line whenever Coach Elison can arrange it. Sophie doesn't hit Dima with the intent to injure, but she does hit him in order to separate him from the puck, to prevent a pass, or to force him into making a rushed decision with the puck.

After the first period, the score is tied at zero, but for the first time in too long, Sophie isn't disappointed by it. It isn't her job to score right now. Her job is to keep Dima's line from scoring, and she's succeeding.

Sophie is pleased as she sits next to Jacobs at intermission. Jacobs, of course, looks alarmed, because Sophie usually sits at her stall, between Merlin and Elsa, during intermissions.

"You're playing well," Sophie tells Jacobs. She's talked

with him between shifts, but there isn't a lot of opportunity for conversation when they're catching their breath. "You aren't letting Ivanov distract you."

Jacobs offers a hesitant smile. "I can always watch him on the highlight reel later."

"Not tonight," Sophie says. "We aren't giving him anything that they can play on the highlight reel."

Jacobs's smile grows. "I scored my first goal off Mikhail Figuli and now I'm in a shutdown role against one of the best goal scorers in the league."

"Not bad for a rookie. Coach trusts you and for good reason. You were solid out there all period. Now, we do it again for another two." Sophie pats Jacobs's knee and returns to her place between Merlin and Elsa.

"Laying it on a little thick?" Merlin mutters.

It took Sophie most of a season with the captaincy to realize people listen to her when she talks and that they believe what she tells them. It's a lot of power to give one person, and she uses it carefully. She doesn't lie to her teammates, and she glares at Merlin for the implication.

"Were you shutting down the league's top goal scorer as a rookie?" Sophie asks sharply. Saying *good job* or *nice shift* after every play or drill causes the words to lose value. Sophie gives out praise when it's deserved, but she also uses it sparingly, and she tries to make sure it's always specific. *Good backcheck on that last play* or *good job seeing the passing lane and getting your stick in there.* She doesn't believe in mindless platitudes.

"I know." Merlin winces and offers her an apologetic smile. "I'm tired and taking it out on you. I've been chasing Schatz up and down the ice all fucking period. Does she ever get tired?"

"We were young once," Sophie says. "You'll have to really search your memory, though."

She laughs as Merlin swats her shoulder.

*

Elsa forces a turnover and skates the puck up the ice. Peets trails behind her, ready for a drop pass. Further back on the play, Figs checks to make sure the officials are focused on Elsa, then he tips Hertz's helmet over his eyes. Figs jabs the hulking winger with his stick and skates up to join the play.

Hertz, who has more muscle than impulse control, chases Figs up the ice. Figs is right in front of an official when Hertz catches up to him and crosschecks him across the back. The official raises his arm for a penalty, and the play is blown dead as soon as Boston has possession of the puck.

Hertz, mad now, shoves Figs, then mouths off to the official, who pulls him away from Sophie's teammate.

Sophie's laughing when Figs skates over to the bench. "Nice," she tells him.

"It's all about knowing what's allowed and what's not," Figs says.

Coach Elison sends the first power play unit out. Sophie takes her place at the faceoff across from Jefferson. She brings her stick down on the puck. Jefferson brings his stick down on her wrists.

There's a flash of pain, and Sophie swears at him as she knocks the puck back. Elsa darts in, grabs the puck, and skates it to safety. Sophie shakes out her left wrist, then her right one as she skates for her position.

They set up their cycle, and Sophie catches a pass from Kevlar and skates around the back of the net. She protects the puck from Jefferson by leaning into him with one shoulder and using her other hand to keep the puck away from him. She makes a one-handed pass up to Elsa as Dubs skates in to help his teammate.

Drawing two Barons to her means Sophie's pulled Boston out of their penalty kill formation, and Elsa has a wide-open shooting lane. With a flick of her wrists, Elsa sends the puck over Blinksy's stick and Hippeli's shoulder, and it lands in the back of the net.

Sophie is the first to crash into Elsa. She hugs Elsa as her arms are still in the air, celebrating her goal. This is how hockey is supposed to be, Sophie and Elsa celebrating after a goal.

It's extra motivation for Sophie to clean up her game. She wants this feeling all the time, not only on the power play.

Chapter Ten

Quebec is on a ten-game winning streak when they fly to Concord. They've ticked over the quarter-mark of the season, and this is what broadcasters will call a "measuring stick" game. Sophie wishes she felt more confident as she prepares to compete against a strong defensive team, backed by the best goalie in the league.

Goaltending has been Quebec's strength since they came to their senses and made Gabrielle their starter. Le-Garrette Thomas is the core of the defense they have in front of her and, with their offseason signing of Nate Summers, Quebec is now finally getting goal support. It makes them a well-rounded team which, in turn, makes them dangerous.

Sophie skates her customary two warm-up laps, the first one on her own and her second with Elsa. Her gaze is continuously drawn to the far side of the ice where Gabrielle stands guard over her goal. Gabrielle's goalie mask is tipped down and from this distance, her expression is inscrutable. It would be the same even if Sophie was closer.

Gabrielle was a tough goalie to beat when Sophie was at her best, and she has twenty-four games worth of evidence that she isn't at her best right now. Gabrielle stops a shot from Summers and steps out of the net, so Johanna Achenbach has a chance to see a few pucks as well.

"Focus on us," Elsa chides, stealing Sophie's attention

away from Gabrielle and the other Bobcats.

"I'm focused," Sophie says. Her dad sent her two-and-a-half dozen clips of Gabrielle for Sophie to study. Sophie worked with her video coach to find and isolate every instance she has scored on Gabrielle in her career in order to review them and make sure she remembered what she did and that she could do it again.

But goal scoring is only partially on the goal scorer. Sophie could take fifty shots from the same spot and end up with fifty different results. If a defenseman is between her and the goal, he might block her shot, but he might screen the goalie and allow the puck to slip through. She might be able to bank the puck off his stick for a deflection into the net.

She has to try.

That is the mandate she's given herself for this game. If the opportunity is there, she will shoot. Maybe, the puck will go in. Maybe, it won't.

Sophie takes a deep breath and releases it slowly. "We can do this."

"Of course," Elsa answers, steady and sure, because while Sophie has doubted herself throughout this season so far, Elsa never has.

*

Gabrielle isn't the only top-tier goalie in tonight's game. Teddy turns away every puck that makes it through the defense as Nate Summers leads a one-man assault on Concord's net. On the other end of the ice, Gabrielle catches shot after shot safely in her glove or she kicks the puck away with a pad save.

The first period ticks by without a goal on either side, and tensions are high as both teams come out for the second period. They exchange chances on the net, then exchange punches as tempers flare and impatience makes both teams eager to do *something.*

Everyone settles down for the third period, but it doesn't matter, because the score stays stubbornly at zero.

Maybe it's because Sophie has been used to not scoring goals, but she isn't as affected as the others as the game ticks into overtime. She hasn't scored, but that's normal for her these days. Her team hasn't scored, but neither has Quebec.

Overtime means sudden death. The first to score a goal wins the game, and it's over, no second chances. And if they run through overtime, there's a shootout to decide things. Part of her is curious to see how a shootout would end with both Teddy and Gabrielle playing so well. The rest of her is determined not to let it get so far.

Sophie has Woodsy on one wing and Jacobs on the other, and their line has the overtime start. Sophie wins the faceoff against Summers, but a Quebec defender steals the puck off Jacobs's stick. Sophie drops back to play defense.

She didn't watch as much tape on Summers as she did on Gabrielle heading into this game, but she has three periods of her own observations. Quebec signed Summers so he would score goals, and they funnel their offense through him. With the game on the line, they lean on him even more.

Sophie cheats her coverage, and she jumps into the passing lane as soon as the puck leaves the Quebec player's stick. She intercepts the pass before it can reach Summers. Sophie has the puck, and she has momentum, and she flies down the ice with both teams chasing her.

It's Sophie against the best goalie in the North American Hockey League.

Sophie has more than twice as many assists as she does goals in her career, but she has scored goals. It doesn't matter that she hasn't done it yet this season, because her body remembers last season and the one before and all the others before that one.

She does a crossover and relies on muscle memory as she watches Gabrielle track the puck. Gabrielle is sharp— she has quick reflexes and an even quicker mind. Sophie fakes glove-side, then snaps the puck high corner.

The puck hits the back of the net, and the goal light flashes red.

Sophie throws her arms up in the air, relief for the win and for ending her fucking goal drought. She holds herself open to her linemates as they crash into her to celebrate, but she looks past them toward the bench. Elsa is on her feet and shouting, and her gaze locks on Sophie's.

You knew I could do it, and I did it, Sophie thinks. She pats her linemates' helmets, clasps her d-men on the shoulder, then she leads them to the bench where they can unite with and celebrate with the rest of the team.

*

Scoring against Quebec doesn't open the floodgates for Sophie. Their next game is against Indianapolis and even though Sophie scores the opening goal, Indianapolis scores the next five. No one cares about Sophie's goals in back-to-back games after such a long stretch without. No one mentions how well Concord played against Quebec, the Titan of the East, after they're embarrassed by the Titan of the West.

Sophie is barely even a footnote in the post-game coverage. It centers on Kensington, it highlights Lexie, and a few broadcasters even look toward the upcoming draft when Emily Skelton will be available.

It isn't the first time Sophie has heard Emily Skelton called *the next Sophie Fournier*. And it certainly isn't the first time Sophie's seen people try to shuffle her to the side in order to make room for a different woman.

Maybe it's because Sophie's older now, the commentary hits harder. Or maybe it's because Figuli is on her team now, and she's spent a lot of the season thinking about what a complete hockey career looks like and what it means to have a legacy.

Sophie isn't ready to hang up her skates, and she certainly won't leave hockey on someone else's terms. She fought to make a place for herself in the NAHL and yes, part of that fight was making sure other women would be able to play as well, but she won't give up her place for them.

After practice and a presser where she answered more questions about Indy and their dominance than her own team, Sophie finds herself at Figs's apartment.

It's a nice place, but she knows he could do better. He could afford a house, but the apartment is a sign he isn't planning to stay in Concord long-term. The pictures hanging on the walls are personal enough that the apartment doesn't feel like a hotel room, but it's the only concession he makes to this being a home.

There are team pictures from every NAHL team Figs has been a part of. There are just as many pictures of international teams from when Figs has represented Slovakia. She notices a conspicuous absence.

"No Team Czechoslovakia?" Sophie teases.

Figs rolls his eyes. The International Hockey Tournament, which had been the NAHL's response to the Winter Games, didn't have enough interest in its inaugural tournament to have the same set-up as the Winter Games. There simply weren't enough high-quality players available to have the variety of the Games. Which led to mash-up teams like Team Czechoslovakia.

"I won't be a part of it next year," Figs says. "No more international hockey for me."

"There hasn't been any pressure to change your mind?" Sophie asks.

"There's been pressure, but I won't change my mind. It's good practice for when the NAHL starts badgering me. I'm retiring before the centennial season, and I know the commissioner won't like it."

Figs is so confident this is his last season. He's sure he'll win the Cup with Concord, then retire. Sophie spent her entire media scrum fielding questions about Indianapolis and their back-to-back Cup wins and how they're hungry for more. Surely, Figs has seen the same articles and coverage and heard the same hype.

"Why didn't you sign with the Renegades?" Sophie asks. "Everyone says they're the next dynasty."

Figs scoffs. "I saw Montreal's five Cups. I saw Quebec's. I know what a dynasty team looks like. Indy has swagger, and they certainly think they're unbeatable, but the moment they lose, and they will lose, they'll crumble. They're fragile. The right pressure at the right time, and they'll shatter."

Sophie wrinkles her nose. Two nights ago, Indianapolis came back from being down four goals in the first period to win in regulation. They don't look like a team on the verge of shattering. She knows things don't always run smoothly in Indianapolis. There are rumors of tension between their two stars, Lexie and Chad. There are whispers about Chad withholding first goal pucks from rookies and pissing off veteran players.

But those are only rumors, and as Sophie knows from personal experience, winning covers all kinds of faults. And Indy is certainly winning.

"I like being a Condor," Figs says, which is as much an answer to why he isn't a Renegade as his previous one. "You and Elsa remind me of when I played with Stucki. When we were in our prime..." He has a faraway look. There's pride in his expression, but there's pain as well, as if he's remembering how their duo ended, with a career-ending injury for Stucki and musical teams for Figuli.

"I'm glad this team will be my last," Figs says.

Sophie hopes she is never shuffled from team to team like Figs was. She knows playing hockey is better than not playing hockey, but she wants to be a Condor for life. She wants to commit to a team and have them commit back to her. Her next contract will all but guarantee she'll be a Condor for life. She has to finish this season and make it through the trade deadline and the summer trading period, but once next season begins, her no movement clause will be active. She won't go anywhere she doesn't want to go.

Playing with Figuli, especially when he's preparing to retire; it makes Sophie think. About his career, yes, but also her own. Figuli will be remembered for decades. Will she be remembered the same way? Will her legacy be that she was the first woman in the NAHL or will it be something more? Will it be records and point streaks and Cups?

"They love you, you know," Figs says.

Sophie looks over at him, curious.

"The team," he says. "The front office. The fans."

Have Sophie's doubts been on her face? There have been more and more fans with nines on their jerseys with no three after it. They're showing up in droves to games in Figuli's jersey. With her drought, Sophie wondered if she was being forgotten. With the influx of articles on Lexie and now Emily, Sophie can't help but think people are trying to set her aside.

"You've done so much," Sophie says, "and people still come after you for not doing enough. If you don't win a Cup, there will be an asterisk next to your name. One of the NAHL's greatest players, shame he never won the Cup."

"There will be an asterisk even if I do." Figs shrugs, unconcerned. "One of the NAHL's greatest players, shame he only won one Cup. But I'm not doing it for them. I'm winning for me. One Cup, and I'll be satisfied." He looks over at Sophie. "What about you?"

"What do I need?" Sophie braces her arms on Figs's island counter. Her father's mantra, what Sophie grew up on, was *if you're not the best, you don't get to play*. But it isn't strictly accurate. Maybe, she had to be the best to make it to the NAHL, but she's here now. She was at the top of her game when she tore her ACL and was sidelined. And even though she had a rough stretch of games to start this season, she wasn't benched.

What would satisfy her? She taps her fingers on the counter. "I would say two Cups, but if we win a second, I'll want a third. How will I know when it's time to stop?"

"You'll know," Figs answers. "You'll feel it. You'll never stop loving hockey, but one day, hockey will stop loving you back. That's when you start thinking about hanging up your skates."

"This is really your last season," Sophie says. She's heard him say it, but she wasn't sure she ever believed it. She was there when Delacroix decided to retire. She talked him into one more season. It was a season she spent playing hard for him, chasing the Cup, but she knew the entire time that there was a countdown on the time she had left with him.

Figs closes his eyes and exhales deeply. For the first time, Sophie looks at him and sees a man who is nearly fifty years old. There are wrinkles lining his face and dark bags under his eyes and when his hair falls forward, there's gray mixed in with the brown.

"All my buddies have retired. I'm the only one left. Some of my rookies have retired. You don't know how much you're loved until you're done. When you're playing, it's always one more goal, one more win. You should've done this, you should've done that. Once you retire, they remember all the amazing shit you did along the way. I blame it on those compilations *TNSN* loves to run.

Anyone can have a kickass career when it's condensed to their top moments."

Exactly. Sophie can never do enough for the fans, for her father, even for herself. She can't stop pushing to be better and do more, because she doesn't want to stagnate or even slip backward. But if she's constantly pushing for more, can she ever be happy?

"They're going to retire your number," Sophie tells Figs.

"League-wide. I've played on too many teams for them to do anything else." Figs laughs and invites Sophie to laugh along. "They'll retire yours as well. Not just Concord. The league itself. Ninety-three will hang in the rafters and no one else will be able to wear it. That's how you know they love you. They won't allow their memories of you to be tainted by anyone else wearing your number."

Sophie doesn't demur. She knows her number will be retired, because of her role as the league's first woman if for no other reason. "But like you said, they don't show how much they value us until we're done."

"Do you play for them?" Figs asks. He isn't judgmental. He's curious.

"A little bit." She can't turn it off completely. She hears what people say. She burns to prove them wrong. For so long, her career was limited by all those people. If she didn't play well enough, they wouldn't allow her entry. She *had* to care. It's difficult to simply turn that off.

"I'm trying to be better about finding balance," Sophie tells him. "Hockey was my entire life, because if it wasn't, I wouldn't be able to keep playing. And then it would be *my* fault. I'm in the NAHL now. I'm the captain of my team, I helped win the first Maple Cup in franchise history. Next year, my ten-year contract extension will kick in. But I'm afraid if I let up, I'll lose it all."

"You can't lose what you've already done," Figs tells her.

Oh. *Oh.* Sophie ducks her head so Figs won't see the way her eyes well up with tears. She can't lose what she's already done. Even if she never wins another award or accolade, she has a career to be proud of. And she *won't* suddenly lose her skill or her talent. Everything she does from today on is a bonus. It *adds on* to her career, it doesn't take anything away.

"I chose Concord, because I recognize the drive in you," Figs says. "You've won the Cup, and you know how hard it is to do, but you have the fire to do it again. I chose Concord, because I believe in you and this team Concord has built around you."

"We're veering into soft territory," Sophie warns, because hockey culture tends toward macho and bravado, and soft is one of the worst four-letter words in their world. Soft is gentle, it's emotional, it's *sentimental.*

Figs scoffs. "I think we're allowed. But if it makes you feel better, I won't offer to hug you."

Sophie chuckles and discreetly wipes her eyes. They move the conversation into safer territory—their upcoming games, and the players Figs knows on each of the teams.

Chapter Eleven

After Indianapolis, the entire team enters a collective slump. They lose, starting a two-game losing streak. It isn't a problem until it's three games, then four. It becomes a pattern, and Sophie sees the defeat on her teammates' faces before they even take the ice for their games.

Sophie had a good talk with Figs, but it didn't magically fix her. In some ways, it's increased the pressure on her. Because Figs *believes*. He believes in Sophie, and he believes in this team, but belief isn't enough to win games.

This is Figs's last season, and if Sophie can't turn her team around, she'll be the reason his career ends in disappointment.

Sophie does her best not to bring her frustration home. Elsa, as Sophie's teammate, doesn't deserve her captain's ire. And Elsa, as Sophie's girlfriend, doesn't deserve Sophie's temper. Sophie takes to calling her dad, because he'll poke at her weak spots until she snaps at him, then he'll yell back at her. It's hardly a solution, and Sophie isn't even sure it's helping.

Their thirtieth game of the season comes against Cleveland. They fall behind in the first minute of the game and never catch up. The game ends 4-5, and Sophie knows her sleep tonight will be haunted by the ping of the puck off the crossbar when she had a chance to tie the game and didn't.

It extends their losing streak, and Sophie hates to lose, but she especially hates to lose against Cleveland. Michael Hayes, her longtime rival and brief teammate, smirks at her after the game. She wants to grab a fistful of his jersey and demand to know what he's done against her that's worth smirking about. She's the one who beat him year after year in prep school. She's the one who Concord chose to keep, and it was Hayes they traded away. She's the one with a Maple Cup and records and a Hall of Fame career. He won a game. So what?

But his win does mean something, because it burrows under her skin. It bothers her after the game, when she does her press. It bothers her when she's home, when she's trying to settle enough to sleep. Concord is losing, and they turn to Sophie to pull them out of this hole. She hasn't yet, and how long will it take before they stop believing she will?

With each loss, she feels as though she's personally letting down Figuli. She's letting down Elsa and Teddy, Theo and Kevlar. She's letting down herself, and she hates it, but all that hate doesn't make the puck hit the back of the net more often.

The day after their loss to Cleveland, Sophie goes to the rink even though they've been given the day off. Sophie isn't the only one with the restless need to play until she figures it out, but Coach Elison forbid them from on or off-ice practice today. They need a reset.

Sophie doesn't go to the rink for practice but to see her coach.

"I don't know what's wrong," Sophie tells him. Coach Elison is behind his desk, and there's a furrow in his brow as if he's also worried about the losing streak. Sophie doesn't sit. She can't. She paces. "If I don't know what's wrong, I can't fix it."

Growing up, Sophie's dad would tape her practices so they could review where she needed to improve. He would put together drills to target her weaknesses, and they spent the weekends repeating the same drill over and over until she was better. She's learned to self-diagnose, with and without video assistance.

But she's at a loss. She's changed her shot, her stick, even her line, and none of it has worked. Worse, she isn't the only one struggling now.

"I need you to fix me," she tells Coach Elison. They haven't had the easiest relationship. He came in after their previous coach was all but fired, because he mismanaged the team, and Sophie in particular. She was hesitant to trust after Butler, and it was Coach Elison who bore the brunt of her suspicion.

They've found a balance that works for them, and now she's asking him—no, begging him, to help her.

"Patience," Coach Elison tells her.

Sophie grips the back of the chair resting across the desk from Coach Elison. She's tempted to lift it off the ground, to throw it, to break and destroy and try to excise this building frustration inside her.

"I have been patient," Sophie snaps. She forces her fingers to unclench. She tries to take a deep breath, but her breath stutters, and she bows her head. What weaknesses is she exposing to Coach Elison right now? How many of them will he use against her when he's with a new team next year?

Sophie's breath comes faster. She feels as if she can't draw in enough air, but the more she tries, the less she pulls in. Darkness spots her vision, and her fingers tingle, numbness spreading into her hands, then her wrists, her arms.

She gasps and shudders, and she can't stop.

Then there's a hand on the back of her neck. The hand is warm, the palm dry, and it's grounding. It keeps her from floating away, but it isn't enough. Another hand curls around her shoulder.

There's a voice by her ear. "Breathe with me," Coach Elison says. He tells her when to breathe in, how long to hold it, and when to breathe out. It's a steady count, and she doesn't have to focus on anything except the numbers and his quiet commands.

Sophie's always been good at following instructions.

Once she can breathe again, Sophie can think again. With thinking comes shame. Sophie twists away from her coach, and he doesn't follow her. He gives her space, and she hates that he does, but she would hate him more if he followed.

Coach Elison leans against his desk. He folds his arms over his chest and regards Sophie for a long moment. When she doesn't speak, he does. "We need to have a talk."

Sophie can't hold his gaze—it's too warm, too understanding, and so she glares at his shoulder. "Isn't that what we just did? You told me to be patient." She almost spits the word. "We're thirty games into the season. How much more patient do I have to be?"

"I'm not sure you understand the definition of patience," Coach Elison says.

Sophie snarls at him, because he's already seen her at her worst. "It isn't a luxury I can afford anymore."

Coach Elison waits, *patiently*, for her to continue.

"My no movement clause doesn't kick in until next season. Neither does Elsa's. If we don't win, they'll trade one or both of us. This is your third season here. If we don't win, you'll be fired. This is Figs's last season in the NAHL. If we don't win, he never lifts the Cup. Everything hinges on us—on *me*—performing, and I'm not. I'm letting everyone down."

Coach Elison watches Sophie as she breathes heavily, winded from her outburst. Sophie can't meet his gaze, but she doesn't turn away from his scrutiny either. She told him the truth. There are no secrets she's hiding.

"I can see why you're struggling," Coach Elison says. "You have a lot on your mind."

Sophie bristles, hearing the censure in his words. "I'm the captain. The team is my responsibility."

"Do you remember what I told you when I first came to Concord?"

Coach Elison told her a lot of things. They had more than one meeting between captain and new coach, because everyone was invested in their partnership working out. But she knows what he's referring to. "You told me keeping your job wasn't my responsibility."

"It's mine," Coach Elison says. "You can lift that weight from your shoulders."

Sophie clenches her jaw and doesn't argue. Can she give up that weight? Can she afford not to?

"Mikhail Figuli chose to sign here," Coach Elison continues. "It was his choice. It doesn't fall on you."

Sophie's eyes fill with tears, and she stares at the floor as if she can will them back.

"Whether the front office trades Elsa before next season is determined by her play. You can lift that weight off your shoulders. Whether you're re-signed is determined by your play, and I know you're in a slump, but you have no need to worry. You're a strong, two-way forward. Your scoring is valuable, yes, but so is your defensive game, and the leadership you bring to this team."

Sophie turns away so Coach Elison won't see as the tears finally spill over.

But Coach Elison isn't finished. "I won't make you a promise I can't keep, but if the decision was firmly in my hands, I wouldn't trade you. Not at the deadline, not during the summer, no matter what the outcome of this season is."

Sophie wipes furiously at her eyes. Crying is an admission of weakness, but hadn't coming here at all been one? She fled to her coach's office, she's had what amounted to a pity party then a breakdown, and—

Shit.

"If you aren't with us next season—" Sophie clears her throat and hopes her voice will be steadier. "This doesn't leave this room, right?" How many of Sophie's secrets did Butler give to Denver? How many of her weaknesses did he share with a team who eagerly exploited them?

"My office is like a confessional," Coach Elison promises.

Sophie nods. When it doesn't feel like enough, she adds, "Thank you."

*

"You were gone for a while," Elsa says when Sophie comes home. There's no judgment in Elsa's tone, no suspicion in the way she tracks Sophie's movement through the hallway, then the kitchen. There's only mild concern, which grows as Elsa studies Sophie's face and the signs of crying Sophie couldn't scrub entirely away.

"I had some things to do," Sophie says. She yawns and doesn't bother to cover it. She's exhausted from an emotional conversation with her coach. "Nap?"

"Nap," Elsa agrees.

They head upstairs together, and Sophie washes her face again, but it doesn't hide as much as she'd like, because Elsa beckons Sophie into bed with open arms and holds her tightly once she's there.

"If you don't want to talk to me about it, I understand," Elsa says, and the words are measured, almost painful as if they aren't what Elsa wants to say. "But you should talk to Dr. Malone."

She should. After Sophie tore her ACL, sessions with Dr. Malone, a sports psychologist, were mandatory. They haven't been mandatory since, and Sophie's sessions aren't as frequent, but she still makes appointments to speak with the woman. With everything piling up recently, Sophie told herself it was better to spend her free time at the rink or studying tape instead of talking. It was a mistake, of course, but she'll make an appointment after their nap.

"What about you?" Sophie asks.

"I'm good," Elsa answers. She huffs fondly as Sophie twists so they're facing each other. But there's nothing but truth in Elsa's gaze and her voice as she repeats herself. "I'm good. Would I like it if we were winning more? Of course. Would I like it if you were back on my line? Yes. But those things will come."

Why does everyone except Sophie believe? Hasn't her faith, her drive been what made her so successful? She would never have made it to the NAHL without it and now, in her ninth season, it's gone? This is not a productive line of thinking if she wants to have a restful nap.

Elsa must agree, because she pulls Sophie even closer and distracts her. "We're going to dinner tonight so have a good nap. Dream about appetizers and dessert."

"We can't have both," Sophie says, because they have nutrition plans to adhere to.

"Which is why you're dreaming about them." Elsa grins and presses a kiss to Sophie's forehead. "Sleep, now."

"So fucking bossy," Sophie murmurs but she doesn't protest.

She feels better after her nap, groggy but rested. She's warm from being under the blankets, and she's stuck thanks to Elsa's tight hold, but Sophie isn't in a rush to go anywhere. She grabs her phone off the bedside table and uses the Notes app to compose a letter to Emily.

All this talk about pressure and expectation, about legacies and careers, it's impossible not to think about Emily Skelton. Half the hockey community believes she's Sophie's successor. They want her to *replace* Sophie, as if there's only space for one of them in the league.

It's bullshit and next year, everyone will see that. Emily will be drafted this summer, and she'll start with whatever team is lucky enough to have her. She and Sophie will compete in the league at the same time. They'll even compete against each other. But—and Sophie needs to get herself used to this now, so she isn't caught off guard by it later—there will be things Emily does that Sophie will never do.

Sophie doesn't put this in her letter to Emily, but she can't help but wonder if Emily will be the first woman drafted first overall. She certainly has the skill for it. It could have been Sophie, and there are times where Sophie bitterly thinks it should have been her. Lexie certainly believed that she should have been the top pick at her own draft, but it was Kensington instead.

Could Emily be the one? The selfish part of Sophie hopes it isn't. The inevitable comparisons already exhaust her. But the part of Sophie who wants to see the league grow and evolve wants to see Emily acknowledged as the best in a talented draft. Sophie has met Emily a few times, has mentored her from a distance, and for Emily's sake, Sophie wants to see her succeed.

It will sting that Sophie can never go back in time and be drafted first overall. The sting is lessened by the fact that the possibility exists for Emily because of Sophie, but it doesn't erase it entirely.

Elsa grumbles against Sophie's neck. "Stop thinking."

Sophie checks the time on her phone. "It's time to be awake." When Elsa only grumbles again, Sophie wiggles out of her grasp. "You promised to take me out. We have to get ready."

This, predictably, gains Elsa's attention. Or maybe she's less willing to laze about in bed when Sophie isn't in her arms. "I made reservations."

"Reservations?" Sophie echoes. "That means fancy."

"Mm-hmm." Elsa somehow manages to look smug, even with her hair a tousled mess and her eyelids heavy with sleep.

"Fine," Sophie says, then she delves deeply into her closet for something appropriate to wear. Normally, when Sophie needs to be dressed up, she falls back on wearing a suit. She wears suits on game days, to formal team functions, and she likes them. But they also mean hockey, and Sophie needs a break from hockey tonight.

If she isn't wearing a suit, it means she's wearing a dress, and here she falters. Half her dresses still have the tags on them. She's tempted to ask Elsa for help picking one out, but she keeps her mouth shut, because she wants to surprise Elsa.

She settles on a midnight-blue dress, only a shade or two away from black. There's a decorative silver belt made of interlocking rings to help give the dress shape and structure. The dress is a hair shorter than her knees which means she has to wear tights. She hates tights. They always feel as though they're falling down, and there's no good way to subtly hike them up.

Maybe she's being ridiculous. A dress and tights, then she has to straighten her hair and do her makeup. It's so much effort and for what?

Sophie scowls at the woman in the mirror.

Her blue eyes are brighter than usual, her makeup causing them to stand out. Her lips are stained dark red thanks to her lipstick. Her dress has thick straps but no sleeves so her arms, muscled from daily workouts, are on display. The body of the dress is fitted, neat seams giving her a shape.

Sophie looks in the mirror and she doesn't see a hockey player. She sees a woman. And yes, there's a year's worth of sessions with Dr. Malone in those two thoughts, but it's true. Sophie is rarely allowed to be all of herself. She's separated into pieces so people can use only the parts they need.

Elsa's always wanted all of Sophie.

"Oh," Elsa breathes.

Sophie turns to see Elsa standing in the doorway to the bathroom. Elsa's gaze drags from Sophie's calves, on display because of the length of her dress, up all the way to Sophie's hair. It's pin-straight, not a hint of wave or curl to be seen, because Mary Beth likes to curl Sophie's hair to make her softer for press appearances. Sophie isn't *soft*.

Elsa's lips part as she stares, and her eyes roam as if she wants to look at all of Sophie at once. Sophie shuffles her weight from one foot to the other. It's Elsa who deserves the attention. She's in an emerald-green dress that has some kind of sheen, catching the bright light of the bathroom. Her blonde hair is piled on top of her head in an explosion of gold curls Sophie wants to reach out and touch.

Maybe after dinner. Sophie won't ruin the time Elsa's put into her look before they go out, but after? After, Sophie can pull the pins out of Elsa's hair until it tumbles down. Sophie can card her fingers through Elsa's hair and pull her in to kiss her. She can—

"This is a bad idea," Sophie says. Guilt presses on her chest, heavy until it's difficult to breathe. "We shouldn't— *I* shouldn't—" Sophie curls her hands into fists and looks away. But because they're in the bathroom, there's a giant mirror, and even though she looks away, Sophie can still see. "I'm in a slump. I don't—" She cuts herself off, because she sees Elsa's jaw clench, and knows Elsa knows what she was going to say.

"You don't deserve this?" Elsa asks, and there's

something sharp beneath the question. Elsa shakes her head. "Tonight is about us." She steps forward until she can clasp Sophie's hands in hers. "You don't have to score a certain number of goals or win a game in order for us to go out. Hockey has nothing to do with this."

Sophie opens her mouth but at Elsa's head shake, she closes it again.

"I know, you aren't playing as well as you'd like." Elsa's softer now, careful, as if she thinks Sophie needs it. "But we aren't hockey. Not this part of us at least. If hockey isn't going well, it's even more important for the other parts of your life to be good. You don't have to be miserable."

Logically, it makes sense, but it goes against everything Sophie's grown up believing. Still, Elsa believes it and she looks at Sophie expectantly, so Sophie nods.

"We're going out." Elsa swings their joined hands. "We're having a nice dinner, and we're going to share a bottle of wine and stay for dessert. If we're feeling daring, we'll hold hands under the table. And when we come home, I'm putting music on, and we're dancing in our living room."

"That's—" *Silly, decadent, a waste.* "That sounds really nice."

"I have the best ideas," Elsa says. She laughs and kisses the outraged look right off Sophie's face. It's a gentle kiss, softer than what they usually exchange, and when Elsa pulls back, she checks them both in the mirror.

Lipstick, Sophie realizes. She laughs and feels lighter. "That's another reason to hate makeup, if you can't kiss me the way I like."

"When we get home," Elsa promises. The heat in her gaze promises a long night of making it up to Sophie, of giving Sophie everything she asks for. Elsa raises Sophie's hand to her mouth and presses another gentle kiss to Sophie's palm. "I love you, not your point total."

Before Sophie can come up with a response, Elsa pulls her out of the bathroom and to the bed. There's a weird pair of nylon socks on it that Elsa tosses at her. "Take off your tights and put those on instead. You hate tights."

"But I'm wearing a dress," Sophie protests. Even as she argues, she does what Elsa said.

"And? You don't wear tights under your shorts when we work out. Bare legs aren't scandalous. Well..." Elsa's gaze turns speculative, as if she's thinking about Sophie's bare legs. Like she's thinking about Sophie's bare *everything*.

"Quit that," Sophie says as a blush rises in her cheeks. "Or we're never going to make our reservation."

"After dinner," Elsa says.

Chapter Twelve

November was a dismal month for the Concord Condors, and December doesn't start on a new note. Teddy struggles in net, their d-core is depleted with injury, and in no short order, they've dropped to sixth in their division. Most of the broadcasters and analysts have written the season off. There are mourning articles for Figs and an equal number calling for Concord to trade him to a contender, so he still has a shot at the Cup. Sophie does her best not to read or listen to the coverage calling for Sophie and Elsa's trades.

Strangely, it's when the team is at rock bottom that Sophie finds her game again.

She has Jacobs, now Cubs, on her left wing and Stenner, a Manchester callup, on her right wing, because Woodsy is out with pneumonia of all things. Woodsy isn't the only one out. A quarter of their forward group is bogged down with the same illness, and their d-corp is still beat up, and it means most of the team is Manchester callups.

On December 15th, Sophie and her team fly to Houston. The coverage headed into the game is that Concord looks more like a minor league team than a NAHL team. They're young, they're inexperienced, and the leadership core is shaken and weak.

Sophie calls bullshit.

Yes, they have several Manchester players on the

roster right now, but they're familiar with Concord hockey, and they have experience playing with one another. In a few games, they'll have the experience of playing with their Concord teammates. And yes, they're young, but youth means speed and it means resilience.

Sophie isn't shaken and she isn't weak. The only people who think Sophie has lost the respect of the locker room haven't been in the locker room.

She takes Cubs and Stenner over the boards for the first shift of the game. Hockey buzzes under Sophie's skin. She always plays her best when she's underestimated and has something to prove.

She wins the faceoff, and Cubs carries the puck up the ice. He's confident enough to bring the puck into the offensive zone himself, and he's skilled enough to protect the puck from Browning as the Houston forward tries to steal it.

Cubs passes to Stenner who rims the puck around the boards for Sophie. She battles a Houston d-man for it and comes out victorious.

Her line doesn't score on the opening shift, but they force Navarro to cover the puck which means an offensive zone faceoff for the next line out. Sophie grabs Elsa's jersey as Elsa's line is sent out. "We softened him up for you. He's shaky left-to-right."

"You say the sweetest things." Elsa grins and pats Sophie's helmet.

"Ugh, save it for later." Peets shoves Elsa away from Sophie and toward Navarro's net.

Sophie sits between Cubs and Stenner on the bench, but she doesn't sit for long. Peets wins the faceoff, and Elsa takes the puck around the back of the net. She draws Navarro to his left post and makes a neat pass across the goalmouth to Gleason. Navarro can't push to his other post quickly enough, and Gleason scores his first NAHL goal.

Gleason stands, stunned and staring at the net, until Elsa barrels into him. Sophie can hear Elsa laughing as she raises Gleason's arms above his head and waves them in an imitation of a celly.

Gleason recovers in time to lead his line down the bench for praise and shoulder slaps from the guys sitting and watching. Once Elsa is on the bench, she stands over Stenner until he slides over and makes space next to Sophie.

"Bully," Sophie accuses affectionately.

Elsa preens and doesn't apologize. She does watch as the jumbotron changes the score and notes the goal scorer and assists. "You should have an assist on that," Elsa says.

Sophie shakes her head. She doesn't need her name written down to know she contributed. Her line forced the offensive zone faceoff. She identified Navarro's weakness. And Elsa and her line capitalized. Sophie is used to changing the course of a game with the puck on her stick, but she can do it even without the puck. And *that* should have every opposing player in the league scared.

"Yeah?" Elsa asks, as if she can read Sophie's mind. She laughs and rubs her glove over Sophie's helmet. "They don't know what's about to fucking hit them."

Sophie grins and leans forward, her elbows braced on her legs, so she can find more weaknesses to exploit in Houston's game.

*

It's 2-1 when Browning, a Houston forward, flies up the ice on a breakaway. He tries to fake out Elmo, who's in Concord's goal because Kolmonen's sick and Teddy's lost his last four starts.

Elmo, Morgan Elwood, doesn't bite on the fake shot, and he easily gloves the real shot when it comes.

"Stick to poetry, eh?" Elmo chirps.

Browning's scowl melts into a look of confusion. "The fuck?" he demands.

Sophie's equally confused, but she doesn't resort to swearing. Elmo, unfazed by Browning's temper, tips the puck into the official's outstretched hand. "Elizabeth Barrett Browning? I went to college, you know. Even managed to learn some shit. Which means I'm better at hockey *and* reading than you are." Elmo smirks. "Now, fly away, little swallow." He makes a shooing motion.

Sophie steps between Browning and her goalie before Browning decides to take a swing. And while Browning was willing to have it out with a minor league goalie, he skates away from Sophie. Sophie doesn't lie to herself. It isn't her intimidation factor which chases Browning away. He's likely afraid of Jonny's retribution if he tries anything against Concord's captain.

"We should have a read-aloud on the plane tonight," Elmo says.

Sophie looks over at her goalie to confirm that yes, he's completely serious, he wants a bunch of hockey players to read poetry to one another. Why not, she decides. "If we win," Sophie says.

Elmo grins and tugs his mask down so he's prepared for the next shift.

"You have no idea what you've done," Stenner says as they skate for the bench. "He doesn't only read poetry, he writes it."

"Elmo?" Carter Martin asks. He's another Manchester callup, and he looks down at the ice at where their goalie is scuffing up his crease. "Do you remember when he was writing haikus and *I made the save* was only four syllables so he just added *Wheeeee!* to the end?"

"He's smart," Elsa says.

"That's cheating," Martin counters.

Elsa shrugs, which says everything it needs to about

her diligence as a student. Sophie takes her seat on the bench and doesn't hide her smile as her teammates begin to light-heartedly grumble about poetry or Elmo's antics. The mood is still lighter than it's been in weeks, and Sophie has a good feeling about this game.

Maybe Elsa was onto something with distractions and breaks from hockey. If Sophie can have them all thinking about poetry, they aren't focused on their mistakes. They aren't even focused on what they need to do. Everyone on the team, callup or not, knows how to play hockey. They need to trust themselves and sometimes, that means thinking a little bit less.

*

Late in the second period, Sophie and Elsa are on the ice together for a power play. Sophie has been buzzing around the net all game, and Elsa knows it. Elsa shoots the puck purposefully wide, and the puck bounces off the boards, and Sophie corrals it with her stick.

Elsa hovers on Navarro's backdoor, but there's a d-man guarding her. Kevlar is up by the blue line, but Sophie will only pass to him if she doesn't have a better option. Cubs jostles with Houston's other d-man in front of the net. Maybe Sophie will pass to Kevlar. They can cycle the puck, wait for a good shot, and—

No.

Sophie has a good shot.

Well, she has *a* shot. Sophie's just above the goal line. There's a sliver of the net open, and earlier this season, she would pass to Kevlar. But tonight, she shoots. The puck squeaks under the crossbar and in.

"Fuck yeah!" Sophie shouts.

*

In the final minute of the game, Coach Elison sends Sophie out with Elsa on one wing and Merlin on the other. It's a callback to a line from years ago, and Sophie doesn't hesitate. She scores the final goal of the game, the one to give them a decisive 6-3 victory.

Sophie isn't sure who's more pleased, herself or Coach Elison.

It's an important win, because it stops their losing skid, and it's Sophie's first two-goal game this season. Just as important, the entire team is in high spirits. They won with their third-string goalie when no one expected them to.

Not even Elmo's read-aloud on the plane can bring the team down. They heckle him, with love, and Elmo just grins and shouts even louder, sharing his own haikus with them but also poetry from people Sophie's never heard of.

Someone, of course, looks up limericks, then everyone tries to find the dirtiest poetry they can. Sophie's pleased with the chaos she's caused, but she isn't finished yet. When they reach the hotel they're staying at in Kansas City, she prints out a few of Elizabeth Barrett Browning's sonnets, and she slides them under Elmo's door.

"You're smiling," Elsa says when Sophie returns from her errand. Elsa looks suspicious as if a happy Sophie is one to be wary of.

"I am." Sophie smiles wider and laughs as Elsa looks truly alarmed. She changes into her pajamas and brushes her teeth. Elsa reels Sophie in for a kiss when she comes back, but Sophie doesn't let Elsa pull her down into bed. Not yet.

Sophie has a mental count in her head, and she's almost to four hundred when there's a knock at their door.

"Are we expecting someone?" Elsa asks. She frowns at the door.

Sophie pulls a sweatshirt on over her tank top. It's

one of Elsa's, but she shrugs and then goes to answer the door. Cubs stands on the other side. Sophie figured he would flee his room, but she didn't think he would have come to hers. Sophie leans on the doorframe and tries to control her smile.

"Please, Cap, you have to help me," Cubs says. "Someone gave Elmo more poems. He's counting all the way he loves me."

Sophie relies on every ounce of her media training to keep a straight face. "And you ran away? Cubs, the reason we have road roommates is to foster personal relationships. A team is only as strong as the bonds between its players."

All along the hall, their teammates are opening their doors and poking their heads out to see what's going on.

Cubs doesn't notice. He's too busy staring at Sophie, mouth open, eyes filled with betrayal. "It was *you*? Why?"

Sophie cracks now, unable to hold back her laughter. This is exactly what the team needed. Something lighthearted, something to remind them that yes, they're professionals, but they're allowed to have fun. "Maybe you can take turns reading so you can show Elmo you're interested in his passions."

"I'm going to give Elsa poems and see how you like it," Cubs says.

"I don't know how to read English," Elsa calls from the bed.

"Bullshit," Cubs fires back, but he knows when he's lost a fight. He sighs, shoulders slumping, then he slinks off to beg someone else to let him crash in their room for the night.

Sophie makes eye contact with Merlin, and she knows he'll handle keeping this poetry gag going for a few more days at least. By then, hopefully, there will be something new to distract and entertain the team.

She shuts the door and looks over at Elsa. "Even the rookies are wise to you."

Elsa responds in Swedish.

"You do too understand," Sophie says. She pulls her sweatshirt off and tosses it on the floor, then she gets into bed with Elsa.

Elsa holds out the bags of ice they made up earlier. Sophie scowls but she accepts them and rests them on the worst of her bruises from the game. She hisses as the cold seeps into her skin. It never gets easier, having to ice.

"Will you set the timer?" Sophie asks. She closes her eyes, even though it means the only thing there is for her to focus on is the cold against her side. It's a sharp contrast to the warmth from where Elsa is pressed against her. Sophie tries to shuffle closer, and Elsa laughs softly, but she obliges.

She cards her fingers through Sophie's hair as Sophie cuddles her. Then Elsa talks in Swedish again. It isn't teasing like earlier. Elsa's voice is soft, and there's a cadence to her words, almost as if—

"Are you reading poetry?" Sophie asks.

"Shh," Elsa hushes.

"Älskling," Sophie continues. "You've called me that before."

Elsa hushes her again and returns to her reading. She keeps it up until the timer goes off, then Elsa sets her phone aside as Sophie goes to empty their ice bags into the sink. When Sophie returns to bed, Elsa turns off the light and pulls Sophie close. She murmurs to her in Swedish again, but this time she isn't reading someone else's words. She uses her own.

*

They have a morning practice, then the rest of their day is their own. They don't play Kansas City until tomorrow, and Sophie knows the team is taking advantage of the free time. She makes plans of her own and drags Elsa along with her.

Sophie doesn't know Jordan Cassidy well. She played against her in the last Winter Games, and they met briefly at the draft this summer. It means tonight could be awkward, and Elsa alternates between grumbling that Sophie's dragged her out to be social and smiling indulgently as if Sophie's outreach to the other women in the league is cute.

Sophie does her best not to snap at Elsa over it, because it will lead to a fight neither of them want. Sophie spent a lonely two years in the league as the only woman playing in the NAHL. She could have had Elsa with her in her second season, she *should* have had Elsa, but Elsa stayed another year in Sweden. Sophie doesn't want to make Elsa feel guilty about the decision, but she also doesn't want Elsa dismissing what Sophie's trying to do now. There aren't as many women in the league as Sophie wants, but she will make sure none of them felt as lonely as she did.

The cab drops them off in front of Up-Down, the bar Jordan chose, and Sophie wonders if maybe this wasn't the best choice after all.

"Be nice," Sophie tells Elsa as they head inside.

"Or what? You'll send me home from our playdate early?"

They both pause inside the building. The walls are exposed brick, giving the place an industrial feel which reminds Sophie of Concord. What catches her off guard, though, are all the games. There are TV screens hosting video games, there are arcade games lining the wall, and there's even skee-ball in the corner.

"I take it back," Elsa says. "This could be fun."

"I aim to please," Jordan says. She saunters up to them in a pair of faded jeans that strain across her thighs and a T-shirt which ends well before her bellybutton. She's relaxed, completely at home here.

"I bet you I can beat you in any game here," Elsa challenges.

Jordan's smile turns sharp. "Loser buys the first round."

Sophie is left to trail after them as they argue over which game they're playing first. She doesn't have to mediate as often as she feared, because the games allow Elsa and Jordan to channel their competitiveness into a more productive avenue than fighting.

When they've exhausted all the interesting games, they head to the bar for food, and the talk turns to Kansas City itself.

"I like it here," Jordan says. She takes her second slice of mac and cheese pizza off its tray. Sophie tries not to eye it with too much suspicion. Concord has an unfortunate tradition of surprise pizza where, when they're feeling bored, they go to a local pizza place and roll some dice or pick toppings out of a hat in order to create a random, and often stomach churning, concoction.

Sophie leaves Elsa to carry the conversation as she's sucked into watching one of the TVs mounted on the wall. There's football on some, basketball on others, but the one closest to Sophie shows the Indianapolis-Chicago game. She frowns as Kensington scores. The camera zooms in on him to catch his sweaty face and triumphant smirk as he celebrates.

"Jackass," the guy next to Sophie mutters. He nudges Sophie with his glass of beer and lifts the glass toward the screen. "I'd like to beat his fucking face in, you know?"

"Has he been causing problems for the Cavaliers?" Sophie asks, as if Kensington hasn't been causing problems for every team this season.

"Him and that bitch he plays with," the guy says. He misses the way Sophie stiffens and shifts away from him as he warms up to his rant. "There are too many bitches in hockey these days. I remember when it was a man's sport."

Unfortunately, the man's loud enough to interrupt Elsa and Jordan's argument over who lives in the better city. They both turn to him with matching glares.

"Nah, now that they let women into the NAHL, you can see how many men just simply don't measure up." Jordan's expression is flinty, and Sophie realizes now that she and Elsa's bickering had been friendly because *this* is what Jordan looks like when she's pissed off. "Is that your problem? It's too hard to measure up?" The words drip off Jordan's tongue like poison, and she accompanies them with an obvious look down at the man's crotch, before she flicks her gaze back up. She laughs as he turns red with rage.

Sophie has a vision of a drunken bar fight and having to call Merlin to come and bail her and Elsa out of a Kansas City jailhouse.

"All right, that's enough," Sophie says. The bartender, a smart woman, bustles over to take Sophie's credit card and hand her some to-go boxes in return.

"Do you think you're some kind of hockey expert?" the man demands, as if he hasn't realized he already lost the fight. "You wear a pink jersey to the games, and you think it makes you a real fan?"

"As long as Sophie Fournier's name is on the back, I don't care what color my jersey is," Elsa says, deciding to join the fight.

And now it's really time to go, before anyone who's an actual hockey fan realizes who any of them are. If this incident ends up on *The Sin Bin*, Sophie will be in trouble with the Commissioner and with Mary Beth.

"Fournier?" The man spits Sophie's name as if it's

something dirty.

Sophie takes her credit card and her receipt from the bartender, adds another ten percent to the tip as her thanks for the speed, then she ushers Elsa and Jordan out of the bar before Elsa starts throwing punches.

Once they're outside, Jordan kicks the metal base of a street sign. "Fucker." She glares at the sign, then at Elsa, then, for good measure, glares at Sophie too. "You didn't get mad."

Because then Elsa really would have punched someone, Sophie thinks. What she says is, "If I fought every person who didn't think I belonged in the league, I wouldn't have time to play hockey. Tomorrow, I'm going to take the ice and play my game. What some guy in a bar in Kansas City thinks doesn't matter."

"You make it sound easy." Jordan continues to glare. "You make everything seem easy."

"It's what I want people to think." Sophie leans against Elsa and allows her to wrap her arms around Sophie and hold her up. "But it isn't. None of this is easy. We all know it. But if we act like it's hard, then the guys in there think they have a chance to win. And fuck that."

Jordan looks up, something like hope sparking in her eyes. "You do have some fight in you, then."

"I wouldn't have made it to the NAHL if I didn't." Sophie doesn't understand what it is with American players. First Lexie and now Jordan seem to think that her media persona is her true self. They should know better. She didn't make it to the NAHL by asking nicely.

Sophie insists Jordan take the first cab they hail, then she leans more firmly against Elsa as they wait for a second.

*

Jordan Cassidy opens the scoring with an objectively gorgeous goal. Then she skates by Concord's bench so she can wave at Elsa.

"Please tell me that didn't just happen," Merlin says. He glances at Elsa to see if Elsa's about to launch herself off the bench at the Kansas City forward.

"It happened," Sophie says. Before she can tell Elsa not to retaliate with a penalty, Elsa's line heads over the boards.

Sophie's on the edge of the bench, concerned, until Elsa scores a goal of her own. It's a grit goal, none of the flash of Jordan's, but it counts on the scoresheet, and that's what Sophie cares about.

Elsa doesn't even look Jordan's way after the goal. She celebrates with her linemates on the ice, then she skates straight for Sophie on the bench.

Chapter Thirteen

Their road trip continues up until the Christmas break. They win against Santa Fe, a positive note, before the team scatters to see family and friends.

Sophie and Elsa's families both fly in, and Sophie is nervous. Their families have never been together like this before. Sure, Sophie and Elsa's mom have hung out on Moms' Trips and Sophie and Elsa's dads have ignored each other on Dads' Trips, but this is different. This isn't hockey.

This is Sophie and Elsa hosting their families for the holidays. It's a big milestone, and Sophie's as eager for it as she is terrified of it. But these nerves, they're normal people nerves. Hundreds of thousands of people all over the world worry about their partner's family meeting their own. At least Sophie and Elsa don't have to worry about offending anyone by traveling for the holidays. As long as they're still playing hockey, they can make everyone come to them.

"Do you think this means we need two in-law apartments?" Sophie asks as she bustles through the living room, straightening pillows and rearranging the decorative magazines. "Armand says it's possible, even if it isn't typical."

"We have enough money to make anything possible," Elsa answers. She watches Sophie fuss from one of the island stools, amused and with no intention of helping. "But no, we don't need two in-law apartments. What if there was a guest suite on the first floor? One or two bedrooms with an attached full bath?"

"I like that," Sophie says. She wants their families to feel as if they have a space of their own when they visit. She also wants to make sure she and Elsa continue to have their own space.

"I'm very smart," Elsa says. "You should let me design the whole house."

"No," Sophie says, because that way lies saltwater pools and rope swings off the second floor.

Elsa pouts and even though it's fake, Sophie stops moving the TV remotes from one side table to the other in order to cross into the kitchen and kiss her girlfriend. One kiss turns into two, then three, and Elsa has a hand up Sophie's shirt when the doorbell rings and Sophie nearly jumps out of her skin.

Elsa laughs at her all the way to the door, and Sophie pats her hair down quickly before she opens the front door and greets her family.

It's a packed house once Sophie's parents, Elsa's parents, then Colby and his girlfriend arrive for Christmas Eve and Christmas Day.

Sophie's mom makes blueberry pancakes for everyone, a Fournier tradition, and Elsa's dad produces matching pajamas for each member of both families. Sophie makes Elsa a cup of coffee and when she hands it over, she sees her mother doing the same for her father and Elsa's dad doing the same for Elsa's mom. Sophie leans against Elsa's side.

"This is good," Elsa says quietly, as if she's reading Sophie's mind.

"It is," Sophie says.

Sophie's family is the first to leave. Elsa's parents

linger, because the flight from Sweden is too long for only a handful of days. They're in the stands for Concord's two games after the Christmas break, then they stay through the New Year's break as well.

Sophie, Elsa, and Elsa's parents go to dinner on Elsa's birthday. They have a small celebration at the house after, and once Elsa's parents retreat to the in-law apartment, Sophie hands Elsa her present.

Elsa's curious as she accepts the envelope. She slides a standard birthday card out of it and glances at Sophie. When Sophie doesn't say anything, Elsa opens the card. There are two airplane cutouts inside. Sophie can't help but search Elsa's face for a reaction. She waited to give it to Elsa when it was only the two of them, because she still hasn't decided if it's a good present or a copout.

Elsa doesn't react, and Sophie can't stand the silence, so she explains. "Our schedules make it difficult to plan things, so I can't surprise you with a trip. I did this instead. The two of us, anywhere you want to go. This summer, maybe."

"It's perfect." Elsa snakes an arm around Sophie's waist and reels her in. "We're going somewhere with a beach. We can go sailing."

"Do you know how to sail?"

Elsa shrugs, as if this is an unimportant detail. Then she grins, light and teasing, and Sophie knows she isn't going to like whatever Elsa says next. "Surfing?"

"Absolutely not."

"You'd look cute in a wetsuit."

"No, I wouldn't," Sophie says.

"You'd look better in nothing," Elsa continues, and it's cheesy and ridiculous, but Sophie still kisses Elsa when she leans in.

*

They go on vacation sooner than Sophie expected. Every year there isn't a Winter Games, the NAHL hosts the All-Star weekend. One player from every team is voted in by the fans, then the NAHL selects the remaining players. For the first time since Sophie came into the league, she isn't going to the All-Star weekend.

Even the season she tore her ACL and couldn't play, the commissioner insisted she attend the festivities in order to appear in photo ops and promote the league. Figs is the fan vote this year, even though he asked them to give him the time off.

Sophie can't lie, to Elsa at least. It stings to be passed over by the fans and slighted by the league, who decides Concord's play has been so abysmal they don't deserve a second player at the All-Star weekend. But suddenly having free time is a bonus, because it means she and Elsa can take a trip.

Sophie packs everything she needs into a small suitcase, then Elsa packs a second one for Sophie and tells her she has to bring it. Sophie doesn't know why she needs two suitcases for such a small trip. Well, she does. Because for some reason Elsa thinks Sophie needs three bathing suits and *five* sundresses. Is Sophie supposed to wear two dresses every day?

Sophie allows herself a few judgmental eyebrows, but she doesn't protest, because this is Elsa's trip, and Sophie's willing to indulge her.

It isn't a hockey trip, but a vacation. They still board a plane, and Sophie sighs as she buckles her lap belt and stretches her legs out. Her feet bump the seat in front of her. "When I retire, I'm not going anywhere for a year. Anyone who wants to see me will have to travel to me."

"The NAHL won't let you become a hermit." Elsa drapes a blanket over both of them, then finds Sophie's hand so she can hold it.

"Shh, don't ruin my fantasy."

Elsa laughs and squeezes Sophie's hand. "In this fantasy of yours, do you live alone? It's hard to be a hermit if it isn't only you."

"You're the one who called me a hermit. I just don't want any more airplanes or buses." Sophie looks over at Elsa. "In this dream, I don't live alone."

There was a time where Sophie didn't think about the future, especially a future without hockey in it. It felt like tempting fate, like disrespecting everything she had worked tirelessly for. But, despite the All-Star slight, Sophie knows she's in the prime of her career. She has several good seasons under her belt already, and she has more stretching out in front of her.

And, when the day does come for her to retire, there are things to look forward to.

*

Sophie allowed Elsa to make the plans, which she regrets as they pull up to where they'll be staying. It's a giant hotel with a water slide curling around the far side. Then Sophie spots all the buildings surrounding the hotel and realizes her first guess wasn't quite right. It's a resort.

"Now, we don't have to worry about anything," Elsa says. They wheel their suitcases down the hall to their suite. "If we don't want to leave the building, we don't have to. There are restaurants, a water park, a spa, even a beach. Everything we could possibly want is in one place."

They reach their suite. The door opens into a living room with a desk and office chair, two couches, and a large TV. A sliding door leads onto a small balcony with three chairs. There's a second sliding door on the balcony which leads into the bedroom. The bed is the focal point of the room and takes up nearly the entire space. There's a door back to the living room and another one to the bathroom.

Sophie pokes her head into the bathroom to investigate. It has a large glass shower with two showerheads, which seems opulent until she spots the bathtub. The tub might as well be a jacuzzi given its size.

"Wow," Sophie says.

"Mmm." Elsa comes up behind Sophie and nuzzles under her ear. "I didn't tell you about the water park, so we need to buy you another swimsuit."

"I already have three," Sophie says.

"And you need four. One for when we start our day with a sunrise swim on the beach, one for a floating lunch in the hotel pool, one for when we end our day relaxing in the hot tub, and then one for the water park."

Sophie turns to face Elsa. "In what world are you awake for a sunrise swim?" She evades Elsa's attempts to pull her back in and heads into the bedroom. "We are not eating in a pool, that sounds unhygienic. And what do we need a hot tub for when we have that?" She gestures to the bathroom and their gigantic bathtub.

"This is my birthday present," Elsa reminds Sophie. She stalks forward and Sophie backs up until she hits the bed. Elsa wraps a hand around her waist before Sophie can fall back on the bed. "We can go shopping now and then have dinner." Elsa slides her hands into Sophie's back pockets and pulls her close. "I'll buy you chocolate cake."

"Are you trying to bribe me into buying a fourth bathing suit with chocolate cake?"

"Is it working?" Elsa asks.

"No," Sophie answers.

"Hmm." Elsa ducks her head to kiss the underside of Sophie's jaw, where she knows Sophie is sensitive. "How about this?"

"I don't—" Sophie breaks off to suck in a sharp breath as Elsa kisses her again. She uses a bit of teeth this time, and Sophie's fingers scrabble at Elsa's back as she tries to pull her even closer. "I don't need another bathing suit."

"You don't need this either," Elsa points out.

The bed is right there, so Sophie twists them and pushes Elsa down on the bed. She straddles her girlfriend, one knee on either side of Elsa's hips. Elsa looks up at her, hair mussed and lips already a darker shade of pink. She looks delighted by this turn of events.

"I do," Sophie says. "I'm on vacation with my girlfriend. I need a lot of kisses."

"How many?" Elsa challenges.

"I'll tell you when I've had enough."

Elsa surges up at the same time Sophie bends down. Their mouths meet in a painful clash. The kiss turns gentler, but it isn't soft, as Elsa kisses Sophie with an intensity bordering on desperation. They have their entire vacation just for the two of them, but Sophie doesn't tell Elsa to relax or back off. Elsa kisses Sophie as if she wouldn't mind staying in this bed and doing nothing else. She kisses as if she'll never grow tired of it.

Sophie gives back as good as she can. They kiss until Sophie's light-headed with it, until they've shoved up each other's shirts but can't get any further until they break their kiss. It's Sophie who pulls away first. She's breathing hard, and she pulls her shirt over her head before she nudges Elsa to do the same.

"One," Elsa says. She tosses her shirt somewhere behind them.

"One?" Sophie asks.

Elsa sits up and kisses Sophie's shoulder as her hands work behind Sophie's back to undo her bra clasp. "Two."

"Keep going," Sophie says. "Two isn't nearly enough."

Elsa kisses Sophie's collarbone and the hollow of her throat. She kisses Sophie's cheeks, and her lips are featherlight, barely a touch at all. Sophie loses patience then, and she pushes Elsa down on the bed, and it's her turn to initiate the kiss.

*

Sophie's new bathing suit is neon pink.

*

The first morning they spend at the resort, they wake up naturally instead of to an alarm. They eat a lazy breakfast and have an even lazier swim in the hotel pool. Sophie rests her arms on the lip of the pool and looks out the floor-to-ceiling windows. She can see the ocean from here, and the waves are steady but small, certainly not a destination for surfers.

"It feels wrong to swim indoors when the ocean is right there," Sophie says.

"Then we go to the beach," Elsa says, as if it's that easy.

It is. They climb out of the pool, dry off, and head up to their room. Elsa insists on showering to rinse off the chlorine from the pool, then they have to change into new swimsuits. By the time they reach the beach, Sophie isn't in the mood to swim. She spreads her towel out and makes herself comfortable with her crime novel.

She makes good progress on her book, even if she had to start over because she doesn't remember what happened anymore. She's a few chapters in when she gives in to the warmth of the sun and decides to take a nap.

She wakes up to drool on her book and someone's hands on her.

"Elsa?" Sophie asks blearily. She hopes it's Elsa, especially as the person's hands skim beneath her bikini strap.

"It's me," Elsa answers. "I'm reapplying your sunscreen, but we might be a little late. You're already pink."

It sounds like a problem for later. Sophie drops her head back to her book and falls asleep again.

*

After a morning spent at the beach, they return to the hotel room to change for lunch. Sophie looks at her back in the mirror. It is pink, but only faintly, and it doesn't hurt when the water from the shower hits her skin. It means she isn't sunburned, but she resolves to be better at applying her sunscreen or wearing her coverups. The best way to ruin a vacation is to end up too sunburned to enjoy it.

Sophie had been curious when she showered solo, because Elsa hasn't shown any inclination to let her out of touching range, let alone her sight, so far this trip. But when she emerges from the shower, there's a dress and pair of sandals on the bed waiting for her. The khaki capris and loose linen shirt Sophie had picked out for herself are nowhere to be seen.

Elsa's already dressed. Her sundress comes with a distracting neckline, and the bottom swishes around her knees when she walks. Sophie looks back at her own dress, then she remembers she doesn't have to worry about staring at Elsa too long here.

They're on vacation, on a beach where no one knows who they are. Sophie looks over at Elsa again. She slides her gaze over Elsa's sandals, platform wedges because Elsa likes to be tall, then upward, taking in Elsa's shapely calves and the hint of quad muscles before Sophie's seeing dress instead of skin. She lingers on Elsa's chest, the way it rises and falls with Elsa's breathing. Her lips curl into a smile as Elsa's breaths come quicker.

"If you keep looking at me like that, we aren't going to make it out of this room," Elsa says.

"You say it like it's a bad thing." Sophie drops her towel, and she smirks a little, as it's Elsa's turn to stare.

*

On their second morning, Sophie insists they go for a run. Elsa convinces her to compromise, and they have a leisurely, barefoot jog on the beach. They chase the horizon until Elsa finally stops and shakes her head.

They walk back on the paved sidewalk. There are other people awake, but when Elsa holds Sophie's hand, she doesn't shake the touch away. Cyclists are taking advantage of the beautiful morning to get a ride in, and vendors set up at their kiosks.

They buy mango smoothies from one vendor and pastries from another. Then they wander, looking at T-shirts and knickknacks as they debate what to bring back for their teammates as souvenirs.

"Maybe we shouldn't get them anything," Sophie says as Elsa looks at tiny snow globes. "Not even one of them has reached out to see how we're doing."

Sophie hasn't talked to anyone she knows except for Elsa since they boarded the plane. She's talked to flight attendants and waitresses and shopkeepers, but none of them know who Sophie is. It means she doesn't have to worry about her image or Concord's or even the NAHL's. Sophie isn't the face of Concord hockey right now. She's a woman on vacation with the woman she loves.

It's nice. Sophie isn't used to nice.

"Maybe they're busy," Elsa says. They make their purchases and head back to the hotel.

"Busy?" Sophie echoes. "Doing what?"

Elsa shrugs and doesn't answer.

When they return to their room, Sophie puts their presents with her suitcase, so they won't forget them.

"What's the plan for the rest of the day?"

"Spa," Elsa answers immediately. "Full massages and then manicures and pedicures."

Sophie frowns as she looks at her nails. There's a bit of sand under them, a side effect of being at the beach. They're uneven, some shorter than the others. Her hands are scarred from various training accidents, and the skin around her knuckles is cracked but not outright bleeding. Her hands aren't delicate, not by any stretch of the definition.

"My nails chip too easily."

"They'll chip here?" Elsa gestures to their suite and the gorgeous view of the ocean out their window.

Maybe not here, but they aren't staying here forever. They'll be back in Concord in no time. Sophie will return to the weight room and the ice. She continues to frown. "I guess we can try."

"Good," Elsa says. She steps forward and brushes a kiss over Sophie's lips.

"You can't kiss me every time I agree with you," Sophie says.

"Positive reinforcement. Tell me I'm the best winger you've ever played with."

Sophie rolls her eyes, but it isn't like it's a lie, so she says, "You're the best winger I've ever played with."

Elsa kisses her. "Tell me I'm the best girlfriend you've ever had."

"You're the best girlfriend I've ever had," Sophie says.

This kiss lasts longer, and Sophie sways into it. When Elsa pulls back, she cups Sophie's face in her hands. Her thumbs reach out and touch Sophie's bottom lip, where Sophie can feel the imprint of their kiss.

"Tell me I'm the last girlfriend you want to have," Elsa says, her voice barely above a whisper.

"You're the last girlfriend I want to have," Sophie says, then she leans in to claim her next kiss.

*

Sophie's fingernails are painted to look like the skyline at different times of day. Her thumbs are early morning, and her pinkies are dusk, and the fingers in between show the sun's progress through the sky. It's clever, but more than that, it's *pretty*.

Sophie can't stop staring.

She's careful not to touch anything for an hour after the recommended drying time, and she resists Elsa's plans to spend the afternoon at the beach. "What if the sand scratches them?"

Elsa smiles as she tucks Sophie against her side. "I'm glad you like them."

"You don't think I'm being silly?" Sophie asks.

"You should do things that make you happy," Elsa says. "Even small things. Especially small things." She kisses Sophie's forehead. "If we're not going to the beach, what should we do instead?"

They do end up going to the beach. Sophie's feeling indulgent, so she wears the pink bikini, and she and Elsa take dozens of selfies. Sophie flips through the pictures that night in bed, and her smile grows with each one. Their skin is sun-pink, and their smiles are wide, and they're happy.

Is this what a future after the Condors looks like? Sophie always thought retirement would mean a death knell. Who was she without hockey to define her? But there are things besides hockey in her life now. One day, when she doesn't have a full season to play, she'll still have this. Well, maybe not exactly this. She can't spend her days on vacation, but she'll have Elsa.

"I love you," Sophie says as Elsa joins her in bed.

Sophie sends one of the beach selfies to her mom, because she knows it'll make her happy, then she sets her phone on the bedside table.

"Love you too," Elsa says. "We have to leave tomorrow."

Sophie is disappointed to leave this behind, even if she's ready to play hockey again. She leans over to kiss the corner of Elsa's mouth. "We'll plan a vacation this summer. It'll be something to look forward to."

"Another beach?" Elsa asks.

"Sure." Sophie's pretty sure she'd give Elsa anything she asked for right now. It should scare her, but it doesn't. Elsa won't ask for anything Sophie isn't willing to give her.

Before Elsa can start thinking too seriously about the summer, Sophie kisses her full on the mouth. There will be plenty of time to plan for later. But for now, they still have another night here, and Sophie wants to make full use of it.

Chapter Fourteen

Sophie is refreshed coming off the All-Star break. She worried all the travel would wear her down, but she's energized, ready for hockey the way she usually is after the offseason. It's amazing what a few days removed from the sport can do for her.

She and Elsa arrive at the rink early so Elsa can hang a keychain in everyone's stall. Sophie puts a shot glass on the top shelf of their stalls and sets a mini-Gatorade next to it. Presents distributed, she changes into practice clothes and hits the weight room for her warmup.

When she returns to the locker room after her bike ride and stretching routine, the room is bustling. Sophie isn't the only one eager to be back on the ice. Her teammates are all here, and the room is loud as stories are exchanged.

"He was a coward and refused to try it," Bechs says, the tail end to a story Sophie missed.

"It was *moving*." Peets crosses his arms over his chest, refusing to feel shamed.

"Imagine falling asleep in a live octopus," Spitzer says. He cackles and ducks as Peets swings his chest protector at him.

Sophie waves and smiles to her teammates, but she doesn't interrupt anyone's stories as she makes her way to her stall. She tugs her shorts down, revealing spandex underneath them.

"Now, lift your shirt up," Merlin says. Sophie raises her eyebrows, but she lifts her shirt up. Merlin circles her with a frown. "No ill-advised tattoos. Stick your tongue out." Feeling silly, Sophie sticks her tongue out, and Merlin sighs. "No tongue piercing, either. When Elsa told us not to interrupt your vacation under threat of evisceration, I thought she was going to get you drunk and coax you into bad decisions."

Sophie slowly turns around to look at Elsa. There isn't a shred of guilt on Elsa's face as Sophie stares her down. "You said you didn't know why no one was texting me."

"I hypothesized that they might be busy," Elsa corrects. She smirks, proud of herself.

If they were still on vacation, Sophie would kiss the expression right off her face. Since they're in the locker room, she settles for a half-hearted glare. "You're a bully."

Jonny pretends to puke.

"Where did you even go?" Merlin asks. "Elsa wouldn't tell us."

"The beach," Sophie answers.

Merlin, the dramatic asshole, gasps and presses the back of his hand to Sophie's forehead. "You went somewhere without ice?"

"It isn't that unusual," Sophie says.

"Figs is the only one who was on the ice over the break," Woodsy points out. "Power move, by the way, using your captaincy to limit your shifts."

"You what?" Sophie asks, curious, and a little mad she never thought to do that. Of course, she's always looked forward to the All-Star weekend. She knows a lot of guys think it's a waste of time or they treat it as an excuse to drink with guys they don't normally see. But for Sophie, it is a proving ground. She is on the ice with the best of the best, and she wants to measure herself against them.

"Wait." Merlin holds up a hand and, miracle of miracles, the entire locker room grinds to a halt. "You didn't even watch the All-Star game. Are you an imposter?"

"You're ridiculous," Sophie says. "It was the All-Star *break*. I took a break."

"From hockey?" Merlin asks, just to be sure. He yelps when Sophie punches his shoulder, then, because he never knows when to stop, he looks over at Elsa. "How did you convince her to go?"

Elsa leans against her stall. Her posture is loose, and her expression is positively wicked, and Sophie's cheeks flush, an automatic response to that look now. Elsa flicks her gaze over toward Merlin. "It was my birthday present."

The locker room explodes into chaos. Merlin refuses to believe it, Bechs wants to know why Sophie won't take him on vacation for his birthday, and by the time Sophie settles everyone down, they're almost late to practice.

*

After practice, their strength and conditioning coach ushers them into the weight room. Sophie partners with Jonny, because they lift similar amounts which makes them good partners. Sophie slides a second plate onto the bar so she can squat, and she catches her finger between the two plates.

She curses and shakes out her hand. When she looks at her fingers, the pain fades to the background as she sees the damage she did to the rising sun. She curses again and glares at her hands until the tears stinging at her eyes fade away.

"Really?" Jonny asks. "You broke a nail?"

Sophie punches his shoulder, hard enough to hurt,

then she adds a second plate to the other side of the bar.

As soon as she's home from practice, Sophie goes to the bathroom and scrubs her nails with the foul-smelling nail polish remover, until every last bit of polish is gone. She didn't cry in the weight room, and she isn't going to cry now, even if she feels hollow, staring at her fingers. Her nails are pink and seem vulnerable without the coat of polish.

"It's stupid," Sophie says. She knows Elsa's standing in the doorway watching, even if Elsa hasn't said anything.

"It isn't," Elsa says. "This summer, we'll get our nails done as often as you like."

*

Concord loses their first game back from the All-Star break. It puts them last in their division, but Sophie doesn't allow herself to wallow. There is a third of the season left. They haven't made an easy path for themselves to the playoffs, but they aren't out of it yet.

Sophie leads the forward group in ice time against Boston, and they win. She has another strong performance against Memphis, and they win. Elsa has a four-point night in their win over New Orleans. They beat Detroit, then they thrash Philly, and chase Pearce out of his net.

They lose to Quebec, but they bounce back with a win against Montreal and another against Orlando.

Then they fly to Cleveland.

When Sophie's team shows up for morning skate, there are people lined up outside the arena with their usual signs. There are the ones where Sophie is roadkill and her body is pecked at by vultures. There are the ones reminding her she was the last pick of the draft. It isn't anything new, but they hit harder today than they have in years.

Sophie pretends it doesn't bother her, and she's dialed in for morning skate. She works with the rest of the first power play unit on their zone entries, because they aren't as effective as they need to be. She takes a few shots on Teddy at the end of practice, because he thinks he's too slow glove-side.

Thoughts of Cleveland simmer in the back of her mind all day, though. In her hotel room, she strips down to a tank top and a pair of shorts for her customary pre-game nap.

"They still hate me," Sophie says as she climbs into bed. When she takes the ice for tonight's game, there will be boos. Cleveland's fans will cheer whenever she misses the net, and they'll cheer even harder when one of their players takes a run at her. "I always thought they'd get tired of it eventually."

"They aren't very bright," Elsa says, and she nudges Sophie until Sophie smiles.

"Ignore me," Sophie says as she pulls the covers up to her chin.

"Never," Elsa says.

They nap and Sophie feels refreshed for the game. It doesn't make it easier to hear the *Sophie sucks* chants as she skates her warmup laps. She waits for the inevitable *Hayes is better* follow-up, but it doesn't come. It's Rizzo that Cleveland pours their love on.

In some ways, that's worse. It means Cleveland doesn't hate Sophie because she's a woman. They hate her because she's Sophie.

Elsa joins Sophie for her second lap. "We're putting you on the board tonight," she promises. "We'll remind Cleveland and their fans why you're the best hockey player in the league."

"Big words," Sophie says.

Elsa grins, her eyes bright behind her visor. "You'll back them up."

*

Rizzo uses Sophie as a measure of her own skill. Every time she blocks one of Sophie's shots or intercepts a pass or makes a good defensive play, she throws Sophie a little smirk. It's needling, but Sophie deals with this better than the crowd. If another player is going to give Sophie this much power over them, she'll use it.

Because yes, Rizzo does stop Sophie from scoring more than once. But a period and a half into the game, Sophie buries the puck decisively in the back of the net. It silences the crowd, and Sophie's feeling just the right kind of reckless, so she skates by Rizzo on the way to her own bench.

"Maybe next time," she says. If Sophie has ten good looks at the net, and Rizzo prevents eight of her shots from going in, that's still two goals Sophie's scored. She doesn't expect to get the better of Rizzo every time, but she'll beat her when it counts.

Rizzo snarls, the fury on her face easier to read without the cages they had to wear during the Winter Games. "I see why they call you a bitch."

Maybe Elsa was onto something when she told Sophie a goal would settle her. Because Sophie doesn't care about Rizzo's scowl or the angry fans or the entire city who is watching and hoping for Sophie to fail. Sophie's team is clawing their way out from the bottom of the standings, and they need big wins and decisive goals to keep the momentum going.

Sophie doesn't mind being the lightning rod for her team. She flicks her mouthguard out and smirks around the plastic. "Naw, you won't fully see until I knock you out of the playoffs."

Rizzo takes a step forward, ready to throw a punch and knock the smirk off Sophie's face. Kevlar pulls Sophie away as Theo steps in between the two women. The fans howl for Sophie's blood. Sophie ignores them as she skates through the fist bump line at her bench. She has a goal, her team is now up by two, and Rizzo's focus will be on revenge, not hockey going forward.

Everything is going exactly to plan.

*

Rizzo abandons her coverage to lay a hard hit on Sophie in the corner. It's the kind of hit where Sophie swears she feels her bones grind together. It disorients her for a moment now, and she knows she'll be aching because of it later.

But Rizzo left her d-partner out to dry, and Cubs takes advantage and tallies a goal of his own.

Sophie doesn't bother with any smart comments this time. Rizzo hangs her head, furious with herself, and doing all of Sophie's work for her.

A few shifts later, Sophie lays a hit of her own, but she targets Hayes, not Rizzo. Hayes has possession of the puck, and Sophie throws her shoulder into his chest and knocks him flat against the glass. Woodsy darts in to steal the puck, and the fans pound on the glass, demanding Hayes drop his gloves and fight Sophie.

Sophie doesn't intend to give the fans what they want. She pins Hayes to the glass for a moment, stares him down so he knows she thoroughly beat him on this shift, then she jumps into the play to see if she and Woodsy can connect for a goal.

They don't manage to score, but they force an offensive zone faceoff, and Sophie's line swaps out for the third line. Sophie skates back to the bench amidst a passionate rendition of *Sophie sucks*. Peets slides over to make a space next to Elsa, and Sophie sits down.

"Was that supposed to make them like you more?" Elsa asks.

"They're never going to like me," Sophie says, because she knows it, even if part of her will always long to have everyone on her side. But she can't. There will always be people who hate her, who doubt her, who would rather see her lose than win, but she can't let them matter. Sophie leans against Elsa's side. "I might as well give them a reason to boo."

"That's my captain," Elsa says, full of pride.

*

After they beat Cleveland, Coach Elison puts Elsa back on Sophie's wing. He pulls them both aside before practice to tell them of the change. Sophie's curious why he didn't announce it at practice or tell Sophie and have her spread the word. Then Coach Elison looks over at Elsa and says, "Don't make me regret this."

Elsa scowls, but she's too disciplined to talk back to her coach. And Sophie realizes the next team they play.

Denver.

It's the only time they face the Boulders this season, and the game is being broadcast on *The National Hockey Network*, instead of staying local. Denver is always a shitshow, and it isn't only Elsa's fault.

Sophie and Elsa both accept Coach Elison's change and his warning, then they head to the locker room to prepare for practice.

Coach Elison isn't the only one worried about the Denver game. But while Coach Elison wants to limit the dramatics, others want to capture them on camera. After practice, Sophie meets with Mary Beth, Coach Elison, Reggie Powers, and Derek Napoli. Reggie Powers is like the Napoli of *TNSN*. He produces a lot of the behind-the-scenes content for the channel, and he sees this Denver game as an opportunity.

"We want you mic'd up," Powers tells Sophie. "There are always fireworks when you play Denver."

Napoli is on the edge of his seat, practically salivating at the opportunity to get sound from a Concord-Denver game to use in an episode of *In the Nest*. Sophie isn't sure what Powers and Napoli are so excited about. The stuff that makes for a scandalous story? The commissioner would never allow it to air.

It's why she shrugs and says, "I'm not opposed as long as I have final say on what is and isn't used." It won't be a secret that she's mic'd up. And whether Sinclair tries to censor himself because of it or he tries to spew even more shit than usual, it'll be a distraction.

"Are you sure this is a good idea?" Mary Beth asks. She ignores the sharp looks she receives from both producers. "Denver games are charged and, given the preseason controversy and that this is the only time we face Denver this season, this game will be especially charged."

Sophie stood in front of reporters this summer and told anyone who cared to listen that she had no interest in playing for Denver. It shouldn't come as a shock to anyone. There's bad blood between Sophie and the Boulders. She broke their captain's nose in her second season. He always has a shitty comment and sharp elbow to throw her way. He ran her hard enough in the finals of the IHT to take her out of the game and effectively end her season. That injury and the shitshow that followed led to Butler's ousting as Concord's coach. Then he signed with Denver.

So, yeah. The game will be charged.

*

Sophie isn't mic'd up for warmups. She isn't surprised when Sinclair takes advantage and finds her while she's stretching. He looms over her as she shifts into a modified butterfly. Colby, Sophie's older brother, would laugh if he saw her lack of flexibility, but he was a goalie, and they're all born with rubber instead of bones in their bodies.

"Coward," Sinclair accuses. "What, you can't play me without someone making sure no one hurts your feelings?"

"I didn't ask for this," Sophie says. She gestures to their surroundings, the dog-and-pony show the NAHL has cooked up. Powers and his team have been hovering since morning skate. She bets a secondary crew stalked the Boulders as they disembarked the plane. "Powers and *TNSN* want a show. Do you plan to give him one?"

"The way you did this summer? This is your fault."

"Oh, are your feelings hurt?" Sophie mimes wiping a tear away. "All I said was that I didn't want to play for Denver. I didn't expect you to disagree. Did you want to be teammates?"

"Bitch," Sinclair snarls.

She's only just starting. Sophie stands up. Sinclair still has a few inches on her, and he's heavier than she is as well. If he wanted, he could hurt her badly. She stands skate-to-skate with him and doesn't flinch. "The C does look better on my sweater than yours. Given the way you can't handle losing to a woman, I'm not sure how well you'd do taking orders from one."

Sinclair gives her a two-handed shove. It's almost gentle for him, but immediately, Jonny and Bowser skate over to support Sophie. One of the officials drifts by as well, ready to intervene if Sinclair or Sophie escalates.

Sinclair glares at Bowser but he reserves his nastiest look for Jonny, who had once been his teammate.

"Is there anything else you want to get off your chest before I'm mic'd up?" Sophie asks. "I'd hate for you to say anything that tarnishes Denver's reputation." When Sinclair doesn't say anything, she allows herself one last taunt. "Maybe I'm not the coward here."

Sinclair steps into her space, and Sophie's aware of Bowser and Jonny crowding closer. She knows there are two officials hovering nearby now. She can only imagine how many cameras are pointed at the two of them.

"You're all talk," Sinclair says. Then he pats her side, where he rammed his stick during the IHT and left her gasping for breath on the ice. She curls her hands and narrows his eyes, and Sinclair smirks, pleased he's gotten to her. He skates away, before Jonny can give in to temptation and haul him off.

"I wish you wouldn't do that," Jonny says. He sticks close to Sophie's side as they skate to the bench. "He hates you enough without you winding him up."

"He started it," Sophie mutters.

Jonny's look is far from impressed. "He wants to finish it too. Don't let him."

*

Sinclair makes up for the fact that he can't say any of the things he wants to say by hitting Sophie as hard and as often as he can. Every time she has the puck she's braced for a hit. He comes at her from behind, and she barely gets a forearm on the glass in time to keep her from going face first into it.

On another shift, Sinclair comes at her from the right, and he jabs his elbow into her side.

One time, he catches her at center ice. It's a brutal body-to-body collision, and they both end up on their asses on the ice. Sophie gets to her feet first.

It's the small victories that count.

*

Elsa scores to open the second period.

Figs scores on the next shift.

Late in the second period, a power play gives them another opportunity, and it's Jonny who converts.

The score is 3-0 headed into the third period.

It's 3-3 by the end of it.

Sophie was on the ice for two of the goals. Her body aches from the abuse it's taken this game, layered on top of the hurts she already had from the game against Cleveland. Coach Elison reads the fatigue on her face, and he sends Kansas's line out to kick off overtime.

"Tell him I'm fine," Sophie tells Coach Vorgen. The assistant coach gives Sophie a look, and she stares back at him, defiant. He shrugs and passes the message along until it reaches Coach Elison.

When Kansas skates to the bench for a change, Sophie takes his place. Woodsy and Elsa join her as soon as they can change out for the third line wingers. Sophie plays freer, more daring, with Sinclair on the bench.

As soon as Denver can manage a change, they put their captain out, and Coach Elison calls for Sophie to return to the bench. It becomes a chess match, pieces moved and pieces protected. Sophie resents the sheltered minutes, but she knows Sinclair is hitting her to hurt. She won't risk losing out on the rest of her season because of her pride.

The game ends with a goal from Spitzer. It gives Concord a desperately needed two points. Right now, the division standings have Quebec in first, followed by Montreal, Boston, and New York City in the final playoff spot. Concord is right behind the Empires, in fifth place. These two points are important, but Sophie frowns when she sees the Empires won their game tonight as well. Concord needs to win, and they need New York to lose if they want to pull ahead in the standings.

This wouldn't be a problem if Sophie and her team had played better earlier this season. But it's too late for regrets. She can't change the games they've already played. All she can do is make sure they win the games still left on the schedule.

*

Reggie Powers is thrilled with the footage and audio from the game. The problem with Sophie insisting he can only use what she approves is that she has to listen to the full playback. Sophie is used to seeing herself play by this point in her career. She's watched more hours of game footage than she's actually played. But listening to herself will always be strange.

She doesn't remember saying half of what she said during the game, and she's hyperaware of every time she swears, because she knows it will have to be censored in order to air on *TNSN*. Still, there's nothing embarrassing or incriminating.

It's obvious that Sophie is dialed in and that her teammates are following her lead. Shift after shift, Sophie barks out observations, gives well-deserved praise, or strategizes on the bench with her teammates. Sophie watches herself give Bechs a pep talk, then he follows her advice and has a strong shift.

She watches as Sinclair crushes her into the boards on a particularly hard shift, and she sees the reaction of her teammates. Then she sees herself return to the bench, shaky but unhurt, and settle them all down. Is this what other teams notice when they watch footage of Condors hockey? Sophie is the heartbeat of her team. Everything runs through her, the offense, the defense, the discipline. No wonder players like Sinclair target her. They think if they can take her out, her team will crumble.

Sophie isn't even sure that they're wrong.

Sophie's always known, even before there was a C

stitched onto her jersey, that she couldn't falter. She is the bedrock of the Concord Condors. She doesn't do it alone or she couldn't do it. She has Elsa on her wing, she has Theo and Kevlar to steady the defense, and she has Teddy in net. This team has been built around a strong core, a group of players who have won the Cup together before.

They're going to do it again.

Chapter Fifteen

Despite the strong performance over the last stretch of games, Sophie is nervous as the trade deadline approaches. Concord had a dismal start to the season, and Sophie personally hadn't been her best. If they were still struggling, Sophie would expect half the team to be traded away.

Even with the recent surge, she can't help but worry. Will the front office recognize that there's something special building? Will they see the momentum and trust this group to continue building it? Or will they make dramatic, devastating changes?

This isn't Concord's last chance to trade Sophie or Elsa if they have doubts, there's still the summer, but it's one of the few remaining. When next season opens, Sophie and Elsa are Condors until they decide otherwise. Sophie didn't go to the All-Star Weekend for the first time in her career this season. Will the front office see that as an indictment? Will they trade her away?

Sophie keeps her phone within reach for the entirety of the trade deadline. Every time her phone pings with a notification, her stomach clenches, then she checks to see what's happened.

Indianapolis shores up an already strong team.

Quebec tweaks their fourth line and adds a veteran center.

New York trades for a new backup goalie.

Concord doesn't bring in any new players. They don't send anyone out either.

When the trade window closes, Sophie is still a Condor. So is everyone else. This is the team she's going to the playoffs with. This is the team she's *winning* with.

Sophie has a four-point night in their first game post-deadline. She notches two goals, then an assist on Elsa's goal and another on Bechs's power play goal.

It sparks a surge because, as always, where Sophie leads, her team follows. They string together a win streak, and they're only a point out of a playoff spot when Indianapolis flies to Concord.

All the playoff talk is centered around the Titan of the East and the Titan of the West, Quebec and Indianapolis. All the broadcasters agree these two teams will face each other in the Maple Cup Finals, but they can't agree on who will win.

Indianapolis has a high-powered offense, led by Lexie and Kensington, but Quebec has the best goaltending in the league. Quebec rarely scores more than three goals a game, but they don't need to when they have a goalie who rarely allows more than two against.

The two teams played each other twice this season, before the Christmas break, and they split them, a win for each team. Sophie's curious which team would win in a best-of-seven playoff round, but it will have to remain curiosity, because Concord, not Quebec, will represent the Eastern Conference in the finals.

Sophie prepares for the game against Indianapolis by setting up in the video room in Concord's practice facility. She's an hour into her review when Figs joins her. He has a bag of takeout with him, and he splits its contents evenly between them.

"Elsa told me I'd find you here," Figs says.

"This is an important game," Sophie says. Every game at this stage is important; they need wins if they want to make it into the playoffs, but Indianapolis is even more important. This game will show them if they're ready for the playoffs.

Indianapolis is already in post-season mode. They steamroll opponents, and they don't let up, even when they rest their top lines and allow the younger, less experienced players to have more ice time. Sophie knows her team will make the playoffs. This game against the Renegades will tell her if they're prepared for them.

"Every game is important in its own way," Figs says. "If you linger too much on that importance, you lose the focus you need to win."

Sophie swivels her chair to look over at Figs. "Philosophy?"

He shrugs. "If you'll take advice from someone who has never lifted the Cup."

"You're someone I look up to, Cup or no Cup."

"And yet, you think only one doesn't validate your own career."

Sophie scowls but she doesn't lash out. Figs isn't saying anything she doesn't already know to be true. "I don't play only for me," she tells him. She leaves a lot out. How in her first season, when she slept in the Wilcoxes' basement, she would lie awake, afraid she'd be sent down to Manchester if she wasn't good enough. And if she wasn't good enough for Concord, would it scare other teams off from drafting women? After all, Concord *took a chance* on her. If it didn't pay off, why would other teams take the risk?

Sophie's never had the luxury of playing only for herself.

"What did you feel watching Engelking lift the Cup?" Figs asks.

It isn't the question Sophie expects. Her lips twist into a bitter smile. "Which time? The first time she won, we were already out. I was glad to see a woman lift it. I was jealous it wasn't me. I was frustrated because I knew she would rub it in my face. The second time was worse. She was the first woman to win back-to-back Cups. The first woman to win two at all."

"Accolades you can't have now."

"You can't be the first if someone's done it before you." Sophie sighs. "Lexie and I are complicated. Everything is a competition to her. She has to win everything: every shift, every game, every season. And I was raised believing if I wasn't the best, I didn't get to play. But we're both women in a league where that bonds us. We're rivals on the ice and linked off of it. We're not enemies but we're not friends." Sophie shrugs. "Like I said, we're complicated."

"What if she wins this season?" Figs asks. "She would be the first woman to win three Cups. Is an accomplishment for one woman an accomplishment for them all?"

"I'm not that selfless," Sophie says. And this is where the strain of being the first woman in the league stems from. Sophie is a Concord Condor, but as the first woman, she's connected to all the women who have come after her. They're scattered across different teams and what's good for one of them isn't necessarily good for Sophie or for Concord, but she can't dismiss what they've done.

But she supposes Figs's point is that when push comes to shove, Sophie is a hockey player, a Concord Condor before anything else. She won't make herself smaller, no matter what kind of gains it would mean for Gabrielle or Lexie or any of the other women in the league. If Lexie wants to lift the Cup a third time, she'll have to go through Sophie in order to do it.

Figs nods at the TV, frozen on one of Lexie's shifts. "You won't find your answers here." He takes the remote and fiddles with it until it's one of Concord's games on the screen. "We beat them by being better than them. Watching their footage only shows how to contain them, but we need to go one step further."

"All right," Sophie says. She picks up her sandwich and takes a bite. "I'm listening."

*

The first period is full of hard hits, driving plays, and a dozen saves that will all complete for the highlight reel when the game is over.

Then the second period kicks off with a greasy goal for Merlin. The goal light flashes, Concord is on the board, and it's like the floodgates have opened. Bowser scores a few shifts later, then Cubs notches himself a goal.

Indianapolis pulls their goalie and replaces him with their backup as Lexie shouts at her teammates on the bench. It isn't Sophie's style of leadership, but it works for Lexie, and it works for the Renegades. They score in the last minute of the second period then score again to open the third. The game's momentum flips, and Lexie punctuates it when she slams home the tying goal.

There is pride etched across Lexie's face as she throws her arms up, celebrating in the face of Concord's unhappy fans. Sophie's had the kind of game Lexie is having. She knows what it feels like to be unstoppable. She's played with the power of knowing that her team won't lose because they *can't*.

Lexie finds Sophie and their gazes lock across the ice. Lexie's expression is fierce, and there's a challenge in the slant of her smile. This is the showdown Lexie thrives in, will against will. But Sophie learned early on never to play Lexie on her level.

At the next TV timeout, Sophie gathers her teammates around her. Coach Elison gives her a nod of acknowledgment and takes a half step back.

"This game is nothing to Indianapolis," Sophie says. "Win or lose, this game doesn't affect their playoff chances. But this game means something to us. A win here, and we're in the playoffs. So why are we letting them outplay us?" She looks around her teammates, and she's proud when they all meet her gaze. None of them are defeated. "We had a strong start. Find that spark again, and this game is ours."

"We got lazy," Kevlar says, adding his voice to Sophie's. "We thought three goals was good enough, and we sat back and watched. We can't do that against a team like this. It's time to stand back up."

"Stand back up," Theo echoes. He rests a hand on Teddy's shoulder. "We hung you out to dry. That's on us, and we'll be better."

"We score this next one for Teddy," Merlin says.

"For Teddy," they all agree.

Sophie takes her line out for the first shift after the break. Elsa's gaze jumps from Renegade to Renegade as she determines their weaknesses and decides how best to exploit them. Woodsy's gaze flits to Lexie, confident on her bench, then to the ice, then back to Lexie again.

"She's beatable," Sophie says.

Woodsy played with Lexie in Juniors, and he's always held her in a high regard. Sophie can't allow him to make her bigger than she is.

"She's in juggernaut mode," Woodsy says. "No one can stop her when she's like this."

"Not one person," Sophie agrees. It's why she won't take Lexie on in a one-on-one battle. On a night like this, Lexie would probably come out of it on top. "But we have a whole team."

Sophie claps Woodsy on the back and settles in for the faceoff.

*

Elsa jams the puck past Moser to give Concord the lead again. It's only one goal, and Indianapolis has already come back from being behind three. Sophie won't allow them to even up the game again. None of her teammates will either.

Kensington weaves through Concord's defense like it isn't even there. He loads up his shot, then the puck is hurtling toward the net. Spitz is suddenly there, and he takes the puck off his shin and it skitters harmlessly to the corner.

On another shift, Lexie barrels through Theo and Kevlar, and it's only Teddy left between Lexie and a goal, but he jabs his paddle out and knocks the puck away from her stick.

When Sophie takes the ice again, she prevents a goal by carrying the puck into the offensive zone, as far away from Teddy as she can manage. She passes to Kevlar, and he slings the puck around the boards. Sophie stops it behind Indy's goal, and she battles with Riley Dennison for possession.

Sophie almost has it when someone crashes into her from the other side. Now, she uses her elbows and her stick to keep both players at bay as she uses her skates to trap the puck. Woodsy calls to her from her left so she kicks the puck out to him. It's his turn to pin the puck, and Sophie hovers nearby, ready to give support when needed.

The puck finally springs free, and Sophie darts in to scoop it up on her stick. She skates away from the cluster of players by the boards. She considers passing to Elsa, then Lexie crashes into her with all the force and grace of a wrecking ball. Sophie hits the boards hard, and Lexie skates away with the puck.

Elsa skates a path to cut Lexie off, and Lexie passes up to Kensington. Woodsy jumps into the passing lane, grabs the puck, and holds it in the neutral zone while Sophie and Elsa skate to the bench for a change.

Only two shifts later, Indianapolis pulls their goalie to give them an extra attacker. It's a frantic final minute, but Concord emerges with the win.

Their celebrations are loud and their smiles are bright as they congratulate each other on the ice. Tonight's win officially puts them in a playoff spot. It might be the final spot in their division, but it doesn't matter. All Concord needed was an opportunity, and now they have it.

*

Sophie and Elsa host the pre-playoffs party at their house. They fill their fridge with drinks and their island counter is arranged with a variety of snacks. Figs gladly dons his crown and does his duty as King of the Grill again. There are mushroom caps, stuffed peppers and onions, and various meats on the grill, and Sophie peers over Figs's shoulder only for him to poke her with the grill brush.

"Quit hovering," he grumbles. "Go find the rookies. The sausages are almost done."

"And the kebobs?" Sophie asks.

"Go," Figs says but he laughs as he shoos her away.

Back when Matty was the captain and the King of the Grill, he liked to buy weird sausages and make people try them. Sophie hasn't trusted sausage since. She scans her backyard and while there are plenty of players standing around with plates of chips and salsa or fruit or those veggie chips Kolmonen's into, she doesn't see Cubs or the other rookies.

She doesn't see them in the kitchen either. She heads down the hall, but the TV room is empty. No one is playing video games with the weather so nice. She does hear whispering, though. Sophie crosses the hall to the memorabilia room. Cubs and the other two rookies are standing in front of the poster-sized picture of Sophie with the Cup hoisted above her head.

Cubs is the first one to turn and look at her. He shuffles his feet and offers her a hesitant smile. "Uh, hi. We were just passing through."

"You're allowed to wander around the house," Sophie says.

Cubs nods and looks back at the poster. "What does it feel like?" His fingers hover over the protective glass as if he wants to touch the Cup himself.

"It's different for everyone," Sophie answers. "Some people say it's the heaviest twenty pounds you'll lift in your life. Others say it's the lightest. I've been told it's never as sweet as the first time you lift it, but if you do it more than once, it means more because you know now how difficult it is to do."

"What about you?" Cubs presses.

Sophie looks at the photograph on the wall. It's in high definition and zoomed in enough that she can see the beads of sweat on her forehead. She also sees the relief in her eyes, almost as bright as her excitement. Her fingers are curled around the metal trophy. The maple leaf the Cup is named after is pointed toward the cameras. On the other side of the Cup is the eagle, added after there were enough American teams in the league to demand something of their own on the trophy.

In the background, Sophie's teammates are fuzzy so that she is in perfect focus. There are other pictures in this room of Sophie with her entire team and the Cup, but this one is about her and her journey. She was the first woman in the league by being the last pick at her draft. She led Concord to the playoffs for the first time in their history and the next year, she captained them to their first Cup win.

She proved thousands of people wrong when she lifted the Cup over her head, and she proved herself right. She was a hockey player, she was the best, and now everyone would know it.

"There was a buzz in my ears," Sophie finally answers. "Everything faded, the crowd still at the rink, the reporters lurking in the background, it was just me and the Cup. I had dreamed about winning it ever since I was a kid. I was laughed at for it. I was told girls can't play hockey and that, even if I did, I would never play in the NAHL. But I did. And then I *won*."

Sophie feels the same stirring of pride. She taps the glass with her fingers. "And then the world came rushing back and I turned around. My team stood behind me. I saw Delacroix, and I knew exactly who I would hand the Cup to first. Benoit Delacroix, he works with the d-men sometimes, he was Concord's first ever player, signed after the team was created. He took a bad hit the season before and missed a lot of time. He wanted to retire that summer, but I convinced him to stay for one more season. I promised him he'd retire with a Cup if he stayed."

In the same season Delacroix was injured, Sophie lost Matty when their captain was traded at the deadline. That summer, when Delacroix tried to retire, Lindy, their starting goalie, was traded. She knew why the moves were happening. Matty was traded to make room for Sophie to step into the captaincy, and Lindy was shuffled to another team so Teddy could become the starter.

The core of the team shifted to younger players, and while Sophie understood, she wasn't ready to lose everyone. She convinced Delacroix to give her one more season, and she followed through on her promise to see him win the Cup before he retired.

Sophie takes a deep breath and pulls out of her memories. It's time to make new ones.

"You'll have to tell me what it feels like to you,"

Sophie says.

Cubs's gaze drifts back to the Cup. "Do you really think…" He stops before he voices the full question, as if afraid to put into words what he badly wants to.

"I *believe*," Sophie tells him. "Do you?"

Cubs nods, his eyes bright and shining, even as his gaze remains fixed on the Maple Cup. He's young enough to believe wanting it is enough. He's still young enough that he's won more games and championships than he's lost. He doesn't know yet the desperation which builds as year after year passes with playoff exits that are always too soon. Every player wants the Cup. Only a few each year actually win it.

Elsa raps sharply on the door, then she pokes her head into the room. "Figs apologizes for sending a search team, rather than a search and rescue. Food's done."

"Sorry, I found them and then got distracted." Sophie ushers the rookies toward the door. "Go, before the only thing left is weird sausages."

Elsa steps aside so the rookies can rush past her, then she enters the room with two plates full of food. She holds the one with three stuffed peppers on it out to Sophie, then laughs and gives her the one with the kebobs instead. Elsa stands close enough for their shoulders to touch and she looks up at the Cup.

"We're doing it again this year," Elsa says.

"First, Quebec," Sophie says.

Chapter Sixteen

Quebec is the top seed in the division, which means Concord flies to them for the first two games. The next two will be in Concord, then home ice advantage alternates for the next three. The playoffs are a race to be the first to win four games.

When it's put like that, it seems simple. Win four games. How hard could it be? But Sophie knows how difficult it is. As motivated as she and her team are to win four, the other team is just as motivated.

And in this case, she's up against Quebec and the best goaltender in the world right now. It feels almost like a betrayal to think it, because Teddy is Sophie's goalie, and she doesn't want anyone else in net for her when they compete for the Maple Cup, but the truth is Gabrielle is better.

But the series won't be decided on Gabrielle and Teddy's records. Concord's defense will help Teddy protect his net to keep their goals against down. And Sophie will lead their forward group on offensive assaults that not even Gabrielle's impressive save percentage can hold up against.

This will be a team effort, all the way through.

"Don't sleep on Nate," Woodsy says.

Sophie looks up from her breakfast. She manages to

blink at Woodsy but nothing more. Her mind is crammed full of scouting sessions and game tape on Gabrielle, and Sophie fell asleep dreaming of scoring goals with a quick release or a deceptive shot, because it takes something extra in order to beat Gabrielle and—

"Nate," Woodsy repeats. "Nathaniel Summers. Quebec picked him up this summer. Lex and I played with him in Juniors."

He used to play with Kansas City. Sophie nods as her brain catches up. "Sniper. Soft hands. He should be better in the shootout than he is."

Woodsy laughs and it's a good look on him, seeing him relaxed and happy, especially when talking about Juniors. "We used to give him shit for it. He's deadly on the breakaway, but when it's only him and the goalie, he loses all that skill."

"Some people can't handle the pressure of the game on their stick." Elsa joins them at their table with a plate piled high with food and two coffee mugs. One of her mugs is already half-empty, as if she needed the caffeine to make it through the breakfast line.

"It's why he and Lex were the dynamic duo," Woodsy says. "He likes the spotlight on someone else, because then people forget about him."

"And Lexie loves a spotlight," Sophie says.

As she's been prepping for the series against Quebec, it's been impossible to ignore the coverage on Indianapolis. They're the favorites to come out of the Western Conference, and Sophie can't look at any hockey site or channel without being forced to see Lexie or Kensington's faces or a clip from one of their games.

"We won't forget about Summers," Sophie says.

*

Nate Summers scores the first goal of the series.

Woodsy nudges Sophie as she watches the replay on the bench. Sophie doesn't sigh but it's a close thing. "Yes, yes, you told me so. We'll be better."

They have to be.

They also have to score on Gabrielle *twice* now, if they want to win the game. *Everyone is beatable*, Sophie reminds herself. She cannot allow herself to put Gabrielle on a pedestal. She won't let Gabrielle beat her before Sophie even takes a shot. Gabrielle is a goalie, and Sophie has an entire career built on scoring against goalies. She can do it again.

The game stays stubbornly 0-1 through the first two periods, even though Concord has two power plays and more than one aggressive shift. Gabrielle is locked in.

Sophie reminds herself that Gabrielle has weaknesses. They aren't glaring, but they're there. The broadcasters are no doubt saying that Concord is going to need a lucky bounce in order to score, but Sophie doesn't believe in luck. She didn't make it to the NAHL because of luck or chance.

Midway through the third period, Elsa streaks down the far side of the ice. The puck is seemingly glued to her stick, because she keeps possession as she dodges hits and dances out of the way of poke checks and backchecks. Elsa cuts a sharp angle and drives the net.

Gabrielle squares up for Elsa's shot. But Sophie drops down on the opposite side of the net. Elsa fakes a shot, forces Gabrielle to commit, then she flings an aerial pass to Sophie. The puck flies over the d-men's sticks. Sophie lifts her own stick and, careful not to raise her stick above the height of the crossbar, bats the puck into the net.

Goal.

Sophie grins, triumphant and pleased, and she pushes through Quebec's players to reach Elsa. It was Elsa's commitment which drew Gabrielle's attention, and it was Elsa's pass which got the puck to Sophie.

Sophie claps Elsa's helmet with her glove and taps their visors against each other. "Now, we need another."

"We'll get it," Elsa promises.

They skate to the bench together and collect the support of their teammates. Sophie makes contact with every player as she bumps their outstretched fists. She scored and so can they. Gabrielle, *Quebec*, is beatable, and Concord can win this game.

Sophie sits down next to Merlin.

"Have you been sneaking off to the batting cages?" Merlin asks. "You aren't switching sports on us, are you?"

"You're stuck with me," Sophie tells him, then she looks up at the jumbotron to watch her goal.

*

It takes overtime, but Figs nets the game winner and sets a record for most game-winning overtime goals scored in the playoffs. One of Ben Granlund's staff members manages to produce a pie plate of shaving cream in time for Merlin to greet Figs with it after the game.

"Is this a hint?" Figs grins, all good cheer, as he wipes the white foam off his face. "Should I shave my eyebrows?"

"You aren't allowed to shave anything," Theo says, as if Figs has somehow forgotten the rules of the playoffs.

When the playoffs roll around, the guys quit shaving. They grow patchy beards and weird mustaches, and the wilder their facial hair is, the more successful their playoff run is. Sophie and Elsa can't do the same. They dip dye their hair instead. Ahead of the first round, they dyed the tips of their hair red. For each round they advance to, they'll dye a little more.

It's easier to tell with Elsa, because her hair is blonde and the red stands out more, but when Sophie looks at the ends of her braids, she sees Condors red, and she feels like part of the team.

*

Gabrielle answers the loss with a shutout in front of a raucous Quebec crowd.

*

"We don't win every game," Sophie tells her team. They're back in Concord, in their own practice facility. They play their first home game of the playoffs tomorrow. Sophie scans the room and makes sure her teammates know she isn't giving them an excuse for how they played in their last game. It's forgiveness. It's a release valve for all the pressure that has been building up.

Sophie has won the Maple Cup, and she didn't do it by sweeping every round. Losses happen. The trick is making sure there's never four in the same series. She makes sure she has the full attention of the room before she continues. "How we respond to losses determines whether or not we win the series."

"Gagnon is beatable," Kevlar says, adding his voice to Sophie's. "We proved it in our first game. We've scored on her before, and we'll score on her again."

"She's over-protective of the five-hole," Sophie says. "Fake five-hole or actually shoot there, make her commit and space will open up for other shots."

"I remember watching Billy's final game," Figs says. He leans back in his stall and closes his eyes as he transports himself to another time. "It was Game Seven of the Finals, Quebec was poised to set the record with six Maple Cup wins in a row, and then the puck slipped between Billy's pads. An overtime loss for Quebec."

"There were riots," Teddy says. "When I told my dad I wanted to be a goalie, he showed me the game and then the aftermath. Couches were thrown through shop windows, cars were set on fire, people burned effigies of William Loiseau outside their homes. I was five. I used to sleep with a fire extinguisher under my bed, because I was afraid people would burn down our house if I didn't play well enough."

Sophie isn't the only one who stares at Teddy in a mix of horror and surprise. She hadn't heard that story before. She knew about Five-Hole Billy, of course. Every Canadian did, and Sophie's brother was a goalie, so it was a story she knew well.

Teddy shrugs. "Anyway, fake five-hole. Even better, score five-hole. If I had nightmares, Gagnon's bound to have some fears of her own."

It's a hell of a game plan.

*

Quebec scores in the opening minute of Game Three. The Concord crowd quiets, and the silence seems to echo after the excitement from warmups and the opening lineups being announced. Sophie feels a spark of anger as the fans all sit down, as if preparing themselves for more disappointment.

They're giving up already? There's still almost an entire game to play. Sophie knows how the past few seasons have gone, early exits in the first or second rounds. But does that mean the fans' doubt is justified? Sophie believes in her team every single season. The fans should as well.

Sophie takes the ice on her first shift after Quebec's goal with rage and purpose simmering beneath her skin. She is a professional hockey player. She has trained her entire life to put the puck in the back of the net. She'll do it again. Not even Gabrielle Gagnon is good enough to stop her.

Merlin has the puck trapped behind Gabrielle's net. Sophie skates in and taps her stick on the ice to let Merlin know she's there. He elbows Bordeaux to get himself some breathing room, then he passes the puck to Sophie.

"Change," she tells Merlin as she guards the puck.

She passes the puck to Elsa and they play a game of keep-away from Quebec's players as Sophie's teammates complete their line change. Once Woodsy joins them in the offensive zone, Sophie launches an assault on Gabrielle's net.

She leaves the puck for Kevlar and plants herself in Gabrielle's crease. She fights Rotrand to hold her position. She holds out against Gabrielle when the goalie pokes the backs of her knees to try to get her off-balance.

Sophie shifts to block Gabrielle's view of Theo as he walks the blueline, the puck on his stick, prepared to shoot. Rotrand shoves Sophie hard enough for her to fall. Her knees slam into the ice.

"Heads up!" Kevlar shouts.

Sophie looks up to see the puck hurtling at her head. She twists enough that the puck clips her shoulder instead. It changes direction and slips over Gabrielle's glove and lands in the back of the net.

Sophie scrambles to her feet and throws herself at Elsa as Elsa laughs and hugs her for the goal. Woodsy crashes into their celebration to give Sophie a friendly facewash, then the d-men join, and Theo gives Sophie shit for stealing his goal.

It's all light-hearted, and Sophie looks around the stadium to see the fans are back on their feet as they celebrate the tying goal.

Believe, Sophie urges, then she skates through the fist bump line at her bench.

*

LeGarrette Thomas becomes Sophie's shadow. Any time she's on the ice, the d-man is there and making life difficult for her. He clears her out of Gabrielle's crease. He shoves her up against the boards so one of his teammates can steal the puck. And he does it all with a damn smile on his face.

His smile is bright and cheerful, and Sophie wants to punch it off his face.

Midway through the second period, Sophie collects a pass from Elsa, then she turns into LG. Her skates and stick get tangled up with his, and they both fall to the ice. They take Theo down with them and by the time Sophie is back on her skates, Summers has put the puck in the back of Concord's net.

Again.

*

Two shifts after Summers scores, Figs cuts an edge so sharp, Rotrand falls on his ass trying to keep up. Figs skates easily around Sorkin and flicks the puck into the net.

Tie game.

Again.

*

There's four minutes left in the game when Merlin is called for a hold in the offensive zone. It's a stupid penalty to take, but Sophie grinds her teeth into her mouthguard instead of yelling, because Merlin sits in the penalty box and hangs his head as if he knows he fucked up.

LG scores for Quebec while they have the player advantage, and Sophie breathes deeply and reminds herself that there's still three minutes left in the game. It's plenty of time to score another goal.

With two minutes left on the clock, Merlin squeaks the puck past Gabrielle. Only a shift or two ago, Sophie wanted to grab Merlin and shake some sense into him, and now she wants to grab him and kiss him.

*

As Sophie and her team head to the locker room for a full intermission before the first overtime period, the broadcasters are no doubt telling their audiences how many times this season Gabrielle has allowed more than three goals in a game.

Sophie doesn't know that particular fact off the top of her head. She doesn't want to know it either. All she knows is that her team has scored three goals on Gabrielle this game already. They can score another. Gabrielle is beatable.

Sophie does her rounds in the locker room and shores up each of her teammates. Those who need the boost, get one. Those who are locked in and ready, Sophie feeds off their energy and allows it to fuel her own determination. It's the Maple Cup playoffs, they're in front of their home crowd, and they're going to win this game.

They're all buzzing as they troop back up to the ice. Sophie takes the top line out over the boards for the opening shift. She lines up across from Coderre, Quebec's captain. She wins the faceoff, but he gets her back before the end of her shift with a nasty slash to her knee. If it wasn't overtime in the playoffs, he'd be in the box for it, but, as always, the officials seem to have swallowed their whistles.

Sophie skates gingerly to the bench and grits her teeth against the worst of the pain. She'll need a shift or two to recover, and the chances of her double shifting this overtime are slim. She breathes out hard through her mouth and waves off the trainer hovering over her shoulder. Sophie's played through injury before. And it's the playoffs. Nothing short of being stretchered off the ice will keep her from playing.

Elsa drops down next to Sophie after she makes her change. There's sweat on her forehead and stray wisps of blonde hair curl up toward her hairline. Her cheeks are flushed and her eyes are bright, and Sophie isn't sure Elsa ever looks as beautiful as she does when she's on the ice.

"Don't do anything stupid," Sophie warns, because Elsa has a reputation for retaliatory penalties, especially when Sophie is involved.

"Now isn't the time for stupid," Elsa says.

Sophie believes her, but she also notes the clench of Elsa's jaw, as if she isn't ready to let go of her rage yet. This is where Elsa plays her best hockey, just on the edge of too much. If she brings this passion to the ice and channels it the right way, Sophie knows this game is Concord's.

She wishes she could take the ice with Elsa as Elsa slings a leg over the boards, prepared for her next shift, but Sophie knows she can't.

"Score one for me," Sophie says.

Elsa meets Sophie's gaze. Her grin is sharp, like the edge of a skate blade. She jumps on the ice and calls for the puck. Peets puts it right on her tape, then Elsa drives into the offensive zone. She pushes her way through Quebec's defense and taps the puck between Gabrielle's pads before the goalie can react.

Five-hole and in, because Elsa can be vicious when she wants to be.

*

After that, Quebec doesn't put up much of a fight. Concord wins Game Four at home, and they celebrate at their favorite bar with the Indianapolis game in the background. The entire bar, hockey players and patrons alike, cheer when Indianapolis loses in a rare and unexpected sweep by Minneapolis.

Two days later, Concord knocks Quebec out of the playoffs.

The two teams which led the league during the regular season are out in the first round. Sophie laughs, high on the win, and joins Elsa in the shower after Game Five against Quebec.

"This is our year," Sophie tells Elsa. She laughs again and ducks under the spray. She can't be this open or this happy when she stands in front of reporters in fifteen minutes, but she can have it now.

"Our year," Elsa echoes, and she pulls Sophie in for a kiss.

Chapter Seventeen

Sophie and Elsa watch Game Six of the Boston-Montreal series from their couch. Whichever team wins the series will be Concord's opponent in the next round. Boston is down 2-3 in the series after a shaky two games. Hippeli, their goalie, was pulled after giving three goals in the second period of Game One. Then, in Game Two, their backup Calvert gave up three goals in the third period and he was pulled.

Hippeli has backed Boston to three wins in a row since. He isn't playing his best, but Boston scores enough to make up for it. Still, Sophie takes careful notes as she watches, because Hippeli is a weakness they can exploit.

The camera zooms in on Dima, because he's the biggest star on the ice. He's Boston's captain, and he's led the league in goals scored since he first came into the league. He's the reason why Hippeli doesn't need to post shutouts. He singlehandedly gives Hippeli the goal support he needs for Boston to win.

Sophie adds that to her mental game plan. *Shut down Dima, force Hippeli to be pulled again, and destroy their faith in themselves until Boston crumbles.*

Elsa nudges Sophie and draws her out of her thoughts. "Drink? Something to eat?"

"I can get it," Sophie says, but Elsa puts a hand on her shoulder to keep her sitting.

"I've got it," Elsa says. She goes into the kitchen and returns with a bottle of water, a protein bar, and an icepack. Sophie groans but she puts her knee up so Elsa can rest the icepack on it.

Sophie's knee is stiff, thanks to Coderre's slash, but it isn't anything she can't play through. Still, she knows better than to ignore an injury. Icing will help, even though Sophie hates it. Sophie grew up in Canada. She knows the cold. But she can bundle up to protect against the chilly winters. She can wrap her fingers around a mug of hot chocolate and watch the snow from inside her house.

The point of icing is to be cold, which means she can't defend against it. She has to let the cold seep into her skin until it isn't just her knee that's cold but all of her. She shivers and glares at the icepack and wishes she'd told Elsa to take a run at Coderre in response. Ugh, no, she doesn't. Elsa's series-winning goal was better than a revenge hit.

"You're cute when you're grumpy," Elsa says. She laughs at the expression on Sophie's face and tucks Sophie against her side. "Of course, you're always cute."

"You're full of shit," Sophie says.

Elsa just laughs and drops a kiss to Sophie's forehead.

They watch the first period, then Elsa returns Sophie's icepack and brings back reheated leftovers for dinner. Sophie isn't particularly hungry, because exhaustion has taken over everything, but she eats.

The broadcast switches to the first intermission report, and Sophie scowls as Bobby Brindle and Kyle Sorkin appear on screen. She's broken records that both these men once held. Brindle still refuses to acknowledge hers, but she's accepted he never will. It doesn't mean she wants to listen to him break down the Boston-Montreal game. Knowing him, he'll be biased in favor of his former team.

"Before we talk about Boston and Montreal, we have

to talk about Quebec's early exit," Brindle says.

The camera catches the tight smile on Kyle Sorkin's face. At least Sophie isn't alone in hating Brindle's guts. Brindle played for Montreal during their historic Cup run, and Sorkin played for Quebec during theirs. The two men's careers overlapped, and they have a deep hatred for each other that was cultivated by years of hockey rivalry. Their media personas are more complicated. Their rivalry is good for ratings, but they usually have a veneer of politeness.

Not tonight, apparently.

"Concord was the better team," Sorkin says, with more grace than Sophie would have in his position. "When Sophie Fournier is at the top of her game, there isn't much that can stop her."

"Mute it," Sophie begs. She doesn't want to hear them talk about her, even if they say good things.

"Five goals in five games," Brindle says, and he must be reading off a teleprompter, because Sophie can't imagine he'd ever willingly praise her skill. "Is it safe to say Sophie Fournier looks like Sophie Fournier again?"

"Who did I look like before?" Sophie asks.

"Concord will play the winner of this series," Sorkin says, "but they're not the only team resting right now. It only took Minneapolis four games to eliminate the highly favored Indianapolis Renegades. What happened there, Bobby? They seemed unbeatable during the regular season, and then they went out with barely any fight."

Brindle shrugs. "They don't make teams like they used to."

The two men share a rare moment of comradery, and Elsa mutes the TV.

"Oh, *now* you mute it," Sophie mutters, but she isn't actually mad. She burrows more firmly against Elsa's side. "What do you think happened?" She didn't watch much of

Indianapolis's series, because she was focused on her own. Did the team have a meltdown? Were there problems in the room?

She isn't sure what led to Indianapolis's collapse, but she knows that kind of exit means there will be big changes this summer. Will Lexie still be a Renegade next season?

"Don't care," Elsa says. "Do you think Boston pulls out the series win?"

"If they don't, it isn't like playing Montreal is new to us."

Concord has faced the Montreal Mammoths more often than any other team in the playoffs. They've also lost to them more often than any other team. Sophie pushes the doubt out of her mind. No matter who they face, Concord will beat them.

*

Boston evens up the series and wins it in Game Seven. Sophie has a day to mentally prepare for the first game of the series. Outside of the playoffs, Schatz is one of Sophie's Team Canada teammates and a player who Sophie mentors. And Dima is her friend, someone who visits her when she's injured and makes her laugh, someone she can call and vent to when the season is stressful.

Inside the playoffs, however, they're the competition.

All two hundred and some-odd pounds of Dima slam into Sophie, and it knocks the breath out of her. She keeps her skates under her, but her lungs burn, and she needs a moment before she can jump back into the play.

She never fully catches her breath on that shift. As soon as she's back on the bench, she plants her elbows on her knees and breathes as deeply as she can.

"Sophie, your line is up!" Coach Elison calls.

Already? Sophie wants to ask. Instead, she sprays some water on her face, then she slings a leg over the bench wall and waits for Kansas to skate in for his change.

Sophie takes the ice and accepts the pass Spitzer slings her way. She notes that Hertz comes on the ice for Boston, which means she needs to keep her head up. With the puck on her stick, Sophie skates into the offensive zone. She circles Hippeli's net, and it buys enough time for Elsa to be on the ice now.

Sophie passes to Elsa and cuts back the other way. She's on the far side of Hippeli's net, ready for a backdoor pass. Dubya, a Boston defenseman, shifts to block that passing lane. Sophie drifts up toward the blueline to make herself available again.

Elsa passes to Spitzer who tries to pass the puck back to Elsa, but the puck is deflected. Zehavi takes off after it, a race between him and one of Boston's forwards. Sophie follows, and she's well into the neutral zone when she slaps her stick on the ice and calls for an outlet pass.

DZ slings the puck up to her. She checks her surroundings. Hertz is barreling in on her, but it means there's one less player defending for Boston. She sends the puck skipping back into Boston's zone, and she braces herself for Hertz's hit.

He slams into Sophie and knocks her into her own bench. "You'll stay there if you know what's good for you," he tells her.

Sophie is folded in two, her skates in the air and all her weight uncomfortably on her shoulders. Two of her teammates help orient her. By the time she's sitting properly on the bench, DZ is exchanging blows with Hertz on the ice.

The officials hover, waiting for a lull in the two men's fight. The crowd roars, wanting blood. Sophie grins and itches to be back on the ice, because this is *hockey*. The officials finally separate DZ and Hertz. Sophie taps her stick against the boards with everyone else as the two players are escorted to their respective penalty boxes.

Elsa scoops DZ's helmet and gloves off the ice. She skates them over to him in the box. They exchange a few words, then Elsa joins Sophie on the bench.

"Are you okay?" Elsa asks, checking in.

"I'm good," Sophie promises. "DZ?"

Elsa grins. "He's ready to do it again."

*

There are another three fights before the game is over.

Elsa has her ass handed her by Dima, but Sophie scores while Elsa and Dima are both in the penalty box. Sophie's goal stands as the lone goal in the game, and Sophie gives Elsa as much credit for it as she gives herself.

Of course, none of the reporters wants to talk about Sophie's goal after the game. They crowd around her stall, because Elsa's hiding in the showers, and Sophie's always a favorite. A few of the beat reporters are trying to wrangle a quote from DZ or Jonny or Theo, the other players who dropped the gloves tonight, but the bulk of them question Sophie.

"What did you think of Zehavi's fight with Hertz?" Marty Owen asks. "Did you think it was an overreaction to a legal hit?"

"What about Nyberg's fight with Ivanov?" Rossetti interrupts. "Will we see you drop the gloves next?"

Sophie sits in her stall and smiles as the reporters all talk over each other in a rare showing of unprofessionalism. Sweat gathers on Sophie's back and drips down into her spandex. Her reporters settle down, then Rickers steps forward with a question.

"Can we expect every game to be filled with this kind

of excitement?"

"If they are, you'll be seeing Manchester against Worcester by the end of the series," Sophie answers. "There's history between Concord and Boston, and we certainly know how to get under each other's skin, but I don't expect every game to be this animated. This isn't mixed martial arts, it's hockey. At the end of the day, we have to play hockey to win."

"Well, that's the quote of the playoffs," Marty Owen says with a huff. "*We need to play hockey to win.*"

Sophie doesn't even let Marty Owen bring her mood down. Her team took the first win in what's bound to be a tough series. They won on the road, in front of Boston's fans, and she knows her team can win another three.

*

While Sophie shows the reporters, and her teammates, her pleasure with the game and the win, she allows Elsa to see something closer to the truth. By the time they're at the hotel, Elsa has a bruise blooming on her face. Sophie hands her an icepack wrapped in a towel.

Elsa looks at the expression on Sophie's face and huffs. "We're doing this, then?"

"Coach Elison's going to address it tomorrow, but it can't hurt for you to hear it twice," Sophie says. She is glad they won, she is glad she was able to score while Elsa was in the box, but Elsa never should have been in the box. And she certainly shouldn't have a bruise spreading across her face right now. "I need you on the ice with me."

"You scored," Elsa points out.

Sophie crosses the distance between them until she can curl her fingers around Elsa's wrist and bring the icepack up to Elsa's face. Sophie holds it there, even as Elsa hisses at the cold. "I *want* you on the ice with me. Let Jonny fight. Let DZ and Theo and all of them drop their gloves. When Dima's a pain in the ass, we score a goal. That'll shut him up."

It won't, because nothing shuts him up, but a goal is better than Elsa in the penalty box. And yes, Sophie knows it didn't end badly tonight. She was able to score, Elsa fired up the team with her fight, and Elsa only has a bruise to show for it. But what about next time?

"Tonight's game got out of control," Sophie says. "That's what Coach Elison is going to talk about tomorrow. If we control the game, we win. We aren't built to have a boxing match in the middle of every game. It isn't our style. I know we won tonight and that this is a minor injury." Sophie brushes her fingers over the icepack. "But we can't count on that happening every game."

It could have easily gone in the other direction. Now that the adrenaline from the game has worn off, all Sophie can see are the worst-case scenarios. What if one of the fights led to one of Sophie's teammates getting injured? What if it was Concord who was scored on while their top players were in the box?

Teddy won this game for Concord. Sophie scored the goal, and the reporters are going to cover all the fights, but it was Teddy who kept Boston from scoring the way they're known to. Sophie and her team can't force Teddy to carry them through the whole series. They need to be on the ice and supporting him.

"You're right," Elsa says. She flexes the fingers of her free hand. "It felt good to punch him." She offers Sophie a smile and she grins when Sophie smiles back. "But it'll feel better to score."

*

Game Two picks up where the first one left off. As the home team, Boston has last change, which means Hertz is on the ice with Sophie whenever Boston can manage it. Sophie weathers the pushes and the shoves, because that's part of hockey. It's a physical game, but Sophie can hold her own.

Still, she gives Elsa a warning look, because fighting Dima is one thing, but if Elsa fights Hertz, he'll aim to hurt her. Elsa scowls but she gives a tight nod. When Sophie looks at Woodsy, he grins and holds up his hands. "I have no intention of fighting outside my weight class."

On their next shift out, Sophie is in Hippeli's crease, and she tries to stuff the puck past Boston's goaltender. He squeezes his knees tightly so the puck can't squeak through. There's no whistle so Sophie jabs at Hippeli with her stick. He smacks her with his paddle in response.

Someone punches the back of Sophie's neck, in the vulnerable place between her helmet and her shoulder pads. She's hit again and shoved to the ice, and now the officials blow their whistles.

As Sophie skates to her bench for a change, Jonny stands on the bench to shout at Hertz. Hertz, when he goes to his own bench, shouts right back.

"If you want a fight, then fucking fight me!" Jonny demands.

Hertz pounds the glass and the *TNSN* broadcaster who has his position between the two benches looks a little nervous as Hertz shouts back. "You aren't worth my time!"

Hertz sticks to his position. When Jonny and Hertz end up on the ice together, Jonny buzzes around him like an angry hornet, but Hertz doesn't drop his gloves. He crosschecks Jonny a few times, no doubt says some things, but he doesn't fight.

He doesn't fight after the next time they share a shift. Jonny returns to the bench, his shoulders tight and pissed off. "Fucking fine," he mutters to himself.

Sophie shares a shift with Hertz, and she takes her fair share of abuse from the man. She aches as she swaps out for Peets, and she'll no doubt have her fair share of bruises tomorrow morning, but it's fine. It's the playoffs.

Jonny doesn't think it's fine. He scowls at the red mark on Sophie's neck, he scowls at Hertz on Boston's bench, then he goes over the boards for a shift of his own. He plays tight, hard hockey, and he lines Schatz up and plasters her into the boards. There's finishing a check and *finishing a check*, and Sophie can't help but draw in a sharp breath as Schatz goes down on the ice.

It's a legal hit, but Schatz is clearly shaken up.

Jonny spits his mouthguard out and points right at Hertz, sitting comfortably on Boston's bench. "Will you fucking fight now?"

Boston's bench, and their fans, howl for Jonny's blood. Schatz's linemates help her up and to the bench. Two trainers take her down the tunnel for an evaluation.

Jonny and Hertz circle each other on their next two shifts, but Hertz still won't drop his gloves.

*

Sophie watches from the bench as Cubs slides a pass up to Bechs. Hertz barrels toward Sophie's teammate, and she screams at Bechs to dump the puck, to look up, but he doesn't hear her in time. Hertz bulldozes Bechs, dropping the smaller player to the ice as if it was nothing.

It happens quickly and violently, and Sophie prays it's one of those situations that looks worse than it is. Boston's fans, who cheered for the hit, grow quiet as Bechs doesn't stir on the ice. The whole rink goes quiet, eerily so. Kansas and Cubs stand on either side of Bechs to keep the cameras from zooming in on him.

Spitzer skates over to the bench so he can help one of the trainers over to their fallen teammate. Sophie's stomach twists. She can't watch Bechs so she looks over at Hertz instead. He's standing, protected, between two officials. The third official keeps Bowser from taking a swing at Hertz, and the fourth official hovers near Bechs, *useless*. Sophie's hands curl into fists.

If the officials let Hertz stay in the game, she'll make him bleed. She doesn't care if she's tossed from the game for it. She doesn't care if Elsa will call her a hypocrite for it. No one hurts Sophie's team and gets away with it.

Bechs sits up with help from the trainer, and Sophie almost throws up with relief. The trainer, Cubs, and Kansas help Bechs to his skates, then they escort him to the bench. The fans and the players all clap for Bechs's health. Sophie's glad he's moving, that he didn't have to be stretchered off, but as Bechs approaches the bench, it's obvious he isn't okay. His eyes are glazed, and he's unable to focus on anything. He looks a thousand miles away.

"Concussion," Woodsy says, next to Sophie. "Fuck."

Sophie pats Woodsy's shoulder, because she can't reach out to Bechs. Then the officials call Sophie and Dima to the ice for a scolding.

"Are you done yet?" Maxime Proust demands. "I'd rather throw players out than watch them leave on stretchers."

Something angry and bitter twists through Sophie as she turns to Dima. "Are you done?" she asks, because it was Hertz who deliberately targeted a player hoping to hurt them.

Dima's expression is no friendlier than Sophie's. "Your team isn't angels."

Proust clears his throat. "Clean up your play, both of you."

Sophie takes his message back to her bench.

*

Hertz is tossed from the game, and his status for the

remainder of the series is now in the league's hands, as they debate suspension.

Boston pulls out the win, though, and the series is tied up. The flight home is subdued.

*

"No flowers," Sarah Keller, Concord's head trainer, says when Sophie asks for an update. "No light and no visitors. Tanner is on complete blackout right now."

"That doesn't sound good," Sophie says. Hertz was given a three-game suspension for the hit. It isn't enough but it's more than Sophie expected he would get. It means Hertz, Schatz, and Bechs will all be absent from the next game.

"Head injuries are tricky," Keller says.

*

Concord loses Game Three.

They're in front of their home crowd, with every reason to play hard and win, and they can't do it. After the game, Sophie is furious and guilty, and both feelings intensify as she watches Teddy strip out of his goalie gear.

Teddy is deliberate and he is careful, but it isn't out of respect for his equipment. He's exhausted, *defeated*, and it's Sophie's fault he looks like that. She and the rest of the team didn't give him the support he needed. And now he sits in front of the reporters, his head bowed and his words quiet as he accepts the blame for every goal allowed and the final loss.

Sophie wants to gather Teddy in a hug. She desperately wants to wipe the misery from his face. She wants to throw all the reporters out of the room.

She can't do any of those things.

All she can do is make sure the team is there for

Teddy in Game Four, the way he's been there for them in every game so far.

She grabs Kevlar after media and tells him, "Teddy's had our back all playoffs. It's time we have his." She trusts Kevlar will spread the word to the rest of the d-corps. Sophie handles spreading the message through the forward group.

*

Boston scores two early goals to kick off Game Four. Sophie shakes her head as a few boos trickle down from the stands, as if it's Teddy's fault. She looks over at Elsa, and Elsa's gaze is hard, and her expression is determined.

Sophie scores on the next shift.

Figs ties the game midway through the first period, then Cubs puts them ahead in the final minute of the period.

Teams rally behind their captains and behind their goalies, and Sophie gives a rousing intermission speech that has the entire team locked in as they take the ice for the second period. They score another three goals in the next twenty minutes.

Boston manages a goal in the third period, but it isn't enough. Concord wins decisively, 6-3, and they tie the series.

*

Game Five is back in Boston. Schatz returns to the lineup, and Boston wins the game. It puts them one win away from closing out the series, but Sophie doesn't allow it to rattle her.

Game Six is tight, three goals scored in the first period, then nothing, until Coach Elison calls Teddy to the bench, because there's only a minute left in the game and

Concord is down by one.

Elsa scores the tying goal with three seconds left on the clock. Sophie slams home the overtime game winner.

The series is tied again, three games apiece. Game Seven will be in Boston, and the winner of the game will move on to the next round. Sophie is locked in. Now, she has to make sure her team is as well.

*

Hertz will be back in Boston's lineup for Game Seven. Sophie doesn't let her fear of him rattle her. She doesn't let her fury that he's playing and Bechs is still on concussion watch affect her, either. Where she leads, Concord will follow. She has to be steady. She has to be unshakable.

Right now, she's in one of the hotel meeting rooms with a book of Sudoku on her lap. The meeting room has been converted into a players' lounge. During the playoffs, the team is essentially on lockdown. They limit their contact with the world outside the team in order to limit distractions.

Sophie tucks her pencil into the binding of her book and closes it. Cubs, who has been inching closer to her for the past five minutes, freezes, as if she won't notice him. Sophie looks around the room to give Cubs a moment to compose himself.

Everyone is occupied. Some, like Figs, are lying down with their eyes closed, not napping but resting. Others are doing word puzzles or coloring, something to keep them occupied that isn't stressful. Kevlar and Theo are working on a drawing together, but they're on opposite sides of the room so they keep folding their paper into an airplane and sending it to where the other is sitting.

Sophie shakes her head fondly and looks back at Cubs.

Cubs *tap-tap-taps* his foot on the floor. "Tomorrow is

Game Seven," he says. He doesn't speak loudly, but the room is quiet and so a few players look over. Bowser and Kansas glance up from their game of checkers. Spitzer smiles and nudges DZ so he'll pay attention.

Sophie, who has learned the art of selective hearing and vision, pretends she doesn't notice the audience. "It is. Are you nervous?"

Cubs shrugs but he's tapping his foot again, an obvious tell. Game Sevens are pressure-filled, adrenaline-riddled games, but Sophie doesn't drum her fingers in time with the frenetic beating of her heart.

"Concord doesn't lose Game Sevens," she tells Cubs. They didn't lose a single Game Seven in the playoffs they won the Cup. They haven't lost any since. They've lost series, but never when the series came down to a seventh game. She doesn't intend to break this streak tomorrow. She smiles gently at Cubs, who is looking even more overwhelmed now. "I'm not anxious, I'm ready. Tomorrow, we step on Boston's ice, and we win."

"Concord doesn't lose Game Sevens," Kevlar repeats from his spot on the far side of the room. "That's our playoff legacy."

Cubs stares at Sophie with wide eyes, filled with awe and fear and a sliver of doubt. He's nineteen and it's his first season in the NAHL. Sophie forgives his lack of faith.

*

Boston opens the scoring, and the crowd celebrates as if they've won the series. Sophie scores to even the game. Dima scores to restore Boston's lead. Elsa scores and Schatz responds. It's back-and-forth like that, not only with goals but with hits, with chances.

The score is 2-3 in Boston's favor when they go into the second intermission. Sophie isn't rattled or worried. She's locked in. She wants to be on the ice *now*. She doesn't need a twenty-minute breather or a fresh sheet of ice.

Elsa pushes Sophie down to sit at her stall. She presses a bottle of Gatorade into Sophie's hands. "Drink," Elsa says.

Sophie drinks.

*

Power plays are rare in the playoffs and when Concord earns one, Sophie is determined to make the most of it. She carries the puck into the offensive zone and drops a pass back for Elsa. Sophie dodges Hertz's hit and turns to see Elsa pass the puck to Merlin.

Merlin shoots without settling the puck. It means Hippeli is still pushing himself into the correct position as the puck flies at him. Hippeli whips his glove up, but the puck skims over the top of it and falls into the back of the net.

Sophie shouts and throws her arms around Merlin and celebrates as a hush falls over the Boston crowd.

*

The game is tied and there are two minutes left in the game when Boston is called for back-to-back icings. The Boston coach calls a timeout to give his tired players a breather.

Sophie taps Cubs's shoulder. She points to the game clock. "Do we win in regulation or overtime?"

Cubs hisses at her and raps his knuckles on the boards.

"We don't lose Game Sevens," Sophie says. It isn't superstition, it's fact. "So, when do we win?"

Cubs doesn't answer before the timeout ends. Sophie

goes over the boards with her line. They'll have their answer soon enough.

*

Spitzer scores to give Concord their first lead of the game.

Boston pulls Hippeli, and the Barons squeak the puck past Teddy with just under a minute left in the game.

The crowd works themselves into a frenzy.

On Concord's bench, Cubs looks as though he's about to start hyperventilating. Elsa takes one look at Sophie, then she draws Cubs to her side and walks with him down to the locker room for intermission.

Sophie's too keyed up to offer anyone comfort right now. This moment, when the game is suspended in balance, is when Sophie is at her best. She's the weight that will tip the game in her favor. She thrives on the pressure, on knowing everyone is watching her to see what she'll do. There's a whole crowd in the stands who want to see her fail, but it doesn't matter. None of them can touch her.

*

Sophie grunts as Hertz knocks the wind out of her. He doesn't linger to taunt her or give her an extra jab. He won't risk it with the game on the line. Sophie regains her bearings and skates to the front of the net to make life difficult for Hippeli.

Boston's goalie covers the puck, then Dubya gives Sophie a push out of the crease. She allows the momentum to carry her part of the way to her bench and skates the rest of the way for a change.

It's Peets's turn now. Sophie rests a hand on Cubs's shoulder as he heads out to join his linemates.

"We don't lose Game Sevens?" Cubs guesses.

Sophie grins and rubs her glove over his helmet, before she sends him on his way.

Peets wins the faceoff back to Cubs who slaps the puck on net, instinct more than anything. The goal light flashes, and Sophie jumps to her feet, already cheering. She throws her arms around Elsa, then she hugs Woodsy and it's a mad scramble over the boards.

Cubs is too shocked to move, still standing where he took his shot from. Sophie laughs as they all surround him to congratulate him on the game winner. They break off to spread the love to Teddy, then there's the handshake line.

At the end of it, Cubs is still dazed, as if the game or the series or maybe even his goal still hasn't sunk in. Sophie has a smile and a hug and a few words for each of her teammates after they go through the handshake line.

When she pulls Cubs in for his embrace, he's the one who talks. "We don't lose Game Sevens," he says quietly.

It isn't a question this time.

Chapter Eighteen

The series between Philadelphia and Cleveland also goes to seven games. Cleveland emerges victorious. Sophie watched the game from the couch in her living room, because she refused to allow either team in her bedroom, even if they're only on a TV screen.

She has a full playoff series against Michael Hayes ahead of her. A full series against Cleveland, a team with nothing but hate and bad memories for her. On the TV, the broadcasters tease an upcoming segment about the Concord-Cleveland Conference Finals. Sophie turns off the TV. She already knows what to expect.

"Bed," Elsa says. She stands and stretches, then holds her hand out to Sophie.

Sophie grasps it and allows Elsa to help pull her up off the couch. Sophie's muscles are stiff from sitting, and almost every part of her aches. It doesn't matter how much she stretches or ices, the playoffs are brutal on her body.

She looks up the flight of stairs that leads to her and Elsa's bedroom and groans.

"We asked Armand for a master suite on the first floor," Elsa says, as if she can sense Sophie's thoughts. "Once we have our new house, we can sleep there during the playoffs."

"It's for one of our families," Sophie says. She begins the slow trek up the stairs, because the sooner she starts, the sooner she'll be in bed. Her knees pop and crack with each step, reminding her that the career she chose is hard on her body.

"Not during the playoffs," Elsa says.

It's true. They'll only need one space during the playoffs, for Elsa's family, and it's best that they stay in the in-law apartment, instead of in the house proper. It's where Elsa's parents are now, close enough for Elsa to stay hello, to wheedle her mother into cooking for her, but it's enough distance that Elsa can stay focused on the playoffs.

Sophie's family, of course, doesn't need a place to stay in Sophie and Elsa's house. Her dad's strict rules mean they'll only watch in person if Sophie makes it to the Maple Cup finals, and if that happens, they'll stay in a hotel. Her dad has always been concerned with distractions to Sophie's games, sometimes to the point where he becomes a distraction.

Elsa tugs on Sophie's hand and leads her into their bedroom. They brush their teeth and change into their pajamas, then fall into bed together. They're on top of the blankets, but Sophie doesn't feel like moving.

Sophie's shirt rode up a little when she dropped onto the bed. It reveals a strip of skin that Elsa frowns at. She curls her hand around Sophie's waist and her frown deepens. "You're too skinny."

"It's the playoffs," Sophie says. Coach Elison keeps practices light, tune-ups and tweaks, nothing strenuous, because the games themselves are tougher than any regular season game can hope to be. The brutal pace means every player burns more calories than they can eat. Sophie does her best to keep up, but it's impossible. The playoffs are a grind. They're a competition of skill, but they're also a test of endurance.

Elsa grumbles but her touch turns from evaluating to teasing as she trails her fingers under the waistband of Sophie's pajamas. Sophie's stomach clenches, and she feels the familiar stirrings of desire, but they're followed by a wave of exhaustion.

She gently pushes Elsa's hand away. "As nice as that thought is, I'm too tired to finish it."

"Yeah." Elsa sighs and rolls onto her back. "We're going on vacation this summer, and all we'll do is eat and sleep and have sex."

Sophie snorts. "That sounds…" Impossible. Unrealistic.

"Perfect," Elsa says, then she laughs quietly at the expression on Sophie's face.

"We have some unfinished business before we can plan the summer," Sophie says.

"We can beat Cleveland," Elsa says confidently.

Sophie nods and musters up the energy to get under the covers.

*

Because of Concord's poor performance in the regular season, they're the lower seeded team in every series they play. It means they fly to Cleveland for the first two games of the series. The night before their first game, Sophie grabs the ice bucket off the table in her and Elsa's room.

She and Elsa don't actually need ice yet, but Sophie likes the excuse to wander the halls and check in with any of her teammates who are also feeling restless. Elsa tosses some quarters Sophie's way, and they scatter on the floor. "Get me something?"

"Anything specific?" Sophie asks as she gathers up the loose change.

"Surprise me," Elsa says.

Sophie slips the quarters into her back pocket and heads out in search of the ice and vending machines. They're in the middle of the hallway, across from the elevators in their own little nook. Sophie isn't the only one on the hunt for ice. Bowser is there too.

If Sophie is wandering the halls because Cleveland makes her too restless to relax, she can only imagine what it's like for Bowser.

"Is it different?" Sophie asks him. "Being back here for the playoffs instead of a regular season game?"

Bowser, who had been leaning against the wall when Sophie arrived, as if he was looking for an escape and not for ice, sticks his bucket in the machine and presses the button. The sound of ice filling his bucket is loud enough to prevent conversation, but Sophie's question still hangs between them when he's done.

Sophie wonders if he'll leave without answering. The two of them aren't close, the way Sophie is with some of her teammates. She doesn't need to be his friend or confidante, but she's here if he needs to talk.

Eventually, Bowser shrugs. "Is it different for you?"

"I thought it would be," Sophie answers honestly. "I played a lot of regular season games here before I ever played my first playoff game. I was prepared for it to be worse, but it wasn't. I guess they hated me so much, they couldn't hate me more."

Bowser laughs quietly, as if he understands. "I don't think it'll be different for me either. I'm on the outside now. It doesn't matter if it's preseason or playoffs. I'm not one of them anymore. That's how it works."

"You're one of us now," Sophie reminds him. She taps the clear panel on the vending machine. "Elsa wants something sweet. What should I get?"

Bowser is caught off guard by the subject change, but

he recovers quickly enough. He looks over the offerings. "Uh, Twix? They're easy to share."

It's Sophie's turn to laugh as she feeds quarters into the machine. "Elsa and I share a shower. We can handle eating from the same candy bar." Sophie punches in the code for a Snickers. They're her favorite, and Elsa will be just as pleased to have the candy as to see Sophie indulging herself.

"You could get two," Bowser says. "She doesn't seem like the type to share."

Sophie thinks about Elsa, sprawled across one of the beds, and waiting for Sophie to return so she can curl an arm around Sophie's waist and cuddle her close. She can't keep the smile off her face or out of her words as she says, "It depends on the person."

"One of them or not?" Bowser asks.

Sophie and Elsa aren't telling their teammates they're in a relationship and, if they were, Bowser wouldn't be the first one Sophie would tell. She grabs the Snickers bar from where the machine dropped it and fills her ice bucket since she has it with her.

She steers her conversation with Bowser back to lighter ground, then they part ways, Bowser for his room and Sophie for hers.

"You were gone a long time," Elsa says when Sophie returns. "Did you find a friend?"

"Bowser was stressing by the ice machine." Sophie tosses Elsa the candy bar.

"Captain Sophie strikes in the hotel hallway?" Elsa laughs and unwraps her candy. She looks over at Sophie and holds the chocolate out. "Do you want the first bite?"

Sophie doesn't pretend she doesn't. She leans over to steal a generous first bite, then laughs as Elsa scowls and brings her arm up to protect the rest of her candy.

"He's ready for tomorrow," Sophie says. "I am too."

"Good," Elsa says. "I like beating Cleveland in front of their own fans."

*

There are boos from the moment Sophie steps onto the ice. The rumble of the crowd's displeasure rattles the glass, but it doesn't touch Sophie. This is the arena she tore her ACL in, then lost almost a whole season. But Sophie is here and she's healthy, and she may have struggled to start the regular season, but she's having a hell of a playoff run.

She stretches next to Teddy, a break from her usual routine. He offers her a smile, as if he knows she's here for her sake and not his. Teddy was their original Cleveland pickup, long before Sophie even knew who Bowser was.

Teddy never won a single game as Cleveland's backup goalie. But he's won a Cup with Concord, and they're going to win another this year.

Sophie moves into her next stretch. Movement on the other side of the ice draws her attention. Michael Hayes goes through his own warmup routine. The 93 on the back of his jersey is bright and bold. It's the same number he wore for the Weston School, when he and Sophie were prep school rivals. He didn't wear it in his short stint in Concord. Ninety-three is *Sophie's* number.

She'll make sure he remembers why she was given first choice of number when they were teammates. She is a better hockey player than him. She always has been, and she always will be.

When the game begins, Sophie takes her place at the faceoff dot. Hayes sets up opposite her. Sophie wins the faceoff by sweeping the puck back to Kevlar. Then she pushes forward, toward the offensive zone. She makes sure to clip Hayes's shoulder on the way by.

Game on.

*

Hayes scores the first goal of the series, and the crowd erupts as if they've won the Cup. *Hayes is better!* they chant. Sophie puts them out of her head and watches the replay of the goal. Hayes stuffs the puck past Teddy, a brute force goal, no skill at all.

"I can do better," Sophie tells Elsa.

"Then do it," Elsa challenges.

Sophie turns to Elsa. She grins. "Get me the puck and I will."

*

There's a firewagon change. Sophie hits the ice and jumps over the puck, because if she touches it with Kansas still on the ice, they'll be called for too many players on the ice. In the time it takes for Kansas and Jonny to haul their asses to the bench, Cleveland has possession.

Sophie crunches McGuire into the boards to separate him from the puck. She pins him there as Woodsy scoops up the puck and takes off. It was a combined hit from McGuire and Hayes that took Sophie out two seasons ago. Knocking McGuire around won't make up for the time Sophie lost, but it feels good.

Sophie leaves McGuire to snarl insults, and she trails Woodsy into the offensive zone. She drops down the far wing, and Woodsy passes her the puck. She watches Cleveland's defense shift, notes all the players and the reaches of their sticks, then she slings a pass to Elsa.

Sophie skates around the back of Strindberg's net. She slaps her stick on the ice twice, and Elsa sends the puck back to her. Strindberg, in Cleveland's goal, squares up to Sophie's shot. There's a big empty space over his right shoulder, but she knows if she aims there, he'll snap his glove up and catch the puck. She fakes high and shoots low. The puck sneaks through the tiny sliver of space between his right leg and the ice.

Strindberg checks his glove for the puck as the goal light flashes behind him.

Sophie throws her arms up in celebration and turns to meet Elsa's gaze. She told Elsa to get her the puck and Sophie would score. And that's exactly what happened.

Elsa skates over to Sophie, wraps her up in her arms, and bumps their visors against each other. "Best," Elsa says, heated and passionate, and Sophie's entire body trembles with the praise.

*

Kansas scores the go-ahead goal in the second period. On the next shift, Bowser blocks a rocket from Olsson at the point. It would've been a sure goal if Bowser hadn't dropped to one knee and taken the puck off his thigh.

The crowd falls silent as they draw their collective breath. And then they boo, louder even than they had been for Sophie. Bowser was met with mixed reactions from his former team during the regular season. He didn't sign with Concord, he was traded, which meant they had some sympathy for him. But now, blocking that shot, he's betrayed them, and they'll never forgive him for it.

Bowser is heckled and booed every second he's on the ice afterward. He looks stunned at first, but he adapts to it, and by the time the third period is well underway, he doesn't seem to notice it.

Coach Elison notices his poise, and he sends Bowser out for the final shift of the game. Sophie notes Bowser's surprise then the brief smile before he heads over the boards to defend Concord's lead.

Sophie watches from the bench as her teammates battle in the final thirty seconds of the game. Peets and Farage, Cleveland's captain, tie up on the faceoff. Jonny and Hayes battle for the loose puck.

It's Merlin who comes up with the puck, and he tries to outlet it to DZ, but Olsson breaks up the pass. The puck deflects to the far boards, and it's a race between Bowser and McGuire to get to it first. Bowser reaches the puck, but he doesn't fling it down the ice for an icing or even an attempt at the empty net.

Bowser traps the puck against the boards with his skate and weathers every elbow, shove, and slash McGuire gives him until time runs out on the game.

"One down," Elsa says as she and Sophie stand to congratulate their teammates.

"Three more to go," Sophie responds.

*

They lose Game Two in front of Cleveland's raucous crowd, then they fly home for the next two games. Sophie feels more settled once they're in Concord. She's learned to play in hostile rinks; she hasn't had a choice. There's something different, though, about playing for a home crowd rather than playing against an away one.

As always, Sophie leads her team onto the ice for warmups. Bringing up the rear is Elsa. Their entire team, bracketed between the two of them. Sophie skates her first lap on her own and Elsa joins her for the second.

Their fans are all on their feet and decked out in red, impossible to miss, as they cheer Concord on.

"They want a show," Sophie says. She waves at a few zealous fans who pound on the glass to try to get her attention. She looks back at Elsa. "Will you give them one?"

"I'd hate to disappoint," Elsa says.

*

Sophie wins the opening faceoff, but it's Elsa who takes the puck and drives into the offensive zone. She plows through the scrambling defense, leans into her shot, then snaps the puck past Strindberg.

The crowd, still buzzing from the opening lineups, grows even louder with the goal.

Elsa doesn't bother with an elaborate celly. She finds Sophie and pins her with a smug grin. "That showy enough for you?"

"More," Sophie demands.

Elsa's eyes flash darkly, but she continues to smile, pleased and prepared to meet the challenge.

Woodsy hovers next to them. "Am I interrupting something?"

Sophie holds her arm out to bring him into the post-goal celebration, but she doesn't look away from Elsa. Elsa's expression promises Sophie anything she wants. Goals, assists, and a thorough celebration once they're home.

*

Back-to-back icings by Cleveland leaves tired players on the ice, but the game is still young, and Cleveland's coach doesn't use his timeout. Sophie and Elsa go over the boards. Elsa pops her mouthguard out, grins, then shoves it back in.

Sophie wins the faceoff, then Elsa goes to work. Elsa shows no mercy as she skates around defenders until they're dizzy, exhausted, and useless. She dangles the puck in front of Strindberg, daring him to poke it away, and when he tries, she wrists the puck over his shoulder.

Sophie crashes into Elsa's side and knocks her into the glass behind the net. The fans pound on the glass behind them, but neither Sophie nor Elsa gives them their attention.

"More," Sophie says.

*

Sophie cradles the puck and does a quick check on her teammates. Concord is on the power play, which means there should be someone less defended. Olsson steps up, as if he thinks Sophie will stay still long enough for him to steal the puck.

Sophie twists around Olsson, and now she's between the d-man and his goalie. Strindberg pushes off his post and squares up to Sophie, prepared for her to shoot. Walker edges closer to Sophie too, and that's two players focused on Sophie.

She can't help her grin as she loads up and then, once both Cleveland players are committed to her shot, she slides the puck through Walker's legs. The puck lands on Elsa's stick on the far side of the net. She has the entire net to shoot at, but she taps the puck softly in, a taunt.

It's arrogant, it's mean, and Sophie slams Elsa into the boards and says, "Yes," as the fans raise their voices and start throwing their hats down on the ice.

*

Sophie doesn't know how she keeps her hands off Elsa during their post-game. Well, she does know. She sets up with her scrum away from where her and Elsa's stalls are. She doesn't even look toward the shower room, afraid she'll be tempted by the lure of Elsa and a shower curtain hiding them from the rest of their team.

Sophie talks up Teddy's shutout, and she praises Elsa's goals, and when she's asked what she said to Elsa to get her fired up, Sophie smiles and lets them draw their own conclusions.

Finally, she and Elsa are home. As soon as the front door closes behind them, Sophie pushes Elsa up against it and kisses her hard. Elsa's in too many layers, and Sophie's fingers are met with fabric every time she tries to touch her girlfriend. It makes her kiss Elsa more desperately, but Elsa doesn't seem to mind.

Elsa's fingers curl around Sophie's hips and press into Sophie's skin, hard enough to add to the bruises already scattered across Sophie's body. The pain is muted, adrenaline pushing it to the side as if they're still on the ice.

Sophie breaks the kiss long enough to say, "That fucking goal," before she kisses just beneath Elsa's ear, the place that makes Elsa growl and squirm against her.

"Which one?" Elsa asks.

Sophie knows exactly which goal was her favorite, but the reminder that Elsa had *three* is enough to make her set her teeth against Elsa's neck. She isn't so out of it that she bites, even if she wants to. Her blood thrums between her ears, and she wants to leave a mark on Elsa, wants the entire world to know that she chose Elsa and Elsa chose her back. This incredible woman who scores series-defining goals. She is Sophie's girlfriend.

"Upstairs," Elsa urges. She pushes on Sophie's hips but doesn't quite push Sophie away, as if she doesn't want to lose the contact.

Sophie grasps Elsa's hand and tugs her up the stairs and into their bedroom. It's a race to get their clothes off, then they fall into bed, mouths finding each other's as their hands wander, greedy with all the skin now on display.

Three goals for Elsa in the game and none for anyone else. No one on Cleveland scored. No one else on Concord did, either. It was Elsa's game from puck drop. Sophie kisses Elsa, just on the edge of too hard, and pulls back before Elsa can kiss her back.

"What do you want?" Sophie asks. "Anything, it's yours."

Elsa rolls them so she's on top. "I want you," she answers and kisses Sophie before Sophie can tell her that isn't a fucking answer.

*

In the end, Sophie isn't sure if it was Elsa's last goal, insulting in how easy it was to score, or the hat trick that breaks Cleveland, but they collapse after Game Three. Concord wins Games Four and Five to close out the series.

They're Eastern Conference champs, and it means T-shirts and hats, then setting their sights on the next, and more important round.

The Maple Cup finals.

Chapter Nineteen

Denver beats Minneapolis to emerge as Concord's opponent in the finals. It's fitting, Sophie thinks. The first Maple Cup Concord won was with Butler behind the bench. Now, it's their first opportunity for a second, and they're facing him.

The broadcasts spin it into something bigger than it is. But Sophie condenses it into something smaller than it is. She captained Concord, while Butler coached. Which one of them will win out this time? Her or him?

Sophie thought that Butler was her coach and on her side. But he was only ever on his own. Somehow, he went from wanting what was best for Concord to wanting what was best for him. He turned the team against one another, then he hung an entire season around her neck so he would still be hirable once his coaching days were over in Concord.

Coming off the series against Cleveland, Sophie can't help but think about Hayes. They were rivals who were drafted to the same NAHL team. Sophie was committed to being teammates, even if she knew they would never be friends, but Hayes couldn't do it. He couldn't play with Sophie and when push came to shove, Concord chose her.

Then, years later, when Butler made it clear that Concord could either be his team or Sophie's, the front office once again chose Sophie. They selected her last at her draft, but they have made it clear that she is the player the franchise is built around. They chose her over Hayes, her over Butler, and, last summer, they told her they wanted her to lead this team for another ten years.

Sophie's team and her front office are united behind her. Now, all she has to do is deliver.

*

Sophie takes the ice in Denver, prepared for the swell of hate. They don't like her here anymore than they like her in Cleveland. She glances at the stands and wonders where her family is. It's the finals now, which means her dad lifted the ban on live games.

Elsa bumps Sophie's shoulder to bring her thoughts back down to ice level. Sophie gives Elsa a nod of acknowledgement. It's going to take everything they have to win this series. Sophie can't afford to be distracted.

She takes her place at the faceoff dot. Butler, with the power of last change, sends Sinclair out to counter her.

"There are no hidden mics to protect you this time," Sinclair tells her.

Sophie ignores him and looks to the official.

She's too slow on the drop, and Sinclair wins the faceoff.

*

After a shift where Rawlings catches Cubs up high with his stick and sends Sophie's rookie to the bench bleeding, Sinclair smashes Sophie into the boards and pins her there. "I guess every Condor is as soft as you. Will you kiss it better at intermission?"

Sophie shoves him off her and puts herself back in the play.

Where she leads, her team follows. She can't allow

Sinclair under her skin, because if he throws her off her game, her team will fall apart.

*

Pickard knocks Sophie off her skates in front of Lenno's net. Her knees slam into the ice, but she keeps her stick down, and she deflects Kevlar's shot from the blueline. Lenno snaps his glove out to stop the goal, and the officials blow the play dead.

As Sophie pushes to her feet, someone crosschecks her across the nameplate and sends her back to her knees.

She looks up and meets Sinclair's gaze. He winks at her.

*

Sinclair is like a burr, stuck uncomfortably to her side all game. He knocks her into the boards and whispers in her ear. He slashes her wrists and laughs. He elbows her in the ribs, where he rammed the butt of his stick when he took her out of the IHT. And then he does it again because, "twice for flinching."

He pokes and prods and jabs until Sophie's patience snaps. Her answering elbowing isn't enough for his dramatics, but the officials don't care. Sophie is sent to the box for a penalty.

Sinclair scores.

*

Concord loses the game. The final score is 0-2, because they pulled Teddy at the end of the game to try to even up the score and Denver scored on the empty net. The loss sits heavy on Sophie's shoulders. Sinclair scored because of her penalty, then Denver scored again as her team tried to make up for her mistake.

Back at the hotel, Sophie takes the ice bucket and finds the ice machine. She doesn't bother to fill it, only sits down in the small alcove. Elsa is in their room, no doubt preparing a lecture on how it was Sophie who lost her cool after so many warnings to Elsa about the same. Or, worse, Elsa's preparing something *nice* to say. Sophie doesn't want judgement or pity. She wants to win.

She runs her hands through her hair, grips the strands, and pulls. It's a dull ache.

She hears footsteps, and she looks up to see Jonny join her in the alcove. He doesn't even have an ice bucket, as if he came here specifically for her.

"I can always fight him," Jonny says. He sits down across from Sophie. He stretches his legs out and winces at some lingering soreness.

"It would only encourage him," Sophie says. She appreciates the offer, but it won't help.

"Yeah, but it would mean five minutes he wasn't on the ice," Jonny says. "And I'd get to punch him. Think of it as doing me a favor."

Sophie laughs, knowing she's meant to. Jonny came to them from Denver. Sophie remembers being angry, because they had to trade away Big Red, who wasn't big or red. His last name was Clifford, and Merlin's always handed out awful nicknames. He was a young player, showed a lot of promise, and Sophie wanted him on her team more than some fourth line bruiser like Jonathan Kellman.

Big Red got into a fight at one of Denver's practice sessions. He took a swing at Sinclair and ended up traded to Seattle shortly after. Jonny fit in better with Concord, defying all of Sophie's expectations. She knew him from games. He was a tough player, more brawn than skill, and he toed the line of legality. But he adjusted to Concord's style. He fought for Sophie against his former team. He's scored more than one goal off an assist from her.

He's a Condor now, not a Boulder.

She knows he would fight anyone on Denver's roster if she asked. She isn't sure if she should.

"Rawlings once told me it wasn't personal," Sophie says. Rawlings is Sinclair-lite. He's as rough around the edges as his captain, he hits Sophie harder than he needs to, and his checks and his insults are always sharply edged. He and Sophie were teammates at the IHT, and it wasn't a disaster, but it was far from comfortable.

"For Sinclair it is," Jonny says. "For Rawlings, it might not be."

"It feels personal," Sophie says. When they insult her, threaten her, try to take her out of the game. She thought she knew hatred from her years competing against Hayes. But Sinclair is a class of his own. "If you fight him, he knows he's gotten to me."

Jonny gives her a flat, unimpressed look. "I think your elbow already told him that. At least this time, I'll be in the box and not you."

Sophie gives a jerky nod. "You're right. I can't let him get to me like that again. I need to be on the ice." She looks over at Jonny, because she knows what she just implied. "You should be too."

Jonny waves off any hurt feelings. "I know my role, Cap. And you know yours. I'll let you fuss afterward if it makes you feel better."

"Deal," Sophie says.

*

Sophie doesn't allow Sinclair to goad her into any penalties in Game Two. Jonny, true to his word, fights Sinclair, and Sophie scores while both Jonny and Sinclair are in the penalty box.

It isn't enough. Concord still loses the game.

They fly home after the game, and Sophie is glad her dad doesn't let her family stay at the house for the finals. Sophie is brittle and fragile. She doesn't have the energy to waste talking through the game with her dad. She needs to focus on finding her game, instead of playing Sinclair's.

The team has a light practice the day after the loss, then Sophie and Figs go to the team's favorite steakhouse for lunch. Sophie thanks the hostess who ushers them back to a private booth, then stares at the menu. She is in her city again. The next game she plays will be in her arena, with her fans in the stands.

And she'll play *her* game.

"We're going to win," Sophie says.

Figs looks up from his own menu. "I'm hardly going down without a fight."

Because this is his last season, and he's claimed he won't retire without a Cup. This is the closest he's gotten in a long time, and Sophie won't allow Figs's career to end on an *if only* or *so close*. It will end with him hoisting the Maple Cup.

"I've never seen anyone get under your skin the way Sinclair does," Figs says.

Sophie's reminded that, in Figs's long career, he played with Denver for a spell. He and Sinclair were teammates. She still remembers the surprise and hurt on Figs's face when she didn't talk to him while he wore a Boulders jersey. How many times has she been told that the logo on the front is more important than the name on the back of a jersey?

"He's a constant reminder that the league isn't as good as I hoped it would be," Sophie admits. "My younger years, they weren't great. I took shit from the other teams and their parents and fans, but I got it from my own teammates too. Nasty stuff. I told myself it was worth it, because I was going to play in the NAHL. I promised myself the NAHL would be different."

Sophie pauses when the waitress comes over to take their drink orders. Figs orders an appetizer as well. Once the waitress leaves, Sophie sighs and taps her fingers on the table. "There's no way to win against players like Sinclair. If I ignore him, he escalates and it's exhausting. If I snap, he knows what buttons to press in the future. If one of my teammates defends me, he knows he's gotten to me. I feel helpless against him."

Sophie can't meet Figs's gaze, afraid of what she'll see in his eyes. Pity? Scorn? But it's true. Worse than the words Sinclair spits at her or the hits he lays or the memory of his stick ramming into her side, this is what gets to her the most. The twisting, nausea-inducing knowledge that there's nothing she can do against Sinclair.

"Win by winning," Figs says.

"It isn't enough," Sophie tells him. "But it's all I can do."

"Win four and then you won't have to look at him or see him for the entire summer," Figs says.

And, as a bonus, she'll be a two-time Maple Cup champion.

*

Bechs returns to the lineup for Game Three, and it's a much-needed morale boost. Jonny ruffles his hair in the locker room and promises he won't let a single Boulder so much as breathe near him, let alone hit him.

It's good to see Bechs in the room, even better to see him smiling. Jonny is more settled with Bechs here, and the Manchester crew swarms Bechs to bring him into their jokes and their warmup.

The entire team is locked in, Sophie notes as she completes her circuits of the ice. Everyone is paired off or in a group. Even the goalies stretch together, shifting into each new stretch in tandem, without ever saying a word.

"We're ready," Elsa tells Sophie.

"We are," Sophie agrees.

She takes a deep breath and lets it out slowly. The series has shifted to home ice, and it's time for Concord to play *their* game. It starts with Sophie. She takes another breath and moves into the next stage of her warmup.

Now that Concord is the home team, Coach Elison has last change. Sophie opens the game by facing off against Sinclair, but when Coach Elison can make it work, Sophie isn't on the ice with Denver's captain.

She battles with Rawlings instead. He hits as hard as Sinclair does, and he has plenty of shit to say between whistles, but Sophie pretends she can't hear him.

On this shift, Sophie was in the right place at the right time, and Elsa sprung her for a breakaway. She skates in on Lenno, and she can feel Rawlings behind her, but she knows she has too much of a lead on him. It's her against Lenno, and the crowd's anticipation grows with each stride she skates.

Sophie comes at Lenno from the left, then she passes to herself to come at him from the right. Lenno pushes off his post, but he's still moving as she settles the puck and evaluates her shot. Lenno has left her half a dozen opens. She brings her stick back to shoot and—

A stick hooks around her ankle and pulls, knocking her off-balance. She falls to the ice mid-shot, and the puck skitters harmlessly to the boards. Sophie twists and pushes to her skates, furious with whoever interfered with her goal. She takes a step toward Rawlings, then she sees Maxime Proust's arm held in the air.

Penalty.

Sophie spots the puck, still by the boards. She races Rawlings for it, but he reaches it first. As soon as his stick touches the puck, Proust blows his whistle to end the play.

Rawlings scowls, but he knows he committed a penalty. And he'd do it again. Any coach would say it was a good penalty, because Rawlings prevented a sure goal. It would be up to the penalty kill to prevent a possible goal.

Then Proust signals a penalty shot.

Well, then, Sophie thinks. Butler shouts from his bench, and Thomas Hawthorne skates over to pretend to pay attention. The ice clears except for a goalie at either end and Sophie at center ice. Proust sets the puck down in front of her.

Sophie looks down the ice at where Lenno prepares. He taps his paddle against one goal post, then the other. Sophie takes a moment to do her own preparations. With a deep breath, the crowd fades away. Another, and the two benches of players fade away. Next, the crowd. It's only Sophie now, standing on the frozen pond in her parents' backyard.

Sophie practiced one-on-one with Colby for most of her childhood. She mimicked the players she saw on TV and even made up some shots of her own. Whenever Colby grew impatient, they would make a deal. They stayed outside until he could stop her. Sophie was very motivated to put the puck past him.

If you're not the best, then you don't get to play. Those were her dad's words to her, and they echo in her head even now. Sophie comes at Lenno from the left. He squares up to her angle.

Do her favorite moves flit through his head? Is he running through scouting reports in his head as he tries to guess which one he'll use? He brings his glove up and adjusts his grip on his paddle.

Sophie crosses over. As she moves from left to right, Lenno does as well. He pushes hard off his post, but she's quicker than he is. He's still moving, gaps exposed, and she snaps the puck past him.

It's the goal she would have scored if Rawlings hadn't

dragged her down. Lenno wouldn't have stopped her then, and he didn't stop her now, even after just seeing the same move. The crowd is thunderous in their approval, but Sophie doesn't look away from Lenno.

I'm the best, she thinks. *You can't stop me. None of you can stop me.* She spares a glance for Denver's bench. Sinclair shakes his fist in her direction. Butler crosses his arms over his chest, his mouth set in a familiar frown.

That goal right there is why Denver tries so hard to take her out of the game. When Sophie is at her best, no one can touch her. Without Sinclair breathing down her neck and Rawlings throwing his body into hers, Sophie can score on Lenno all game long. And so Denver throws out its bruisers, and they try to knock her off her game.

No more.

Sophie will play *her* game, and good luck to Denver trying to keep up.

*

Rawlings steps up to challenge Sophie. She taps the puck between his legs, picks up her own pass, and blows past him. He hooks his stick around her wrists, but she passes to Elsa before he can impede her play.

Elsa shoots with a goal scorer's precision, and Lenno looks over his shoulder to see the puck in the back of his net.

The game ends 5-3.

*

Concord wins Game Four to even up the series, then they fly to Denver and lose Game Five.

Game Six, back in Concord, is the first elimination game of the series. Sophie feels a familiar rush of adrenaline as she takes the ice for the opening faceoff. Her back is up against the wall. What will she do about it?

Sophie loses the opening faceoff, but she jumps onto defense. She hounds Wimberly and backchecks to break up his developing play. Woodsy scoops up the puck, and he flings a pass up to Elsa. Elsa settles the puck, then Sinclair knocks her off balance and steals it.

It sets the tone for the first five minutes of the game.

It's a frantic back-and-forth. Each bench is full of tired players, all breathing hard to regain their breath, and the score stubbornly stays at zero for both teams.

Figs is on the ice with his line, and Sophie can't help but worry. This pace isn't his style. And, at his age, she worries he'll not be able to keep up. Figs has the puck, and he slows the pace down. He skates up the far side of the ice, and he holds the puck out in front of him, daring his defender to try to take it.

Kirkland steps up to try and Figs spins around him, leaving Kirkland behind as Figs carries the puck into the zone. He passes to Peets and drops down near the net. The puck cycles and ends up back on Figs's stick. He shoots and scores.

Figs leads his line by the bench for fist bumps from their teammates. The home crowd chants his name. His lips quirk up in a smile as he sits down next to Sophie. "I'm not going down without a fight," he tells her.

"Neither am I," Sophie says. They bump their fists again, not to celebrate a goal but a pact that promises another one.

*

Kevlar scores the game's next goal.

Then Theo. DZ adds another, and suddenly the score is 4-0.

Denver does their best to rally in the third period, and

Rawlings even manages to score, but it isn't enough. The game ends with a win for Concord. It means a Game Seven in Denver.

The locker room is jubilant after the game. The d-corps talk shit about the forwards, and Merlin can only splutter, because the defense had three goals this game. Bechs is the first to toss a dirty sock, aimed for Spitzer's head, and soon dirty laundry is flying in every direction.

Sophie laughs and leans against Elsa's side as they watch the chaos unfold.

In two days, no matter what, the series is over. The finals are over. The *season* is over. One game left and it will decide everything. Sophie's fingers shake as she pulls her jersey over her head, but she isn't sure if it's with nerves or excitement or a mix of the two.

"Hey, Cap!" Bechs calls to her from his side of the locker room. His eyes are lit up, his pupils blown with adrenaline. "What do you want for your birthday this year?"

Sophie's birthday is in three days. Depending on the schedule and how long the playoffs go, her birthday sometimes falls during the playoffs. This year, her birthday is the day after the final game of the playoffs. She'll either be celebrating or...

"A hat would be nice," Sophie says, playing along. Winning the Cup means skating a lap with the trophy on the ice. Later in the summer, each player will have a day or two if they're lucky to celebrate with the Maple Cup. They don't get to keep it. What they do keep, however, are T-shirts and hats and even rings emblazoned with the Cup.

"You heard the captain," Bechs shouts. He jumps onto the bench, so he towers over everyone else in the room. "We're winning a hat for her!"

"Idiot," Peets says, but he laughs as he smacks Bechs's calf with his towel.

Bechs wobbles and Jonny steadies him before he can fall and end up with a busted wrist or something worse. Jonny meets Sophie's gaze, and he grins at her before he coaxes Bechs down off the bench.

"A hat?" Elsa whispers in Sophie's ear, quietly, only meant for her to hear. "That's what you want?"

A hat and a T-shirt. A day with the Cup. A ring to memorialize the occasion. Sophie wants it all. And, as daring as she feels, she isn't sure she's daring enough to say it.

"What about a kiss?" Elsa asks.

Sophie's body stills. It makes the beat of her heart seem loud. She looks at Elsa; it's impossible not to. They've joked about it, how they could kiss on the ice after winning and no one would blink an eye. It would be teammates being teammates, because victory kisses are a thing, just like pouring champagne into one another's mouths and falling asleep in a drunk heap at the afterparty.

She could kiss Elsa. In public. And no one would suspect anything.

"We're winning," Sophie says. The last time she won, Elsa was her teammate. Their win was a triumph and the culmination of a difficult season. Sophie had promised Delacroix a Cup before he retired. She promised herself she'd win it for Elsa so Elsa would know she made the right choice to come to Concord and play with Sophie.

This time, Sophie will win it to cement her legacy. She'll win it with Elsa as her teammate and her girlfriend.

"Shower," Sophie says, and Elsa's eyebrows climb up to her hairline, as if she thinks Sophie is going to haul her into their private shower and kiss her now. Sophie gives Elsa a small push. "Go. Before I do something stupid."

Elsa frowns as she realizes she's being sent to shower alone, then she laughs, delighted, because she knows she's under Sophie's skin. Sophie pushes her again, but she's smiling, fond, and she silently promises that once they're home, Sophie will kiss Elsa for as long as she wants. Or, at least, until they fall asleep.

Chapter Twenty

The night before Game Seven, Sophie dreams of the game. There are only a few seconds left on the clock, and the score is tied at zero. Sophie feels the time draining, and she knows she needs to act. She has to score, has to win, and so she shoots the puck.

Her shot goes wide of Denver's net. The puck careens off the boards and skips down the ice in the other direction until it slides under Teddy's pad and ends up in the back of her own net.

Sophie stands on the ice, unable to believe what's happened. Butler skates over with the Maple Cup and he hands it to Anthony Sinclair.

"I don't lose Game Sevens," Butler tells Sophie.

Sophie wakes up with a gasp. She pulls out of Elsa's grip and slides out of bed. Her tank top sticks to her back, damp with sweat. The air in the room is too thick; it suffocates her. Sophie stumbles to the bathroom and splashes lukewarm water on her face.

Butler isn't Sophie's coach anymore. She has a new coach, a better one. Coach Elison doesn't drop the weight of an entire franchise on her shoulders then watch her struggle with it. He helps her with her responsibilities. And tomorrow, led by Sophie and Coach Elison, Concord is going to win its second Maple Cup.

Sophie won't leave Denver without it.

*

Sophie gears up for Game Seven the way she gears up for any game. Her hands are steady as she tightens and adjusts her gear. She tapes her socks with practiced movements. She looks up to check on her teammates, and she spots Figs untaping his own socks. Balls of tape litter the floor around his feet as if it isn't his first time.

Bechs, normally a ball of energy before games, nudges Figs's shoulder and holds out a fresh roll of tape. Figs looks down at the discarded tape around him and accepts the rolls from Bechs with a half-grimace, half-smile.

"Thank you," Figs says quietly. "I've never played in a Game Seven final before. I didn't realize there were many firsts left for me in the league."

Sophie doesn't mention the obvious, that he still hasn't won a Maple Cup. She can't imagine what it's been like for him to have come up short over and over and now be on the brink of what he wants. No wonder he's nervous.

*

Sophie's first shift ends after securing an offensive zone faceoff. She passes Peets on her way to the bench, and she pats his shoulder. "Be quick on the draw," she tells him.

"Not too quick." Peets grins. "I would hate to get thrown out."

Sophie laughs and finds her spot on the bench. She sits next to Elsa and watches Peets takes his place for the faceoff. Peets wins it, but Rawlings fights hard for possession afterward, and he gains it.

Rawlings springs Wimberly, who skates faster than Figs can keep up with. Wimberly fires the puck at Teddy.

Teddy bobbles the puck, and it jumps out of his glove and falls into the goal. Teddy kicks the puck out, but the damage is done.

Denver drew first blood, and their crowd swells with noise as they celebrate. Teddy skates angrily around his net to clear his head as the crowd switches to chanting his name in a singsong taunt.

Figs skates to the bench with slumped, defeated shoulders. Sophie has a few words on the tip of her tongue, but Cubs gets to him first.

"We're Condors," Cubs says as he pulls Figs down to sit next to him. "That means we don't lose Game Sevens. There's a whole game left. We're going to win."

Sophie tucks her smile away where no one will see it and turns her attention back to the ice.

*

They go into first intermission down by one. Sophie isn't discouraged, she has the same faith as Cubs, but Teddy is down on himself. He sits in his stall with his elbows on his knees, and his head hanging low. Sophie forgoes her usual spot between Elsa and Merlin to sit next to Teddy instead.

He doesn't look over, but he knows it's her anyway. "I don't want a pep talk," he says.

"What do you want?" Sophie asks. If Teddy doesn't want sympathy, she won't give it to him. She's adaptable that way. "Do you want the goal back? I bet that's what Bobby Brindle is saying on the broadcast right now."

"I can't have the goal back," Teddy says. He huffs and runs his fingers through his hair. "Lenno will be stingy tonight. Especially after last game. He won't let in another four."

"We won't need four," Sophie says confidently. "And it's cute that you think Lenno will *let* us do anything. He won't. But we'll still score. He can't stop us."

Teddy doesn't even give Sophie a pity smile. "I need to be better."

"You already have been. It wasn't a good goal, but it was early in the game, when you were cold. You've been strong in your net since. Keep playing how you did in the last eighteen minutes of the period, and we'll be just fine."

Teddy purses his lips.

"What, you don't think we can score two goals?" Sophie asks. She pats Teddy's knee. "You have our back in every game. It's our time to have yours."

*

Lenno is on his stomach after he threw himself over the puck. The puck is somewhere beneath him, and Sophie pokes at him with her stick. Could she push him into his net before the officials blow the play dead? Sophie pokes Lenno again, and she's pulled into a headlock for her trouble.

There's a scuffle after the whistle is blown. Sophie twists out of Sinclair's hold in time to pull Elsa out of the fray before she can take a penalty. Sophie and Elsa skate to the bench as someone signals for a TV timeout.

Merlin tosses Sophie a water bottle as the team gathers around Coach Elison.

"Sophie's line is staying out. Pick up where you left off," Coach Elison says.

"With the headlock?" Merlin asks.

Coach Elison doesn't crack a smile. "Put the puck on net."

"Never a bad idea," Bechs murmurs.

Sophie laughs and swishes some water around her mouth. They'll start with an offensive zone faceoff. Sophie will win the faceoff and everything else will fall in.

Coach Elison hands Sophie his whiteboard. "It's your call," he says.

Sophie takes the whiteboard and draws up the play she has in her mind. She makes sure the five of them who will be on the ice understand it, then the timeout ends.

Sophie wins the faceoff. She sketched out two directions for the play, one if she won the faceoff and one if she lost it. But she wins it, and Kevlar slides the puck across the blueline to Theo. Theo holds the puck until Sophie plants herself in front of Lenno's net.

Theo shoots purposefully wide, and the puck bounces off the boards. Sophie races Kirkland for it. She beats him and muscles him out of the way. She flings the puck at the net, which isn't part of the game plan except that it's never a bad idea to put the puck on net.

Lenno kicks the puck away, but he kicks the puck back to Sophie. She settles the puck and shoots again. This time, the puck gets past Lenno. Kirkland growls and shoves Sophie away from his net, but it's too late.

The goal light is on, and they have a tie game.

Sophie looks down the ice at Teddy. One goal down. Now, they only need a second.

*

Denver didn't make it to the finals by giving up when a game is hard. They respond to Sophie's goal by playing harder. Sinclair knocks Sophie around on every shift. Rawlings launches a one-man assault on Teddy's net and has four almost-goals by the time the time runs out on the second period.

Sophie's goal may have tied the game, but Teddy's play kept the game tied.

She sits next to him at intermission again. This time, he rolls his eyes at her. "Don't say I told you so."

"I won't." She raises her arms over her head and stretches. "We have your back."

"And I have yours." Teddy's posture is loose. He doesn't look as though he's trying to crawl inside his pads and hide. "You owe me another goal."

"Me personally?" Sophie asks. "Or am I allowed to bully Elsa into it?"

"That I would pay to see." Teddy laughs. "Maybe bat your eyelashes at her."

Sophie punches Teddy's shoulder, lightly, and through his pads she doubts he feels it.

*

Despite a full effort from both teams, no one scores in the third period. Both teams head to their respective locker rooms afterward for another intermission before they enter overtime, sudden death hockey.

Sophie drinks half a Gatorade and hands the bottle to Elsa for her to finish. By the end of the third period, Coach Elison had shortened his bench. Sophie expects the changes to carry through into overtime. Figs won't see much playing time. Neither will the rookies.

Sophie will. Elsa and Woodsy, as her linemates, will. This series, after six games and a full regulation three periods into a seventh game, will be decided by a single moment. A single play, a single goal. The stakes are as high as they can be, which means Sophie will be on the ice as often as Coach Elison can put her out there.

She breathes in. The responsibility settles on her shoulders. She breathes out, pushing away the pressure. This is where Sophie thrives, and she won't let her team down. She won't let herself down.

*

An entire overtime period passes without a goal for either side. Then a second. They're in their third overtime period. If they play the full twenty minutes, it will be as if they played two games back-to-back.

Sophie is exhausted. Her muscles quiver when she sits and her lungs burn when she breathes, but there's nowhere she'd rather be than on the ice.

There's a TV timeout, and Sophie is grateful for the small break.

"Well, it's officially tomorrow," Merlin says as they gather around Coach Elison and his clipboard.

"Happy birthday," Bechs tells Sophie.

"It all makes sense, now," Merlin says as everyone turns to Sophie. "You wanted to drag this game into your birthday."

"Birthday goal for the birthday girl?" Elsa asks. She slings an arm around Sophie's shoulders.

Sophie leans against Elsa, but it's Coach Elison's gaze she meets. "This next shift. I have a good feeling."

Coach Elison takes her at her word. He sends her over the boards with Elsa on one wing and Merlin on the other, the line Sophie played with during her first Maple Cup win. On the backend is Theo and Kevlar. And Teddy, steady and sure in their net. The six of them were part of the original Concord team that won. Sophie has played with them for years, and if there was any time to end this game, it would be now.

Sophie sets up across from Sinclair for the faceoff. He's too exhausted to think of witty insults. They battle for the puck, each trying to gain the advantage. Elsa darts in to break the stalemate. She takes the puck and skates into the offensive zone.

Sophie trails her in and slaps her stick on the ice. Elsa passes to her. Sophie takes the puck around the back of Denver's net and notes how Denver's coverage shifts and how her own teammates move to get themselves open. From here, Sophie can see everything.

She slides the puck up to Kevlar at the point. He makes a quick pass to Theo. Theo takes the time to bring his stick back, then he unloads with a bomb of a shot. Sinclair drops to block it, and he grunts as he takes the puck off a place with minimal padding.

Merlin is first to the rebound, and he passes the puck to Sophie. She's by the hashmarks, her favorite place to shoot from. She shoots, bar down and in.

The goal light flashes.

Stunned, Sophie doesn't react at first. Then she drops to her knees, because her body can't hold her up anymore. She scored. Game-winning, overtime goal in Game Seven of the Maple Cup finals. She won the game. She won *the Maple Cup*.

"You're not done yet," Elsa says, and she hauls Sophie to her feet.

Sophie's muscles quake from overexertion, and she's flushed and sweating from a hard-fought game. But standing in Elsa's arms, the sensations feel normal. Sophie sees Elsa's grin, bright and happy, because they *won*, and Sophie's reminded of something they giggled about in the offseason.

She leans in and kisses Elsa before she can second guess herself. She kisses Elsa on the mouth, at the far end of the Denver Boulders' stadium. Objectively, it's a terrible kiss. They're both sweaty, and their visors are in the way, and Sophie starts laughing in the middle of it.

She turns away from Elsa, and Kevlar is standing right there so she kisses him too. It's a shorter kiss, a victory kiss with nothing extra, but it normalizes what she and Elsa did. Merlin, of course, slobbers all over Sophie's cheek, and she elbows him before she seeks out her next teammate.

They huddle together, exuberant and exhausted, leaning on each other as it sinks in that they're the 2020 Maple Cup champions. Sophie was on the ice for the end of the game. She scored the goal to win it all, but it still doesn't penetrate her brain.

They go through the handshake line, and Sophie politely ignores how upset the Denver players are, and she doesn't rub the victory in Butler's face, no matter how tempted she is. She hugs her teammates at the end of the handshake line, then settles them down as the commissioner comes onto the ice. Behind him trail two sets of white-gloved attendants. One pair holds the Maple Cup between them. The second holds the Alain Benoit, the trophy given to the MVP of the playoffs.

"Congratulations to the Concord Condors, this season's Maple Cup champions," the commissioner says. The remaining fans in the stand boo, as much for the commissioner as for Sophie's team. "Before I present the Maple Cup to Concord's captain, I will award the Alain Benoit to this year's MVP."

The commissioner clears his throat and pauses, but the effect is ruined by another round of boos. To his credit, he doesn't look irritated. "This year, the Alain Benoit is presented to Concord's captain, Sophie Fournier."

Elsa laughs and pushes Sophie forward with two hands. Sophie looks over her shoulder at Elsa, surprised, but then she's looking forward again, so she doesn't trip on her skates and faceplant. The Alain Benoit. MVP. *She's the best.* Sophie started this season on a slump. Her sluggish start continued until everyone was speculating this was the new normal for Sophie Fournier. She wasn't invited to the All-Star game. There was talk of trading her before her new contract kicked in.

And now, she's a Maple Cup champion and the Alain Benoit winner.

The commissioner takes the trophy from the pair

holding it, and he presents it to Sophie. They hold the trophy between them, and Sophie finds the nearest camera and smiles. An interminable amount of time later, she's free to skate back to her team.

She hands the Alain Benoit to Elsa, because then she has to skate back to the commissioner, this time to receive the Maple Cup. The Maple Cup is as beautiful as the first time Sophie saw it. Her fingers twitch at her sides. She wants to take it *now*, hold it close, and refuse to give it back. It's hers, she earned it, but the commissioner is prattling on about the season.

There's *another* photo op, and it takes all of Sophie's willpower to keep from ripping the Cup out of his grasp. Then, finally, the commissioner steps back, and the Cup is Sophie's. She hoists it above her head, and the crowd on the ice, the family and friends of Concord's organization, raise their voices and celebrate with Sophie and her team.

Sophie skates a lap around the rink, her legs rejuvenated. The Maple Cup is hers again. She wasn't a one-hit wonder. She led her team once, she led her team twice, and now it doesn't seem so impossible that she might do it again and again.

She turns the corner on the last straightaway, and her team is clustered together, waiting for her. She puts on a burst of speed, because Figs has waited for this moment long enough. She won't make him wait any longer.

There are cameras everywhere, local and national reporters all hoping for the perfect shot. Sophie pretends they aren't there, and she holds the Cup out to Figs.

Figs glances at Elsa, as if he isn't sure why he's the first one Sophie's presenting the trophy to.

"It's yours," Sophie says. She presses the Cup into Figs's hands. He looks stunned, as if he still isn't sure it's real. He kisses the gleaming metal, then he hefts it above his head and shouts.

Sophie drifts to Elsa's side to watch as Mikhail Figuli takes his victory lap with the Maple Cup.

*

After all the babies have been put in the Cup and the older kids have hugged it and all the pictures that can possibly be taken have been taken, the staff ushers everyone down to the locker room. T-shirts, hats, and champagne all wait for them in the room.

They'll start their party here, continue it on the plane, then it'll be an entire week of celebrating in their city. It will be messy and amazing, and Sophie lingers on the ice as her teammates all eagerly race each other down. Because yes, they will party hard, but a week is hardly anything when compared to the months they spent competing for the Maple Cup.

Sophie will have a day with the trophy this summer. She'll plan it down to the minute, and she'll share it with local kids and her entire extended family, but it's only one day. She'll have pictures to remind her of it. There will be video from the parade, and there will be articles noting what she and her team did, but at the end of the summer, they have to give the Cup back.

When the new season begins, what she and her team did will be a mark in the history books, as everyone competes to be the 2021 Maple Cup champions.

"It's your birthday and we won the Cup." Elsa curls an arm around Sophie's shoulders. "You aren't allowed to be sad."

"I'm not sad. I'm *reflecting*." Sophie tries to sound smart and mysterious, but Elsa laughs at her which means she didn't succeed.

"Reflect later, celebrate now," Elsa tells her.

"Two isn't enough," Sophie says. She isn't sure why she thought it would be. She isn't sure it's possible to ever win enough to be happy.

"Of course not," Elsa says. "The day you settle for enough is the day you hang up your skates. But we're two-time champions. We celebrate it tonight. We celebrate it for the whole summer." She laughs and coaxes Sophie to laugh with her. "And then we spend the next ten years playing together and winning again. Condors forever."

That's been Sophie's motto, or maybe dream, for years. And this fall, when their ten-year extensions and no movement clauses kick in, she'll have it. Sophie leans against Elsa's side. "Career Condors. You and me, for-ever."

Elsa looks around to check that all the cameras and fans are gone. Then she leans in and kisses Sophie. It's sweet and soft, nothing like their victory kiss. When she pulls back, she holds her hand out to Sophie. "Let's go fill the Cup with champagne and then dump it on Merlin's head."

Sophie laughs and grasps Elsa's hand.

Acknowledgements

As Sophie's journey comes to an end, I want to say thank you to the people who have supported me along the way. To my family, who stuck with me even through the early drafts; to Lis and Ray, my writing support group; to NineStar for giving this series a home; and to all the readers who have enjoyed Sophie's growth.

About K.R. Collins

K.R. Collins went to college in Pennsylvania where she learned to write and fell in love with hockey. When she isn't working or writing, she watches hockey games and claims it's for research.

Twitter
@kcollins1394

Other NineStar books by this author

The Sophie Fournier series

Breaking the Ice

Sophomore Surge

Lighting the Lamp

Home Ice Advantage

Power Play

Glove, Save and a Beauty

Grounded

Line Chemistry

Connect with NineStar Press

Website: NineStarPress.com

Facebook: NineStarPress

X: @NineStarPress

Instagram: NineStarPress

Bluesky: NineStarPress

Threads: @NineStarPress